MW00453793

Angela's Song

A Novel

AnnMarie Creedon

Book One
"Lady of the Angels"
Series

Full Quiver Publishing, Pakenham, Ontario

This book is a work of fiction. The names, characters and incidents are products of the author's imagination. Any similarity to actual events or persons living or dead is purely coincidental.

Angela's Song
copyright AnnMarie Creedon
Published by Full Quiver Publishing
PO Box 244
Pakenham ON K0A2X0
Canada

Cover photo by Delena Soukup
Cover design by James Hrkach
ISBN Number: 978-0-9879153-1-3
Printed and bound in USA

NATIONAL LIBRARY OF CANADA CATALOGUING IN PUBLICATION

Published by Full Quiver Publishing
A Division of Innate Productions

For Joe

1

I am in a meadow. Barefoot, I can feel the soft grass under my feet and there is the fragrance of flowers in the air. I hold my hand over my brow to shield my eyes from the sun and, off in the distance, I see Devin. My heart starts to race and I run toward him. When I catch up to him, his back is to me. He is very still. I walk around to see him and he is staring straight ahead, looking through me as if I am not even there. "Devin? Devin, it's me, Jel. Look at me, honey," I plead. I reach up and touch his face, the handsome face that has smiled at me and kissed me so many times. It is cold and hard, like granite. I pull my hand away, repulsed. "Devin!" I yell. "Look at me! I'm right here!" Frustrated, I grab his shoulders and start to shake him and he disintegrates into a pile of rubble at my feet. In the distance I hear an ambulance getting closer and louder...

It's my alarm ringing. I smack the snooze button and look up at the ceiling. I'm disoriented and I can feel my heart racing. *What happened to Devin?* Then reality sets in: Devin is dead, I am a widow and I have three children to wake and get ready for school. I let out a long, cleansing breath.

I should be getting up, but I lie there, thinking of all the things that need to get done today. I make a mental list. *Meeting with Fr. Sean, make calls for the Elizabeth Ministry meeting on Wednesday, catch up on the books for the Women's Auxiliary, laundry, ballet lesson, dinner, pay bills*. The memory of Devin takes a back seat to my list now, and I have the strength to get out of bed and shower. As I am toweling off, I hear a knock at the bathroom door.

"Mama, can I wear my leggings and a skirt today?"

It's Rosie, my sweet nine year old.

I wrap the towel around me and open the door. She is in her pajamas, holding a handful of clothes. Her black, curly hair is mussed and there is still sleep in her hazel eyes. She leans in for a hug. "Yuck! Wet towel!" she says, making a face.

I brush the hair from her eyes. "You can wear them if you wear boots, not shoes. It's going to be cold today, Rosebud."

I throw on some black sweats, my uniform lately, put my hair up into a ponytail and head over to the boys' rooms. I knock on Sam's door. "Samwise, you up?" I call.

The door opens and he pokes his head out. "Getting dressed, Mom," he says, sleepily. He has matured quite a bit over the last year and, with his sandy colored hair and handsome features, he looks so much like Devin. His eyes are brown, though, where Devin's were hazel, but Sam's eyes are expressive, like his father's. *Don't think of Devin*, I tell myself. *Don't think of anything*.

Ben is just coming out of his room as I reach it. He gives me a hug. He has been hugging me a lot lately, but he makes sure it's when no one is looking. Ben is the creative one in the family. He has a journal, which he sketches and writes in all the time. He wants to write screenplays someday. Ben is always observing people and I think that makes him very sensitive to their needs. He seems really in tune with mine, especially since Devin's accident.

"Thanks, big guy," I whisper. He looks down at me and smiles. Ben favors me in looks. He has fair skin, with olive undertones, dark brown eyes and thick, black hair. Both my boys, Sam, at 15 and Ben, at 12, have surpassed their mother in height. I am thankful for this, because I top out at five feet tall on a good day.

Down in the kitchen, Sam makes himself a grilled cheese, Ben pours cereal and Rosie eats oatmeal while I assemble lunches. I always make a batch of egg salad on Sundays so we have something on hand in case I haven't gotten out to buy lunch meat. Today is an 'egg salad' day. I need to add shopping to my to-do list.

We have hugs and then the children head out the door. I watch them walk to the end of the street, Rosie between her two brothers. They have been extremely protective of her since Devin has been gone, and I close my eyes and say a prayer of thanksgiving for that.

After throwing a load of laundry in, I grab a cup of coffee and start making my shopping list. When I am done, it is time to leave for my meeting with Fr. Sean.

Fr. Sean has been at our parish, Our Lady of the Angels, for about six years now. The first thing he did as pastor was to preach a series of homilies on the Church's position regarding artificial birth control. I had never heard before that the Pill and IUDs could cause abortions and that there is, actually, a natural way to space births that works with a woman's body, not against it. Needless to say, there were parishioners who left in anger over the controversial subject. It had the opposite effect on me. I wanted to know more. I wanted to know why. I wanted to know the Church that I had been brought up in. I began talking to Fr. Sean, who recommended Natural Family Planning classes for Devin and me. Getting off the Pill and learning about Church teaching regarding birth control was the beginning of a personal conversion for me. Because of this, I have a special place in my heart for Fr. Sean. I love him dearly, much like I loved my father, although this priest is at least five years younger than I am.

I knock on Father's office door. He opens it and motions for me to come inside. He's on the phone and holds up one finger to let me know he is almost done. I sit down and Father settles his large frame into the leather chair behind his desk. He is the definition of Black Irish; dark thick hair, fair but ruddy skin, dark eyes set close together. He wears rimless glasses and always wears his cassock, even on his days off.

He hangs up. "How's things?"

"Not bad, Father. Sam has been doing a great job since you had those talks with him about being the 'man of the house.' He's taken responsibility for things and is a big help to me now."

"Glad to hear it," he smiles. "So, have you spoken with Jim lately?"

"Not really. The last youth group was cancelled because of the snow and I haven't gotten in touch with him." Jim is the youth minister for our parish and I volunteer to help with that ministry.

"He is discerning whether or not to enter the diaconate program."

"Really?" I'm not surprised. Jim's wife, Chloe, passed away from cancer three years ago. He and Chloe were both devout, but since then he has really gotten deeper into his faith. This would be a logical next step for him.

"Yes, well, if he does do it, he won't be able to handle youth group. The training is rigorous. So, I was wondering if you would think about taking over youth group if he decides to go for it, which I think he is leaning toward doing. It would be a paid position, but you would need training, which the parish would pick up the tab for. What do you think?"

"I love youth group, Father. It wouldn't feel like work."

This is exciting, I think, *and a little extra money wouldn't hurt, either*.

"That is why I asked. Jim does an excellent job. You know how he runs the program and you're good with the kids as well."

Father explains that I would need to enroll in a three-year training program with the Lay Formation Institute, which is run by the diocese. Upon completion of the program, I would have a certificate that qualified me to work for the diocese or at a parish in a number of ministries. The classes are two hours, one day a week.

"Do you think you could manage that?" he asks.

"I have been leaving Sam to watch the kids once in awhile and he is doing a great job. I think he could handle once a week, Father."

"What about *you*? You should think about letting some things go so you don't overload yourself, Jel. These classes are in-depth. You're going to have to do reading and even some homework."

"I'm positive I can do this," I say, confidently.

"Well, give Jim a call. He has taken a few of the classes and has decided to do the three-year commitment. Maybe you can carpool."

I nod. "So, are these classes intensive?"

"Believe me, they are. Oh, here," he says, spinning his chair around and taking several small books off the shelf behind his desk. "Remember last time we were talking about working on your prayer life? I thought these would be a help to you.

He hands me the books across his desk. They're biographies of Edith Stein, Gemma Galgani and Gianna Molla. I don't recognize the names.

"Who are they?" I ask.

"Women who lived lives of heroic virtue. In many ways they were able to imitate our Lord. I thought reading about their lives may be a source of inspiration for you." He leans back in his chair and tents his fingers. "God's calling you to be a saint, Jel. He calls all of us."

I have to keep myself from snorting. *Me...a saint? Not likely.*

After I leave Our Lady of the Angels, I do my shopping, then head home. I'm tired. This morning wasn't the first nightmare I have had, and the lack of sleep is taking its toll on me. I pour a cup of coffee and make my calls, then settle down to work on the Women's Auxiliary stuff. While I am putting on a pot of chili, I give Jim a call.

"You spoke to Father?"

"Yeah. When were you going to tell me?" I say.

"Sorry, there has been so much in my head lately regarding this that I'm just, you know, preoccupied. So, you want me to drive? The first class is next Thursday. I would need to pick you up at 6:00."

"Sounds good. Are we set for youth group this Sunday?" I ask.

"Yeah, but can you make some of those killer brownies? I wanted to do brownie sundaes for a snack."

"Of course," I agree and we sign off.

I decide to tackle the laundry. As I am folding, I come across a very old tee shirt that used to be Devin's. Ben has been using some of his father's clothes and I think he snagged this to sleep in. It is a white tee with a picture of Plymouth Rock on it; the words 'Rock On' are printed on the back. I close my eyes and remember Devin wearing this shirt. It was before the kids were born. We still lived in Queens at the time and we took a road trip up to the cape.

Devin loved the beach. I never liked it as much, which is odd, since I grew up on the water, but I prefer to hunt for starfish or scallop shells, than to lie on the sand, sunning myself. Devin loved to just flop and soak up the rays. I remember on that trip he humored me by taking me to Plymouth to see the historical sites. I was so disappointed that Plymouth Rock wasn't as big as it had originally been because people had hacked pieces off over the years. Also, it was behind a wrought iron fence, so you couldn't even touch it. "See, Jel? It's just a rock, after all," he remarked.

But he alleviated my disappointment with a lobster dinner that evening. We went to a place in Bourne, just under the bridge, called *Granny's*. We picked out our own lobsters. I remember that I struggled with mine, so Devin cracked it for me and got me extra butter from the waiter. The place was known for its pies, so he ordered two slices to go and we took them down to the beach with a bottle of wine and watched the sun set. The next day, I let him sleep late and drove back down to Plymouth and bought him this ridiculous tee shirt as a joke. He laughed and told me he would embarrass me by wearing it as often as possible, in my company. I hold the shirt up to my face. My eyes begin to water but I blink the tears away. The pain is still so raw, even after a year.

The children walk in at 3:15. I sit down with the boys for a snack of coffee and some chocolate chip cookies and we chat about their day while Rosie changes into her leotard and tights. Moments later, she skips down the hall, bounces onto a stool and begins to wolf down her cookies.

I run my fingers through my daughter's tousled curls as I catch up on how her day went, enjoying the brief reprieve from activity. It's momentary, however, as I glance at the clock and realize we need to leave. So, I hug the boys, make them promise to do their homework and we head over to the dance studio. Today, for some reason, none of the other parents stay, so I have the waiting room to myself. I nod off while the students practice arabesques at the barre.

After dinner, we all play a couple of rounds of Apples to Apples. My boys humor me because this is family time and they know it's important to me. I am grateful that the boys are so close in age, that they are really best friends. They have other friends, but prefer to spend time together. That has made it easy for me to keep them close to home and involved in our family rather than off doing Lord knows what with who knows who.

After saying a quick bedtime prayer with the children, I tuck Rosie in and the boys head to their rooms to read for an hour. I write out the bills, then fall exhausted into bed.

My fatigued brain avoids thinking about life and I am thankful to be able to go straight to sleep.

2

It is the first day of class, and the kids and I eat an early dinner. I made macaroni with broccoli. It's not my kids' favorite meal, but it's cheap, nutritious and easy. Rosie and Ben help me get dinner on the table. I let Sam off the hook with dinner prep because he is studying for a science test. After dinner, I go over the rules for when I am gone, and thank them in advance for behaving well so I can take this class. The kids think it is comical that I am back in school at my age.

"Maybe Mom will have more sympathy for us now that she is going to have to do homework," Ben jokes.

"Don't count on it, Mr. Man," I say, gently squishing his cheek between my thumb and forefinger.

A car horn sounds from the driveway. "That's Mr. Phaff," I say, as I hug them. "Remember what I said and call me on my cell if anything at all comes up, okay?"

"Ciao, te amo," we chime together, as I throw on my jacket and head outside. *"Goodbye. I love you."*

"How are things?" asks Jim, as I slide into the front seat of his car. Jim likes to drive with his jacket off. He's wearing a sweater. Jim is always wearing a sweater. He even has lightweight ones for the summer that he wears with shorts. His sandy brown hair isn't starting to gray or even thinning, which gives him a youthful look, even though he is in his late 50's.

"I don't know...the same, I guess."

He thinks for a moment. "Jel, there will come a time when it will pass from being the *focus* of your life to being a *part* of your life. There will always be a kernel of sadness at the loss, but you will be able to live with it. You'll see."

I'm so thankful for my friendship with Jim. He has been sort of a mentor to me since Devin died. Jim helped me with the mountain of paperwork I had to deal with, and also helped me work on getting all my finances straightened out. Since Chloe's death, he has retired and spends a lot of time with his five kids, a daughter and four sons, who are all grown. They are a close family. He is also an excellent youth minister. Jim really knows how to get the kids excited about their faith. He brings instruments and lets them jam to Christian music, has them work on skits, write poetry, all kinds of creative stuff, and the kids respond to it. They enjoy being able to express their faith with their peers. I've learned a lot from youth group myself, in fact. I hope, when the time comes, I can even come close to filling Jim's shoes.

We pull up in front of the school and head up the stairs. Jim leads the way. In the classroom, which is actually the school library, there are about a dozen others. In the front of the room is a screen with a Power Point presentation set up and to the left of that is a white board, with the words 'Theology of the Body' written on it in blue marker. I notice a man sitting at one of the tables going through some paperwork. He looks up, smiles at Jim, and then returns to his paperwork.

"Who's that?" I whisper, leaning in close to Jim.

"That's our teacher, Jack."

There is something about this man that captures my attention. His coarse, loosely curled black hair is peppered with gray. It is tousled, but not messy looking. His nose is straight and his eyes are dark and deep set. He reminds me of a sculpture I once saw of a Greco-Roman wrestler in a museum. I take a look at his hands. No wedding band. *What am I doing? Am I attracted to this man?* I try to squash the feeling, but I find myself staring at him and wondering what kind of personality he might have.

Suddenly, I am aware that I am wearing sweats and no makeup. *Ugh! What was I thinking going out of the house like this?*

"Let's sit here," I say to Jim, pointing to two chairs at the back table.

"Don't you want to sit up front?" Jim asks.

"Back is fine," I say, slipping into the chair and trying to make myself invisible.

Jack stands up in front of the class and introduces himself. "I'm your teacher for this course which is 'Theology of the Body.' My name is Jack Bartolomucci, but I will spare you the pain of trying to pronounce my name. Please, just call me Jack," he grins. "This is a five-week course, based on a series of 129 talks given by Pope John Paul II in the late 1970's and early 80's. The original title of these talks was *Man and Woman He Created Them,* and they address the goodness of our bodies and the great and beautiful mystery of spousal love."

There is a distinct eastern accent in his way of speaking and I wonder if he could possibly be from New York. Jack steps up to the podium and rubs his hands together as if he is about to begin a challenging task.

"We all know the story of Adam and Eve. God created Adam, then He took Adam's rib and created Eve, who spoke to the serpent, bit the apple, gave it to Adam and the result was original sin, right?" Jack leans forward and grips the podium. He lowers his voice conspiringly. "Well, what if there was more to it than that? What if lots of stuff went on before the fall? What if what went on before the fall reveals to us what God's original plan was for humankind? And," he pauses, dramatically, "what if there was a way to get *back* to that original plan? To *live* it? The Theology of the Body is the blueprint for that plan."

***

After the kids are tucked in, I go in my room and slip into bed. Just as I am closing my textbook from reading over the homework, my phone rings.

"Hey, Jelly, how was class?" I hear the effervescent voice of my best friend, Marissa.

Marissa lives two houses down with her husband, John. Smithville is a strange conglomeration of subdivisions, rural and semi-rural homesteads. It's a small town of only about 6,000 souls, situated between Kansas City, Missouri, to the south and St. Joseph, to the north.

Marissa and John's only child, Jesse, is grown and lives in St. Joseph. Visually, Mar and I are an unlikely pair. I have light skin with olive undertones, almond-shaped, dark brown eyes and hair to match. My body is busty and hippy and I am at least six inches shorter than my friend. Marissa is tall and waif-like, with clear blue eyes, a straight nose and full lips. Her short brown bob is perpetually tucked behind her ears and, inevitably, there is a flyaway strand which falls down over one eye. A large part of Marissa's beauty comes from the fact that she has no idea how striking she is, and also because the love she has inside radiates out from her like the rays of the sun.

"Intriguing," I answer.

"Hmm. Are you going to tell me everything you learn so I can transform my marriage?"

"Are you kidding? You and John have the *best* marriage...what could possibly need to be transformed?"

"Jel, the eight miscarriages; you know-- you nursed me through four of them-- and the pain of those have, at times, taken its toll on us. We are always open to ways to communicate better and to grow closer."

Tears spring to my eyes. "I love how you and John have a plan. Dev and I, we just sort of lived our lives and let things happen. After class tonight I can see that that was a big part of our problems."

Marissa's voice softens, "Things weren't actually *bad* between the two of you, were they? I mean, you would have told me, right?"

"I didn't think anything was really wrong with us when

Devin was alive. But tonight's class made me look back on our marriage and I'm starting to realize that maybe we could have had more..."

"More what?"

"Well, the teacher spoke about how sex is holy and good; that it is sacred and a reflection of God's love for us. It's just...that sounds so incredibly beautiful," I try to swallow the lump in my throat. "Dev and I never looked at it that way. Sex for us was simply a way to satisfy our mutual arousal. We jumped into bed with each other almost as soon as we met. After we married, the lust wore off and we sort of just started living separate lives because we no longer had all that much in common." I begin to weep.

"Aw, honey, I'm sorry," says Marissa, gently.

"Maybe I shouldn't be taking this class," I say, sniffing. "I don't know if I really want to deal with this right now."

"No," says Marissa. "Take the class, Jel. It's all the *other* stuff you do that needs to go."

***

This week, I find myself dressing up a little for class. I decide that it is time to burn the sweats. What have I been thinking wearing them all the time? They look like bags on me. I fish out some nice, boot cut jeans and a Daisy Fuentes top; a white, blue and gray print. I even put on earrings and some lipstick.

"You look pretty, Mama!" Rosie says as I grab my books.

"Think so?"

"Yes! I like it when you wear nice things. You should dress like that all the time. Wear blue more, too. I like blue on you."

"I will take that under consideration," I say, and give her a kiss and a squeeze.

I remind Sam and Ben of the rules and make them

promise to clean up from dinner before I get home. I hear Jim beep the horn in the driveway.

"Ciao! Te amo!" I yell over my shoulder and sprint down the steps.

"You look nice, Jel," says Jim as I get in the car.

Wow, tonight is just a love fest for me, isn't it?

We are a few minutes early and Jack is already in the room, checking his computer to see if the Power Point is working. He's wearing a pair of tan chinos with a black knit turtleneck, a brown tweed jacket and matching loafers. *Goodness, he is so attractive.* It's just the three of us in the room when Jim gets a phone call and excuses himself. My heart starts to beat faster and I feel a blush spread over my cheeks. I don't know what to do to fill the time, so I rifle through my pocketbook as if I am searching for something. I hear Jack clear his throat.

"So... Jel?"

I look up and I think I am smiling, but my face feels frozen. No words will come out, so I nod.

"Are you originally from Kansas City?"

Relax...relax! He's just making small talk. Be yourself, you idiot!

"No, actually, I am also from the east coast," I say.

He feigns shock. "You didn't pick up my *accent,* did you?"

"Well, it's also the *way* you speak, your inflection...and your dry sense of humor; very New York."

"Jersey, actually. Bayonne. And you?"

"I was born in Queens, but I was raised mostly on Long Island. Isn't it funny that no matter where you go you are bound to meet an Italian from the New York area?"

His eyebrows go up and I notice that he's trying to suppress a smile. "You're Italian?"

"My maiden name was Rezza."

"That'll do." He glances down at my left hand. "So, is your husband also from New York?"

"He was...yes, um, originally from upstate." I take a deep, cleansing breath. "Devin was killed a little over a year ago by a drug addict in a hit and run."

"I had no idea...I'm sorry," he says sympathetically.

He opens his mouth to say something else and is interrupted by another student, a woman, who wants to ask some questions before class. He sends an apologetic glance in my direction as I slide into my seat.

My heart is still pounding as I ponder Jack. He is brilliant and has a great sense of humor; he seems easy going and that curl that keeps falling down over his forehead is just *so* charming. I feel like a schoolgirl. But then I glance down at my wedding band and begin to feel guilty. *How am I supposed to feel?*

A few more students filter in, followed by Jim. He has the goofiest smile on his face. *What is going on with him*, I wonder?

Jim sits down next to me and whispers, "That was my daughter on the phone...she's expecting!" He smiles and laughs. There are tears in his eyes. His daughter, Katie, just got married a few months ago, and I know how hard it was for Jim to be without Chloe during the wedding and preparations. This is the perfect gift for him. The promise of a grandchild, especially now, in the bleakness of winter, will be a ray of light. I squeal and give him a big hug.

"Everything okay back there?" I hear Jack say. My face turns bright red. I hadn't realized he was at the podium ready to start teaching. Jim gives a thumbs up sign and Jack begins his lecture.

***

As I am making sauce for tonight's lasagna, Marissa calls.

"Feel like doing laundry?" she asks.

I think of the two baskets waiting for me in the laundry room. Marissa and I sometimes haul our laundry to each other's houses to fold it together.

"Can you come here? I have a pot of sauce on the stove."

"Be there in five," she says.

As the two of us fold, I say, "Mar, I am thinking about taking off my wedding band and putting it on a chain and wearing it around my neck."

"Honey, that's a big step for you. I think it's a good one, though," her lips curl slightly. "What brought this on?"

"Well, I...I think I may be open to the possibility of dating at this point in time."

"You met someone." She doesn't ask me, she tells me.

"How did you know?"

"I know you inside and out, my dear. And besides, I am glad to see you have traded in the sweats for real clothes. If anything, this guy is having a positive effect on your wardrobe. Now ask him if he agrees with me about you cutting your hair."

Devin liked my hair long, so I've always worn it that way. Marissa, on the other hand, thinks it will look better shorter. She has really been hounding me to cut it, especially recently. "Big step...not ready yet, but I *am* thinking about it, okay?"

She rolls her eyes. "All right, all right...who is he?"

"The teacher at the class."

Marissa's eyes grow wide and she leans in toward me. "Seriously? You can't date him, can you? I mean, it would be inappropriate for a student to date a teacher. He's probably not even allowed."

Sighing, I say, "I didn't think about that. Besides, it is such a long shot. All we've done so far is have one conversation, but it turns out he is from the east coast and he's Italian!"

"You know, Jel, if you have this attraction to him, maybe it is a prompting of the Holy Spirit, maybe not. Why don't you pray about this and ask Him for some guidance?"

"And what if I don't get an answer?"

Marissa adds a folded pair of jeans to her pile, tucks her hair behind her ear and puts one hand on her hip. "You may not get a voice from Heaven, but you may receive an answer through events that happen. Be open. This time, you do the *right* thing, understand?"

I sigh. I know Marissa always has my best interests at heart. I decide to take her advice and pray about this, but I don't know if I trust myself enough to hear the answer. The possibility of getting to know Jack is exciting, but, inevitably, my thoughts turn to Devin.

"You know, Devin thought the Church is repressed and holds people back, but I've been reading this stuff and all I see is freedom and beauty. It's amazing," lowering my eyes and twisting the wash cloth that is in my hands, I whisper. "I only wish I would have known this from the beginning..."

Marissa puts down the shirt she has begun to fold and hugs me. "But now you do," she says, "and that's what counts."

***

Tonight is my third class and I am going through my closet trying to come up with something to wear. I pull out a plain black crew neck sweater. I can either wear jeans or my black dress pants. I go with the jeans again, but this time I wear black mules instead of sneakers. I add some silver hoop earrings and put on my lipstick. Instead of my usual ponytail, I slather my hair with styling gel and blow it dry upside down to add volume.

Ugh! Now it looks messy. I grab a barrette out of Rosie's drawer and clip the top up out of my face. Better.

Jim shows up at 5:50. "Hope you don't mind getting there early," Jim says as I get into his car.

"Not a problem."

He looks at me with a lopsided grin. "What?" I say. He just shrugs.

Jack is already there when we arrive. He is standing at the podium, reading over his notes. He looks up as we come in and smiles. "You must be eager to get to class."

Jim laughs. "I had a meeting and the timing was off. Not enough time to stop home, so I picked up Jel and we headed straight here." He fiddles with his phone. "Aw... crud... I forgot to return a call. Be right back."

I have the sneaking suspicion that Jim staged this as I watch him leave the room.

"So, uh, were you able to get to the homework this week, Jel?" Jack asks, coming out from behind the podium and sliding into the seat next to mine.

"I did," I answer. "But I am afraid I didn't do as good a job as I would have liked. My kids had a busy week and I had to juggle."

"It must be hard being a single parent. How many children do you have?"

"I have three. Two boys: Sam, who's 15, and Ben who is 12. My daughter, Rosie, is nine. They are good kids. I am amazed at how well they are dealing with the loss of their father. Sometimes I feel like it is they who are a comfort to me rather than the other way around. I think it is true what they say about children being more resilient than adults." *Why am I telling him all of this?*

"I understand what they've been through. I lost both my parents when I was four."

"Really? That must have been hard, being so young."

"Well, fortunately my aunt and uncle took me in. They were unable to have children of their own and so they were as thrilled to have me as I was to have them. I am blessed to have had them in my life, for many reasons." His eyes get a faraway, dreamy look, which makes me think he loved them deeply.

Students begin to come in and take their seats. "Jel, I'm sure you did a fine job on the homework. You're a good student."

Jack smiles and walks to the podium to start class.

Jim slips into the seat Jack just vacated. I punch him in the arm. "What?" he says, eyes widened in false innocence.

After class, Jim tells me he has a question for Jack, so I gather my stuff up and walk up to the front of the class with Jim.

Jack, who is erasing the white board, turns and sees the both of us waiting. "Something I can help you with?"

"Yes," says Jim, "Why is it that the Church waited so long to come up with Theology of the Body? It seems to me there should have been some teachings on this stuff before the 80's; that it would have been helpful to people."

Jack leans one arm on the podium and crosses his left ankle over his right. "Marriage is a sacrament and so sex within its context is good and holy. The Church has always taught this. What John Paul II did was to look at the basic teaching and expound upon it..."

Jack's voice trails off as he shifts his weight to his other leg and ponders for a moment. "JP II added his own insights and discoveries on the subject to help people understand its beauty. He worked in words just the way an opera singer works in notes. Pavarotti would take a basic melody and add embellishments and soon it became a masterpiece...absolute beauty to the listener. John Paul added his own embellishments and created a work of art."

"So no one really thought to delve deeper into this subject before JP II did?" asks Jim.

Jack nods. "Mostly, yes." Then he glances over at me and our eyes meet. He holds my gaze for a couple of beats and I hope he doesn't hear my heart pounding; or worse, that it doesn't burst right through my sternum and smack him square in the face.

"Did you also have a question, Jel?"

"I...uh..." I clear my throat to give myself time to calm down. "Are there any books you can recommend for teens...teen boys that will explain this at their level?"

Jack's eyes light up and his love for this subject shines through the smile that slowly spreads across his face. "Absolutely! I have two favorites...here." He takes my notebook from my arms. "I'll write them down for you."

His head is bent over the podium and as he writes, I think, *If he knows so much about love, why isn't he married with a brood of kids right now?*

He hands my notebook back to me.

"If your boys aren't readers, there are some resources in DVD format, but I prefer the written word myself; for learning, anyway."

"Oh, I don't have to worry about that. My boys read books like other kids eat French fries...one after another," I laugh. Jack's enthusiasm makes my nervousness disappear tonight.

"So, what do they like to read?"

"Well, they are big into history, fantasy, mythology. They've read Heroditus, lots of Norse and Greek mythology. They live and breathe Tolkien and Lewis. I mean, I enjoy them, too, but Sam and Ben have read all of the appendices to *Lord of the Rings*. They've pretty much memorized the family genealogies of the elves and Hobbits. Seriously, who else but my boys and JRR himself would know that Galadriel is Arwen's --"

"Grandmother," we say together, and then laugh out loud.

"Well, *you* I guess, then." *Oh, my...this is a man I would really like to get to know.*

He grins. "They sound like boys after my own heart."

"You know, I usually don't admit this, but my oldest son, Sam, is named after Samwise Gamgee. In fact, it's his nickname. I was so drawn to Sam's loyalty and deep love for Frodo in the story that I wanted my own son to have those qualities, and so I gave him the name."

I hear a beep. It is Jim, playing with his phone. Oh,

Jim...I forgot about *him*.

He looks up from his phone and breaks into a goofy grin. Suddenly, I feel self-conscious.

"Go on," he says, "I'm not one to break up an intense conversation on the subject of...uh...literature." He winks at me and I shoot him a look that could pierce body armor.

Jack clears his throat. "Well, it is getting late. I'm sure you need to get home to your children, Jel, so I won't take up any more of your time."

I want to crawl under a rock, but I force myself to look up at Jack and smile. "Thanks again for the suggestions. I will definitely work on getting those books and discussing them with my sons."

Once Jim and I are safely out of earshot, I hiss, "I should throttle you, Mr. Sarcastic!" Jim just laughs and gives me a friendly squeeze.

3

I am bummed. Tonight is our last class. The car ride to school is a quiet one. Jim spends most of it on the phone with his daughter discussing some furniture he is going to buy for the nursery. I settle back in my seat and think about Jack. I've been doing a lot of that lately. I wonder if he will teach any of the other classes I am going to take.

There is a detour because of road work, so we arrive at class about a minute before it starts. When I walk in, Jack comes right over to me.

Gently, he puts his hand on my arm and says, "If you have some time, may I see you after class?" Stunned, I nod and then take a seat and pull my notebook out of my bag. I can't concentrate on the class at all. *What could he want to see me about?*

At 8:00, he says, "Well, that about wraps up this class. I'll do you all a favor and let you go early, if there are no further questions. But before you leave, I have an announcement to make. I will no longer be teaching for the Lay Formation Institute. The Bishop has asked me to fill in for Fr. Pierre at the Diocesan Youth Ministry Office. I will begin that on Monday."

"But what about Fr. Pierre?" asks a classmate. "Why has he been removed from Youth Ministry?"

Jack shakes his head slightly and grips the podium tighter. I can tell that he is put off by the insinuation. "He hasn't been removed at all. Fr. Pierre asked to return to Haiti to do some missionary work and the bishop approved the request. I'll be in contact with him while he is gone. I have also been asked to start a Theology of the Body program and do some other projects, so you'll see me around. Now go, and preach to all nations," Jack says, relaxed now and smiling.

"Wow, hate to lose him as a teacher, but he's good at this TOB stuff," says Jim. "Ready to go?"

"He asked to talk to me after class."

"Hmmm..." Jim raises an eyebrow.

I roll my eyes at him. "It's probably to correct my substandard work," I say. "Meet you at the car?"

Once the room empties out, Jack strolls over to me and sits down. "These are the two books I recommended to you for your sons. I found extra copies and thought maybe you would like to have them."

"Thanks so much, Jack. That's very generous of you." It *is* generous...and thoughtful. But I am fighting disappointment as I stand up and begin to gather my stuff.

"Jel...when was the last time you had a good slice of New York pizza?" he asks, getting up out of his chair.

I look up at him, surprised. "Pizza? It must be ten, no, more than that...oh, what does it matter...*forever ago*."

"There's a place in Overland Park that makes delicious New York pizza...how about grabbing a slice right now?" he asks, and reaches out to take the books from my hands. "They're open till 10:00 on weeknights, which would give us just enough time," he says, and then waits, his head bent toward mine, expectantly.

My mouth goes dry and I can feel my heart racing. The schoolgirl feeling is back, and here is Mr. Handsome asking me out and carrying my books. Then reality hits... Jim is waiting for me in the car.

"I would love to say yes, Jack, but Jim drove me here, so I have no way of getting back up north." I wonder if Jack can hear the disappointment in my voice.

"Well, I can drive you home. It's no problem at all. Do you want to go talk to Jim about it while I pack up here?" Jack says, taking his notes from the podium and slipping them into a folder. "But...but if it's too last minute, I understand."

I walk out of the classroom and then, when I know I'm

out of Jack's vision I run out the door to the car, mostly to burn off all the nervous energy that has built up.

"He wants to go for pizza," I pant. "He says he'll drive me home. What do I do?"

"Go."

"Just like that? Just go?" I practically yell at Jim, because I am so surprised by his reaction.

Jim looks very serious. "Jel, I can tell you like this guy. Go out with him. Have *fun,*" he sighs. "It's time you had some fun." Then he peels off, leaving me no choice but to stay.

I call home and tell Sam that some of the people from the class are going out because it's the last class and to tuck Rosie in for me. He is good about it, but puts Rosie on so I can tell her.

"I'll be home before midnight, so don't worry about me turning into a pumpkin, okay?" I hear her giggle. "Be good for Sam and Ben, sweetie. And get to bed on time; you have school in the morning."

I thank God for my kids and how good they have been and get ready to head back up to the class. I give myself a little pep talk about being myself and not being nervous. When I get there, Jack is putting the strap of his laptop bag over his shoulder. He picks up my books and my bag and walks toward me. "So, what does the lady choose...pizza or no pizza?"

I'm a nervous wreck, but I manage to force a smile. "Well, my ride ditched me, so here I am."

I stay a step behind Jack as we descend the stairs. Now that I am actually going out with him, I wonder if I've made the right choice. When Jack gets to the bottom of the stairs, he turns and looks up at me. His smile and the sparkle in his eyes tell me that he is happy to be with me. This makes my stomach do a flip flop and my legs turn to noodles. He holds the door open for me and, as we walk to the parking lot, his forearm brushes mine. Suddenly, I have a fantasy that the next thing he does is put his arm around me and pull me close.

What am I doing? This is two people who have something in common going for a slice of pizza. This is not *a date. It's a slice of pizza.*

Jack drives a Ford Focus. *He must be frugal.* Devin's maxed-out credit cards come to mind and I think that frugal is probably a good thing. The car smells fresh and clean and slightly sweet, like good soap. When Jack turns the key in the ignition, classical music wafts through the interior. The front seats are neat, but the back seat is covered with books, notebooks and folders.

"Looks like you're starting your own library back there," I say, slipping the texts he gave me into my bag.

He laughs. "Well, I never know when I'm going to need a resource when I'm teaching a class, so I just haul them all around with me."

"It's better than what's all over my van. We've got track shoes, karate equipment, ballet slippers, water bottles and probably some old sweat socks. It's not as bad now that the kids are older, though. For years it was Cheerios, Goldfish crackers and spare diapers."

"So, besides driving your kids to their activities, what do you do, Jel?"

*What do I do? What **do** I do?* "Well, um, I volunteer at church. I'm co-president of the Elizabeth Ministry and I help with the blood drives and youth group and I am treasurer of the Women's Auxiliary. That keeps me busy along with being a chauffeur, a cook and all the rest of it."

I tell Jack all about the work we do with The Elizabeth Ministry. Marissa helped found the chapter and we have worked together on it ever since; helping women overcome grief from miscarriage or the death of a child. We also deal with other issues, like a having a child diagnosed with special needs, complications in pregnancy or an adoption.

"I'm always cooking someone a meal or watching

someone's kids," I say. "It's a busy ministry."

We come to a strip mall and Jack turns in and parks in front of a storefront called NY SLICE. He turns off the car and runs over to open my door for me. Again, he holds open the door as I walk into the pizza place. It smells wonderful and suddenly I am very hungry. There is a short line and when we get to the counter the man behind it throws up his hands and yells, "Ciao, Giacomo! Che fa?" The man looks to be in his late 40's and has a slight resemblance to the actor Danny Aiello. He walks around the counter and he and Jack embrace. It's a guy hug with all the requisite patting on the back.

"So, he brings the lady...and who do I have the pleasure of meeting?" Frankie asks, extending his hand. His accent is thick and I can tell he is from Queens. This man is so friendly and jovial that I can't help but grin.

"This is Jel. Jel is a New Yorker, Frankie," says Jack. "An *Italiana* from New York. Jel, this is Frankie D'Amico. He owns the place."

"It's nice to meet you, Frankie," I say, shaking his hand, "Mmm...the pizza smells delicious! Tell me you use a coal-fired oven!"

He grins. "The lady knows her pizza! Yeah, coal, just like in the city." He sweeps his hand through the air in an arc. "It's all authentic," he smiles, proudly. "What'll you have?"

I order a slice of spinach pizza, my favorite, and an iced tea. Jack orders two slices of pepperoni and two bottled waters. Frankie tells us he'll bring it to the table.

Jack helps me out of my jacket and hangs it up, then we sit down at a corner table. Jack is facing the wall, but I have a good view of the place. It's adorable. Frankie took the red and white checkered tablecloth theme and used that as a basis for his decorating. The flooring is white with red tiles randomly placed, so as not to look too much like a check. The walls are a deep, cool red and the trim is painted white. The tables are white and gray marbled Formica, complimented by red vinyl-covered chairs and booths. Black and white prints of New York City and Italian celebrities adorn the walls. Above us is a large print of the Brooklyn Bridge. In the background I hear Frank Sinatra. Perfect.

"I like it," I whisper to Jack. "Thank you."

Frankie comes over with the tray and sets our meal down. Then he pulls a chair from another table, slides it over and takes a seat.

"So, I'm originally from Woodhaven. Where you from, Jel? And what kind of an Italian are you, with a name like Jel?" he laughs.

What a small world. "Woodhaven? For a short time we were practically neighbors," I smile. "My family lived in Richmond Hill when I was an infant and then my father moved us out to Shirley, so I basically grew up on the island. To answer your second question, Jel is a nickname my late husband gave me and it seemed to stick. Everyone calls me that now. But my given name is Angela. My father used to call me his angel girl."

Suddenly, Jack begins to cough. Frankie jumps up and slaps him on the back. "You okay?"

Jack holds up his hand and nods. "Sorry, went down the wrong way." But he looks shaken and I wonder what could have unnerved him. When it is obvious that Jack is fine, Frankie excuses himself to get back to the counter and I am happy to have Jack to myself again.

"Recovered?"

"I think I'll live." He seems thoughtful. Then he reaches out as if he wants to take my hand, but stops just short of doing so. "Angela...would it be all right if I called you Angela?"

It has been a long time since *anyone* has called me Angela and I am not sure how I feel about this. I look up at

Jack and study his face. He is so earnest and open. There is something about this man that draws me in. I find it both exhilarating and frightening at the same time.

"I'm going to be honest with you. I love my given name and I have never truly been fond of my nickname. It would be nice to be called Angela again."

"Angela...Angela Rezza." *Oh my... he remembered!*

"Angela Marianna Rezza...Cooke." I roll the *r* in Marianna like my parents did.

"And your father called you his angel girl." The tender look he gives me makes my insides melt. At this moment, a bunch of loud teenagers burst in and the noise jolts us back to reality.

Jack picks up his pizza and says, "Behold." Then he folds it and holds it at an angle over his dish. The top of the slice is straight and the bottom part droops a little; a couple of drops of oil drip out.

"Just like home!" I exclaim and dig into my slice. The crust is firm, but not too crispy. It is browned on the bottom and dusted with cornmeal and flour. There is a minimal amount of sauce and I can taste that Frankie uses real mozzarella. The aroma and the flavor take me right back to my childhood.

As we eat, Jack tells me about his life. His aunt and uncle were schoolteachers at the Catholic school he attended. His mother was an only child and his father's only sibling was the uncle that raised Jack.

"So, you have no other living relatives?" I ask, trying to keep the pity from my voice, yet realizing that, although I have a few relations still living, I don't keep in touch. If it weren't for my own children, I'd be in the same boat as Jack.

"It can be a real cross," he says, wistfully. "On holidays I usually do some charity work, or spend some time with my good friends, Chris and Christina and their family. I miss the traditions, though. It's hard to do them for one."

"No fish on Christmas Eve, then?" I ask, sadly. Traditionally, Italians abstain from meat in deference to the Word Made Flesh being born at midnight on Christmas Eve. But it is not a fast, it's a feast and usually all present pitch in to make the meal.

"Tell me you still do that?" he marvels.

"I do, but I've pared it down because it is just the five...uh, four of us. I make shrimp scampi and baked clams and fry some flounder. And, of course, I make the calamari." I pronounce calamari the way I learned to say it growing up. I usually have to catch myself when talking to anyone from the Midwest, and make sure I pronounce it 'cah-lah-mah-ree" so they know what I am talking about. It feels good to know that Jack will 'get' what I am saying.

"I'll bet you're a good cook."

"I don't know about that...but I cook from scratch all the time. I love cooking for my kids and making holidays special."

I am enjoying the evening so much that I don't notice the time pass. Looking around, I realize we are the only ones here. Frankie comes over with a tray on which sits a plate of tiramisu, two forks and two cups of cappuccino.

"On the house," he announces, "We are closed, but it takes awhile to clean, so you're welcome to stay as long as you don't mind that we turn up the music." He winks. "The fun begins after the doors are locked."

I look down at the plate of tiramisu. "It's like heaven," I say, but I'm not so sure I am talking about the dessert.

"You haven't even tried it yet," says Jack as he cuts a small piece, raises the fork, then he hesitates. I can see what he is thinking. He wants to be romantic and feed it to me, but that may be going too far at this point. To let him off the hook, I pick up the other fork and take a bite. The mascarpone cheese is silky and the cake is saturated with Kahlua, but not soggy. It *is* heavenly. As we nibble, the music increases in volume. Rosemary Clooney is singing

Tenderly and I can hear someone from the kitchen singing along, off key.

"So, do you bring women here often for the after hours excitement?" I ask, playfully.

"Never," he answers, then stands up and extends his hand. "Would you care to dance?"

I feel flustered. "I haven't danced in years...I don't even know if I remember how."

He takes my hand. "I'll teach you." And he twirls me around gently. Then he puts my right hand on his shoulder and takes my left hand and we begin to dance. He is very graceful.

"You are a wonderful dancer, Jack."

He groans and rolls his eyes. "Blame my aunt for that. She insisted I take lessons while all the other boys were in the street playing stick ball."

"I'm thinking it paid off in the long run."

"So all those fights I got in over this were not for naught?"

I shake my head. "I think you can safely say, 'you showed them.'"

Dean Martin is crooning *Innamorata* and a couple of the workers from the pizza place join us out on the floor. I can feel that it is getting very late, but I don't want to leave. However, I steal a glance at the clock behind the counter. 10:45. *Yikes!*

Reluctantly, I look up at Jack. He reads my mind.

"I'd better get you home."

We thank Frankie and he makes us swear we will be back soon before he'll let us out the door. The temperature has really dropped and I am shivering as I slide into the car. Jack removes his jacket and drapes it over my legs, then gets in the car. "I'm going to let it warm up for a minute," he says, rubbing his hands together vigorously.

"Thank you for taking me to Frankie's tonight, Jack. I had forgotten how much fun it is to dance!"

He puts the car in gear. "So, if you didn't go dancing, what did you and your husband do for fun, if you don't mind my asking?"

I think. "Devin, uh, worked a lot, so we didn't do much," I sigh. "Well, when we first got married, we loved to travel. Devin wasn't interested in going overseas, but we went to Napa and did the wine thing and we went to the Florida Keys, lots of places for weekends."

And then, what?

"We moved out here just before Sam was born. Devin was in sales at the time and it was his goal to become Sales Director at the TV station, where he worked. Once he got the promotion, the work increased and so did the business travel. So we just fell into a routine where Devin worked and I raised the kids. On the weekends he would watch sports, catch up on yard work and take the boys to their games. He wanted them in baseball and football. Rosie kind of got the short end of the stick there."

The words come out like vomit. I can't stop them. "Sometimes Devin would dust me off and take me out to a business dinner. Those were...oh, who am I kidding? I *hated* those things. And you know what? The boys hate team sports. After the accident they gave them up. Sam does karate now and Ben runs track. He's a sprinter," I sigh. "I don't want to give you the wrong impression of Devin. He was a good man and a good provider, but somewhere along the line we stopped being a 'we' and started living separate lives..."

Jack lets out a deep breath and doesn't speak for awhile. "And where was Angela in all this?" he asks softly.

"I don't know."

We are on 169 going north through Smithville. "Tell me where to go," he says.

I tell Jack to turn right on 180th Street and go up F Highway. "It's beautiful up here," he remarks as we turn into my driveway.

He puts his hand lightly on my back as we head up the steps to the front porch. Jack stops just short of the top step, so that I am almost face to face with him as I finish my climb. I turn and look up at him, expectantly. He says nothing. Then he takes my hands in his, still saying nothing. He seems to be searching for words.

A feeling of alarm rises in my chest. *Is he NOT going to ask me out again?*

"Angela," he says softly. "I really enjoyed spending time with you tonight. In fact, I have never felt more comfortable with any other woman I have ever known." He pauses...a long pause.

"But...?" I say, trying to sound calm.

"I would love to see you again..." His voice trails.

"I'm sensing another '*but*,' Jack," I say, struggling to keep my voice even.

"Angela, I don't know how well I will be able to explain this, but I think this isn't the right time for you to be dating someone."

Shock and outrage begin to simmer inside me, but I say nothing, because at the same time I have the incredible and almost uncontrollable urge to kiss Jack.

"I think, at some point in your life, you got put on the back burner. You seem to spend a lot of time fulfilling other people's needs, but not your own." Jack stops to think for a second. "You know how Jesus said 'Love your neighbor as yourself?' Well, you have done plenty of loving your neighbor and almost no loving yourself. I think you need to find Angela and learn how to love her first before we can consider starting a relationship."

It feels like I just got punched in the stomach. I pull my hands out of his.

"Oh, so you're my *shrink* now?!" I yell-whisper so I don't wake the neighbors and the kids. "Jack, you charm me into going out with you tonight, you act like...I don't know...you...you're brilliant and handsome and funny and

I have not been able to stop thinking about you since the second we met, and then you take me home and analyze me and tell me you don't actually want to see me after all? And I'm supposed to be okay with that?" I am out of breath because I am struggling to keep from hitting him...or kissing him, I can't tell which.

He puts his hand gently on my cheek, which makes me feel like I am going to melt, and I fight the feeling.

"Angela, I am so sorry. I'm not trying to hurt you. I want you to understand..."

Too late. I *am* hurt...and angry. I feel tears welling up in my eyes, which embarrasses me and then I become even angrier because I am humiliated by the crying. Then, before I even know I am doing it, I grab him by the shirt, pull him toward me and kiss him hard, right on the mouth. He resists initially, then begins to yield, catches himself and resists again, although not as strongly.

"Wha...what ..?" he stammers.

"How *dare* you make me care about you!" I slap his face. "And then treat me like some kind of a...a...nut case!" I begin to sob, and I'm so ashamed of my lack of control that I turn my back on him and put my head against the front door. I am fumbling for my keys and I feel his hand on my back once more.

There is pain in his voice. "Angela, this isn't how I planned --"

I cut him off. "Yeah, well, *life* doesn't always turn out like we plan it, does it? Believe me, *I* know."

I finally find the key, but after several attempts I still can't get it into the lock. I throw the keys on the ground in frustration and begin to cry again. Jack picks them up and gets the key into the lock for me. I try to push the door open, but he holds it and won't let me. He takes my hand and puts a card in it.

"What is this," I snarl, "a shrink's phone number?"

His voice full of emotion, Jack says, "If you are ever in

trouble or need anything, you call me and I will come. That is a promise. I never intended this evening to be a good-bye. I have waited a long time for a chance at love and I know that now is not the time for you, so I am willing to keep waiting until the time *is* right."

I am a mess. I wipe my eyes and sniff, but I can't bring myself to look up at him. "What if I never call?"

He puts his hand under my chin and tilts my head up so I have no choice but to look into his deep, brown eyes. In my anger, it is difficult to gaze into the compassion I see there. I don't want him to be kind. I want him to be a jerk so I can shut the door and forget about him for good.

"I'll wait, anyway." Jack whispers. Then he strokes my cheek one more time, turns and slowly walks to his car. I get the door open and rush inside before he drives away, not wanting to watch.

Holding back the tears, I look in on the kids. They are all asleep soundly. Robotically, I make my way into my bedroom and put on a nightgown, wash my face and slip into bed. I set the alarm and plug my phone into the charger. A thought comes to me and I text Fr. Sean, hoping he'll see it first thing in the morning.

Can I c u after Mass? Important. Jel

I shut the light and sink down into the blankets; only then do I allow myself to cry. Replaying every detail of the night in my mind, I work to get past the anger and hurt and try to make sense of what Jack said to me. Reluctantly, I admit to myself that he has a point. I have always defined myself by what I do, not who I am. I seem to need to be good at everything and get approval from others all the time. *How is it that this man knows so much about me?*

Another wave of sadness comes. The only other time I have felt this alone was when Devin died.

I think about what Fr. Sean has taught me since then and I begin to pray.

God, please help me. I am in so much pain. When Devin died I thought that was it for me, that I would be single for the rest of my life. But then Jack shows up and my life is turned upside down. He sees something in me that needs to be...what? Healed? Changed? Lord, you can do this. You can change me. You can heal me. Show me what it is, Lord. Please speak through Fr. Sean tomorrow and show me your will. Bless him, too. He is a good priest and a good friend. And my kids. And Devin...and Jack, even though I am really, really, really mad at him.

The alarm rings. I know I should get up but I smack the snooze button anyway. Then last night pops into my sleepy brain and I feel like staying in bed. I hit snooze twice more before I even consider getting up.

God, please help me get out of this bed, because I certainly can't do it on my own strength.

Immediately I hear children stirring. The bedroom door opens and Rosie bursts in, eyes full of sleep and hair all mussed. She wraps her arms around me in a delicious hug.

"Morning, Mama!" Her smile is like sunshine. "I missed you last night."

Sam appears in the doorway. "Yeah, she made me read her four chapters of *The Silver Chair*, because she said she couldn't sleep without either you or a long bedtime story. She milked it good, Mom," he chuckles. "Did you have a nice time last night?"

"Last night? ...yes, I did." *Well, at least the first half.* "Thanks for watching your sibs, bud. Where's Ben?"

"Shower."

"Showtime," I say and we all head to the kitchen.

I can't get breakfast down, but I manage a cup of coffee. While the kids get dressed I pack lunches and check to see that homework gets in the backpacks. When we are all together in the kitchen, I tell them how proud I am that they stayed home and behaved responsibly when I was gone.

"Let's splurge on Chinese tonight to celebrate how awesome the Cooke kids are."

"Don't forget the Crab Rangoon," Ben grins. He's the only one who eats it, so sometimes we forget to order it.

"I will especially not forget the Crab Rangoon," I say, glancing at the clock. We're running late and the kids have missed the bus. I'm going to have to drive them. "All right, prayers, hugs, then school. Let's go."

We all pile into the van and I drop them off at school on my way to Mass. The two younger ones lean in for a kiss as they get out. Sam stopped doing that after Devin's accident. I guess he feels it's not manly, but I miss it.

"Ciao, te amo," we all say to each other and they are on their way. *Bye, I love you.* As I pull out of the school parking lot my phone beeps.

C U after Mass. Fr. S

My thoughts return to last night on the ride to church. I am full of regret. But there is no way I am calling Jack. I drive north on 169 and make a right into the parking lot and see Our Lady of the Angels Church looming ahead of me. So much of my life is tied to this church that it feels like an extension of home. I walk in and bless myself with holy water, then genuflect and sit in my daily Mass seat, on the right side of the church, near the icon of St. Michael the Archangel. Kneeling down, I make the sign of the cross and try to pray. No prayers will come, so I just sit and remain still. The thought pops into my head that maybe I shouldn't be receiving communion since I am still so very angry with Jack, so I decide not to and hope that Fr. Sean will help me shed some light on this whole thing.

***

"So what's up?" says Fr. Sean, settling into the leather chair behind his desk. "I have to say, I am intrigued. You text me in the middle of the night and show up to Mass looking like you've had very little sleep."

"That bad?"

He grins. "Not bad, just tired."

"I went out with Jack Bartolomucci last night."

Father's eyebrows go up, but he says nothing.

"He took me to a pizza place that is owned by a guy from New York. He said since we are both from back east he thought I'd enjoy it. So we go and we have a great time, Father. It was, actually very romantic. He told me all about his childhood and we talked for a long time, and I thought we really connected, but then when he drove me home things fell apart."

"Fell apart? How so?"

"Well, that is when I got angry at him. And then I kissed him."

Fr. Sean puts his hands on the arms of his chair and raises himself slightly, in surprise.

"You *kissed* Jack Bartolomucci?!"

"You know, Father, I am thinking that this needs to be a confession. Can we make it a confession?"

"Let me get my stole," he says, the shocked look still lingering on his face, while fishing around in a drawer. He pulls out the purple satin stole and drapes it around his neck and makes the sign of the cross.

"Bless me Father, for I have sinned. I kissed Jack Bartolomucci, and then I slapped him."

"You slapped him?" he asks, incredulous. Then alarm spreads across his face. Father lowers his voice. "He did something to you that warranted slapping?"

"No, he didn't, really...well, sort of, at least I thought so last night but today I'm not so sure."

Fr. Sean sighs and rubs his forehead. "I'm confused, Jel."

"Okay. Everything he did and said led me to believe he was going to ask me out and I really got my hopes up. But then he told me that, although he *wanted* to ask me out, he *couldn't* because I'm not ready."

"And then you kissed him?"

I nod. "And then I slapped him."

He lets out a long sigh and looks up at the ceiling. I can't be sure, but it seems like he is praying...or rethinking this meeting with me; I can't tell which.

"Jel, I happen to be acquainted with Jack. He is a sincere person and doesn't do things on a whim. I don't think he was toying with you, do you?"

"No, Father," I admit. The anger starts to dissipate because I am beginning to really examine what happened. Now remorse starts to set in and I feel tears well in my eyes. "He said that I have spent so much time doing things for others that I've lost myself in the process and I need to find myself before I have a relationship..." I sigh. "...I shouldn't have smacked him...or kissed him."

"Ah...probably not the best reaction. But you have been through a lot, and your emotions are still sort of right under the surface. You've held it together pretty well, Jel. It's understandable that you are going to have some, uh, lapses in judgment. It seems to me that you are truly sorry for the way you behaved, so just call and apologize."

Scary thought. I honestly don't want to do that (my pride talking), but I know he is right. "If I promise to apologize at some point when I think I can do it in a way that I am composed enough to do it, would that be okay?"

"If you're not ready, but at least willing, I'll absolve you. Now, I want to explore what he said to you. You know, I have been praying to the Holy Spirit to be able to help you and I think the Holy Spirit spoke through Jack last night."

"Are you *kidding* me?"

"He got to the root of the problem, Jel. I have been hinting since Devin's death that you need to ease up on the volunteering and take some time for yourself, but you have come up with a million excuses as to why you need to keep going. Unless you make some changes, you're going to wind up crashing and burning."

He must have seen my face because he said, "I don't want to hurt your pride, but I think for your own health you need to slow down."

I am angry and I feel out-of-control. I really need some guidance and Fr. Sean is offering it. It's probably a good idea to take his advice since I don't have a plan of my own. Still, my pride is rearing its ugly head and I can't commit. Lowering my gaze, I look down at my hands because I don't want to look Father in the eye. He sits quietly, giving me the time I need.

God help me. What am I scared of? Free time? Relaxation? Or facing myself? I really haven't done anything for myself in a very long time. I thought that was what I was supposed to do: live for my husband and kids, be a good person by helping others...or maybe I was just keeping busy so I didn't have to really look at my life and any problems I may have been having.

"Even Jesus took time away and went into the desert by Himself to pray," Fr. Sean says softly.

Something inside me breaks and I am finally able to say out loud what I have been running from. "Devin and I didn't have the best marriage," I whisper.

"Do you feel guilty about that?" he asks, gently.

His words reach something deep inside me and more tears come. I am wracked by sobs as the pain comes to the surface. The realization that my husband died before I could do anything to fix my marriage is almost too much to bear. He was a good man; he deserved better...we both did, and so did the kids. Now I will never know what could have been. The finality of that feels like a shackle around my heart, constricting it, breaking it.

Father Sean gets up and stands before me and blesses me by making the sign of the cross in the air. "Let it out, Jel," he says, and begins to pray over me. I can't hear what he is saying, but his fatherly presence is a comfort to me and the sobs begin to subside. I feel a release of emotion and finally a warm peace floods my body.

He sits in the chair next to mine and hands me a box of tissues.

"Jel, listen to me. God does not want you walking around with this guilt. He wants you free from it. I can see He is working on you. He loves you so much and I think you know that intellectually, but you haven't truly accepted it in your heart. Maybe part of the reason for that is this guilt. Instead of a traditional penance I am going to give you some spiritual guidance that you need to follow every day. Do you think you can do that?" I nod, weakly.

"First, you need to give up all ministries except youth group, but even that I want you to share with someone. Jim can get someone else to help him with one session a month and you can help with the other. Then, I want you to pray to the Holy Spirit and ask Him to bring to light any emotional wounds you may have and to heal you of them. Every day, come to daily Mass and, afterwards you pray like that in front of the tabernacle, got it?"

"So, I just abruptly quit *everything*?" I ask, dabbing at my eyes with a tissue.

"Yes, and do this daily prayer. Then what I want you to do is to take some time each day and do something special just for you. Go for a walk or get a coffee; sit and read the paper, whatever, but it has to be something you do just for you."

"That seems kind of selfish to me, Father."

"No, it is you learning to love yourself. Jel, loving yourself doesn't mean being selfish, but it does mean having a *sense* of self and feeling the reality of God's love for you. Look, you can't give what you don't have. If you don't love yourself, how can you truly love others? You're running on empty, Jel and it is going to take its toll sooner or later and your children will be the ones who suffer."

He pauses, takes off his glasses and rubs his eyes, then balances them once again on the bridge of his nose. "In the book of Ecclesiastes it says that there is a season for everything. Sometimes there *is* a season for self-denial. But it is not that season for you. Now is the time for you to spoil yourself a little bit and learn to feel the joy that comes from the unconditional love of God."

When I get home the first thing I do, before I lose my resolve, is to send e-mails to all my ministries asking them to find replacements for me. I use the excuse that being a single mom is more than I can handle and I need a break...not necessarily a lie. Walking into my bedroom, I lower myself onto the bed. I should be doing laundry or dusting the ceiling fans, but I force myself to try to relax. I contemplate what happened in Fr. Sean's office and face the realization that he is completely right about everything. Silently, I thank God for him and his presence in my life, and then I drift off into a deep sleep.

It is noon when I wake up and the events of the morning flood my consciousness. My brain is in overload and I don't want to think, so I turn on Devin's clock radio. It is still tuned to the classic rock station he liked to wake up to. Derek Farr, the lead singer of Gray Dawn, an 80's hair band, is singing:

It's easier to do
Than to be
Cover my eyes
Blind myself to reality
Can't stop for a minute
Allow myself to be naked
Won't be able to take it
I'd die from the pain...

I feel like God is speaking to me through this song. That is what I'm doing...racing through life so I don't have to face it. I haven't actually been living life as much as drifting through it. Then the realization comes that if I am ever going to feel joy, I am going to have to let myself experience the pain I have been avoiding and let God heal me.

God, what are you doing to me? Are you speaking to me through this music? Classic rock, Lord...really?

***

"Honey, you look terrible...what's going on?" Marissa says, standing in the doorway of her house. My sweet friend looks like an angel to me, especially after the night I've had.

Sitting at her kitchen counter with a cup of coffee, I tell Marissa the entire story of last night and this morning.

Her jaw is on the floor as I finish up. She lets out a long sigh. "Oh, my word. I've been trying to tell you this stuff for a year. They are right and it's good that you're finally listening."

My eyebrows practically fly off my head. "Really? Why...why don't I remember?"

She shrugs. "I don't know...all in God's time. Maybe now is the time He chose for you to get this message. Maybe now it's time to heal."

4

Fr. Sean moves his chair closer to his desk and absent-mindedly runs his finger under his collar. "So, let's figure out what we need to do for Lent, Jel. Let's set some spiritual goals for you."

Ash Wednesday is in a couple of weeks and I am here in Fr. Sean's office for spiritual direction.

"Well, I have been doing the prayer in front of the tabernacle and, I have to say Father, it is helping, although it is painful. God seems to be showing me my role in what went wrong in my marriage; in not having an attitude of service toward my husband. I mean, Dev didn't either...we didn't make each other a priority."

He smiles, compassionately. "All of this is good. He is purifying you. He wants to forgive you for these things and He also wants you to forgive yourself. Now, what about adding some more prayer to your day?

"I started using Magnificat. It came in the mail the other day, Father. It said it was a gift subscription...was that you?" Magnificat is a small magazine that prints the daily prayers of the Church. When used routinely, it keeps a person completely focused on God and immersed in scripture.

"Oh, Jel, I wish I could afford to buy all my parishioners Magnificat subscriptions, but I can't. Could it have been a relative?"

"No."

"Well, just be thankful and offer up some prayers for the one who sent it." He flips through a folder and pulls out a sheet of paper. "Here is the Litany of Humility. I'd like you to pray this daily as well."

"You're killing me, Father," I say.

"With kindness," he laughs, "You're going to like the next bit of direction I have for you, Jel. Continue pampering yourself. Don't give up anything for Lent."

"Father! Is that even allowed?"

"I'm your spiritual director; you're supposed to do what I tell you because I pray for you and I ask the Holy Spirit for help, and what I got was that you're supposed to bask in God's love this Lent and allow Him to show you how precious you are. Let him spoil you. Are there things you have wanted to do for yourself that you held back on?"

"Well... lots of stuff, Father."

"Go for them, within reason, of course. I don't mean ditching your kids and going to Vegas or anything," he chuckles. "But pamper yourself. Allow yourself to feel loved. And by all means, keep up with daily Mass, prayer, scripture reading and litany."

"If you won't let me give anything up, can I at least fast on Fridays instead of simply abstaining from meat?"

Fr. Sean grins. "I'll allow it. Jel, I can't wait to see how God will work on you. He loves you so much and He really wants you to know it."

***

Today my self-pampering activity was to take a nap. I allowed myself to sleep for an hour in the late morning and, I have to say, it was luxurious. Rubbing my eyes, I climb out of bed. My stomach is growling, so I head to the kitchen. As I eat a tuna fish sandwich, I make a list of things I have wanted to do for myself, but have been putting off.

1. Get makeover
2. Redecorate house
3. Exercise
4. Read
5. Haircut?

Once I am done, I wash up, put on my sneakers and walk the half mile to Marissa's. We live in a semi-rural area near the lake. There are several subdivisions close by, but the houses in our neighborhood, if you can call it that, are rather far apart, because we all have over an acre of land. There are no sidewalks on the street we share, which is a county road, but I like that the walk to see my best friend gives me a bit of a workout.

Marissa's house is a sprawling ranch with a walkout basement. Her husband, John, is a carpenter and did most of the finishing work himself. As Marissa lets me into her cheerful foyer, I pull my list out of my pocket. She looks it over.

"Ambitious," she says, with an enthusiastic grin. "And I see you haven't ruled out the haircut."

I roll my eyes. "I put that in to placate you," I chide. "Do you still know that woman who does the estate sales?"

"Maureen? Yeah! I can set up a meeting, if you want."

I smile. "Yes, it's time to get rid of the pretentious furniture, I think."

Marissa gives me a squeeze. "That means getting rid of everything Devin, honey."

Shaking my head, I say, "I'm keeping the bedroom and the kids' rooms, of course, but everything else will be sold. The Cooke Family is officially going casual."

Marissa's brows come together. "Jel, don't you think that if you would have asked Dev, he would have compromised on the furniture?"

"He would have," I nod. "I know he would have, but I wanted to let him have his way. I thought that was being a good wife to him."

Marissa sighs, "Being a good wife means communicating your needs to your husband and compromising, if need be. One person shouldn't swallow the other one up."

"Devin didn't swallow me up, I let myself get absorbed by him...and everyone and everything else. My life is apparently a train wreck. At least everyone I know thinks so and now I have to fix it," I say, the anger surfacing in my voice. "You know, Mar, there is something I don't get. You are a pretty busy woman yourself. How is it that you can get so much done all the time and be everything to everyone and not melt down, like me?"

"Well, you have to make God a priority. As soon as I open my eyes I pray and I keep going back to Him throughout the day, so that He's my focus. Then everything else seems to fall into place." Marissa tucks a wayward strand of hair behind her ear, puts her hand on her hip, then cocks an eyebrow. "Didn't Father give you some books on this stuff?"

Sheepishly I admit I haven't even cracked them open yet.

"Well, one of your goals was to read," she mock punches my arm, "so get on it, girl."

***

I must have heard Ray Charles on the radio singing "Hit the Road Jack" at least five times in the past two days. How guilty it makes me feel when he sings about how the woman treats him so mean.

I decide that it is time I made my apology to Jack. I can't bring myself to call him, so I head over to the card store. I spend 37 minutes looking for just the right one. Puppies, kittens, children, flowers...ugh...nothing seems appropriate for the card I want to send. Finally I come across one that has a black and white image of a medieval-looking circular staircase. The photo is taken from above and you can see how the staircase winds around itself, reminding me of a nautilus. The picture evokes a feeling of peace and seems right for my apology to Jack. I head to the register, purchase the card, then make my way to the parking lot and get in my van. I know that I will never complete the task if I take the card home, so I fish a pen out of my pocketbook and compose an apology:

Dear Jack,

I want to sincerely apologize for the way I treated you the night we went to Frankie's. What I did and said was rude and completely uncalled for.

I hope you will find it in your heart to forgive me.

Angela

There...short, sweet and to the point. But something is nagging at me and I open my Magnificat to the prayers I said this morning. I remember that there was a quote from scripture that stood out to me. There it is, from the book of Isaiah. *'By waiting and by calm you shall be saved, in quiet and in trust your strength lies.'* For some reason I am compelled to add it to the card, so I write, 'Is 30:15' underneath my name. Before I lose my nerve, I stuff the card into the envelope and seal it, then head to the post office and mail it. As I am driving home, I wonder what Jack will think when he opens the card and I say a quick prayer that it will bring him peace.

5

I'm thrilled with the results of the tag sale. I netted enough to furnish my living room, dining room and rec room and add a pretty good pad to the checking account.

Using mostly Craigslist and inexpensive stores like Hobby Lobby and Target, I was able to create spaces that reflect me and the kids. My one splurge was a deep, soft brown leather couch and matching chair that I bought at a furniture outlet for the living room. I got contemporary end tables and book shelves in a dark wood and an area rug and curtains with deep red and pea green tones. I put matching pillows and a throw on the couch. I didn't go for what was stylish, but what I personally like and feel comfortable with. Instead of being formal and pretentious, the living room is now cheerful and comfortable. The kids enjoy it more now, because it is not so formal.

In the dining room I replaced the ornate set with a casual counter height table and high back stools that seat eight. For the window, I made a valance out of a deep red chenille fabric. I can't sew, so I used stitch witchery and according to Marissa, the results were good. On the walls, I added sconces of brown wrought iron that have cut glass beads hanging from them to catch the light. For each side of the dining room window, I found two Bouguereau prints, of women holding water jars, for a song. I bought stock frames for them at Hobby Lobby and had mats cut to fit. These prints remind me of the Bible story of the woman at the well. I love that story because Jesus is so gentle and kind to the woman, yet he leads her to the realization of how her life has gotten off track. Lately I really identify with that story.

I enlisted the kids' help in the rec room. We decided it should be a place where their friends would like to come and hang out, so we designed it accordingly. The boys repainted the walls a creamy beige and freshened the white trim. We got some white book shelves from Target to store games and music and I moved Devin's Bose stereo down as well. We found two wooden trunks; one on Craigslist and one at a thrift store and spray painted them white for Rosie's toys. We added a futon and lots of large cushions for the kids to lounge on. While out shopping at a craft store one day, I found some very large letters, so I bought WWJD and spray painted them a deep red and hung them on the wall above the compact refrigerator and microwave we had bought for sodas and popcorn. The boys found a couple of Lord of the Rings posters on eBay and we framed and hung those as well.

To add to the rec room walls, I went through all our photographs and found pictures of Devin with the kids and framed them. It was easy to find images of him with the boys. All I could find of him and Rosie was a picture of Devin holding her in the hospital after she was born. Poor Rosie. She never really had a profound relationship with her father. As a matter of fact, Devin mostly paid attention to Sam, because Sam is quite a lot like his father. Devin never understood Ben's creativity and pushed him hard into team sports. I know it was his way of trying to bond with his son and he did the best he could, but I feel sad for the kids nonetheless. Rosie needs a father figure. *Lord, I don't know what you have in store for me, but I think my kids need a father figure in their lives. If this is your plan, please help me see what your will is and be obedient to it.*

There is a rhythm to my life now. I have taken Fr. Sean's advice and incorporated prayer throughout my day. Now it is easier to focus on the important things and let the trivial stuff slide. I'm amazed at how much time I spent on busy work before my talk with Father. I was worried about giving up my ministries, but other women stepped up right away. I guess God knew I needed this time and arranged for everything to fall into place.

I love being home during the day and focusing my attention on my family. When Devin was alive, I tended to keep busy so I wouldn't have time to think about how we'd grown apart. Then, when he died, I kept myself busy to keep my mind off of his death and the guilt I felt about it. Now I pray and work for my children, taking time out to take care of myself. The only time I spend away from the kids is during my Thursday night classes, and once a month during Youth Group, but even then I am with the boys. The end result is that I am happier and more relaxed and my family functions as a cohesive unit. The children have picked up on my cues and even they seem more content.

***

Spring is creeping up on us. The snow has melted, the days are milder and tiny buds are peeping up from the soggy earth. I remember last year being so angry at the onset of spring. It was as if nature itself had staged an all-out assault on me. I felt dead inside and anything that even hinted at life was completely repulsive. This year, I welcome and embrace it. The pain from Devin's death is still there, but I feel that I can live with it now, whereas before it had consumed me.

With the change of seasons, the idea of renewal blooms in my brain and I decide that it is time to get that makeover. I have always used makeup that I bought at the drugstore, but now, at 40, I decide that it is time to get serious, so I take the drive to Dillard's. There is a perky young girl named Selena behind the Origins counter.

"I'm a single mom and I need a whole new look," I tell her.

Selena wraps me in a burgundy cape and proceeds to scrub, buff and moisturize my face until it feels like a baby's butt.

"And now for some color," she says, brushing

foundation on my skin. "What are we thinking...subdued or glam?"

"I think I'll start with subdued and come back another time for glam," I say.

"You have dark eyes and hair and a light olive complexion, so you should be wearing cool colors," says Selena, "I noticed when you came in you had peach tones on. Get rid of that stuff. From now on it's light or dark pink, plum or a cool red...that's it."

"Seriously?" I ask, "I have always worn the warm colors. I thought since I have brown eyes..."

"No, no, no...it's a common mistake. I'm telling you, you're a Winter, if I ever saw one...*not* a Fall. Trust me, I have read the book *Color Me Beautiful* from cover to cover. I know. If you use these shades, they will bring out your natural beauty." She brushes some eyeliner on my left eyelid.

"Ever think about going short on your hair? It would really highlight those beautiful cheekbones of yours."

I chuckle. "My best friend is constantly hounding me about cutting my hair. You know, I just may do it."

Selena applies a lip pencil in a metallic red called *Pearly Jam* and then holds up the mirror for me. I am astounded. I look fresher and more...me.

I leave with anti-aging moisturizer, foundation, two lipsticks, an eye pencil and mascara. On the way home I stop at Marissa's and wind up staying for coffee.

"Oh! Look at you!" she squeals.

"I don't look too glammed up, do I?"

Marissa shakes her head. "No. Simple," she smiles. "It's like more of your inner beauty has come out. Good changes, Jel."

Looking into her coffee cup, she asks, "And speaking of changes...tell me where are we in the process of calling Jack?"

I sigh. "I still don't think it's the right time, Mar."

"Are you praying?" she raises one eyebrow.

"Yes...yes, I really am praying, but I'm getting nothing."

Marissa walks over and hugs me. "Then keep praying. God will give you an answer when it's the right time."

"I hope so," I whisper.

6

"Marissa," I lament. "Why did I say yes to her? This is such a stupid idea." Cherie from the funeral luncheon committee had called and talked me into going out on a date with her brother-in-law, who is coming to Kansas City on business for a couple of days this week. His name is Ted, he's 43, lives in L.A. and he scouts out prospective real estate for a national big box store.

"No. You're doing Cherie a favor by helping entertain her brother-in-law while he's in town. Maybe you'll make a new friend in the process. Besides, Cherie's husband is a really nice guy. How bad could his brother be?"

"Well, for one, he is 43 and not married."

"You're 40 and not married," Marissa points out.

"I think I'm going to call her and tell her I would feel comfortable if it was a double date, given it's my first foray into the dating realm," I say.

"Good idea, although that's not true, technically."

"You mean Jack? Jack was a slice of pizza. This is a date."

If Jack was just a slice of pizza then why do I feel guilty to be going out with someone else?

The kids are at Marissa's and I am dressing for my date with Ted, Cherie and her husband, Tom. I slip on my black dress pants, a blue and black dress top and my black mules. I add some red lipstick, silver hoop earrings and a healthy dose of gel to make my hair nice and full. I should be excited about this, but I have been dreading this evening and I don't know why. Maybe I am just a killjoy. I am trying to muster some enthusiasm when the doorbell rings.

"Ted?" I say, slipping my pocketbook over my shoulder and walking out the door. "Nice to meet you."

I smile and extend my hand.

He is average height, with neat black hair that is thinning slightly. His teeth are straight and white and he is very tanned. His eyes are a clear blue that should be attractive, but I think I may detect some insincerity behind them.

Ted doesn't shake my hand, but leans in and kisses me on the cheek, dangerously close to my mouth. I take a step backward to make a point. He doesn't notice because he is checking me out. Apparently, he likes what he sees because he says enthusiastically, "Nice to meet you too, Jill."

"It's Jel."

As he lets me into the passenger side of his Cadillac Escalade, I ask Ted, "Where are Cherie and Tom?"

"Meeting us at the restaurant."

"Oh," I say, disappointed, "So, where are we going?"

"The barbecue place in Zona Rosa," says Ted, signaling and merging onto 152 heading west.

At least we are going someplace I like. Zona Rosa is a big shopping district outside the city proper. It is chock full of restaurants, retail shops and upscale lofts. More than an outdoor mall, it is like a city unto itself. It is one of my favorite places to go and walk, because the window shopping distracts me and I can get some good cardio in.

Cherie and Tom are already at the table when we arrive. Everyone orders barbecue but me. I am nervous and afraid the heavy food will kill my stomach, so I order a chicken Caesar salad instead. Cherie and I chat about the goings on at church for a few minutes, and then the guys start to reminisce about their childhood. Ted seems relaxed and more down to earth when he is talking with his brother, so I let my guard down a bit and try to enjoy the evening.

Surprisingly, dinner turns out to be pleasant and when it is over, Ted suggests we all go for a walk. Tom and

Cherie decline. They have to wake up early to get their kids to soccer in the morning. I toy with the idea of begging off, but I like to walk and it is a nice night. Besides, maybe Marissa is right; maybe Ted and I will become friends. I feel bad that I haven't actually given him a chance.

We begin our walk and immediately Ted puts his arm around my waist. I move over, but the sidewalks are busy and I can't get completely away from him.

"Do you want to stop in somewhere for a couple of drinks?" he asks.

"No thanks," I say, "I'm enjoying the walk. It's a beautiful night, but I'm going to need to get home soon. I also have to deal with kids' activities tomorrow." This is not a fabrication. The kids are having friends over...in the early afternoon. We are walking past the parking garage and Ted takes my hand and leads me inside. Before I have time to think about what he is doing, his hands are all over me and he is kissing me passionately. I pull back and he laughs, then leans in and kisses me again. I move away from him again, this time taking a giant step backward. "Ted, I barely know you. I'm not comfortable doing this." He smiles at me and I think of a hungry wolf staring at a brace of rabbits.

"Then let me help you relax," he says, wrapping his arms around me tightly and kissing my neck.

I start to shake and fear rises inside my chest. *What if he won't stop?* "Please, Ted. Let me go. I can't do this," I say, the alarm apparent in my voice.

He looks up, annoyed. "What? You were serious?"

I nod while extricating myself from his embrace.

"I took you out; I paid for your dinner...what did you expect?" He says, gripping my upper arms tightly.

"Honestly, I thought I might make a friend," I say and wriggle out of his vice grip.

"Are you from another century? Don't you know how

this works, Jel?" Ted's face is beet red and I think that it will be mere seconds before smoke starts to come out of his ears.

Taking a cleansing breath, I say, "You know, I thought I did, but apparently I don't. So, let me make it up to you, Ted." I fish a twenty out of my wallet and stuff it into his breast pocket. "Here is reimbursement for my meal. I guess that lets me off the hook for the physical pleasure I was supposed to provide, doesn't it? So, we're even. And, to sweeten the deal, I will save you the drive home, so you don't have to worry about the gas money you might have wasted."

He starts to say something, but I hold up my hand. "You know, Ted, I had a pretty nice time tonight and I thought maybe we could be friends. I apologize for not realizing this was some sort of business transaction." Then I turn and walk as fast as my feet will take me into Marshalls and make a beeline for the fitting room. Once I get into a stall, I fish my phone out of my pocketbook and call Marissa.

"Oh, my! Jel! Are you okay?"

"Physically, I am unscathed," I tell her, "but I hit a snag and I need you to pick me up at the Marshalls in Zona."

"Leaving now. I'll call when I am in front."

Then I sit down on the bench in the stall and cry.

***

With a plate of my homemade pumpkin bars in hand, I let myself into Marissa's house and find her sitting at the kitchen counter in front of a pile of bills, poring over her checkbook.

"Hey, Bud, that's no way to spend your birthday," I say, as she looks up from her bill paying. Her eyes grow wide and she lets out a whoop. Standing up, she throws her arms around me.

"You did it! I can't believe you finally did it! Honey, you look ravishing!" she says, as I spin around.

"Well, when I had that date from hell with Ted, he remarked that he liked my hair, so I figured that was my cue to get it all cut off," I say, wryly.

"That, and not your best friend badgering you for years? Hmpf," she sniffs, in mock indignation.

"Shut up and make the coffee," I jest.

"Okay, Posh."

"Huh?"

"Your haircut is just like Victoria Beckham's. You know, real short and stacked in the back and kind of like a bob in front? Except yours is fuller and more feminine, in my opinion...Spice Girl," she chuckles, bumping her hip against mine.

"Call me that again and I will never bake you another pumpkin bar as long as I live."

"I give."

7

The call I have been dreading comes at 9:57 a.m. on a rainy Thursday in late May.

"Mrs. Cooke? This is Desmond Jones from the Missouri State Attorney's office. I'm just calling to inform you that Mr. Jenkins' sentencing hearing is scheduled for next Wednesday at 11:15 a.m. Will you be able to make a statement?"

So here it is...the last piece of my former life, falling into place. I know what I have to do, but I hesitate.

"Mrs. Cooke?"

"Yes, Mr. Jones, of course I will be there. Should I arrive early?"

"Get there a few minutes early, to be on the safe side. Things can run over, and it is possible that it could run much later. Never can tell."

As I hang up the phone, I start to feel nauseous. All the emotions of the past year churn inside me like a rough sea. I want to do this and I know I should do this, but I am going to need some help on Wednesday. I can ask Marissa, but I am going to need her in case things go long and the kids need someplace to go after school.

I need guidance, so I close my eyes and pray a silent prayer of the heart, a union with Jesus in His passion. I give the heavy feeling over to God and breathe deeply and evenly. I can feel tears running out of the corners of my eyes, but I continue to breathe and unite my pain with Jesus on the cross. Slowly the heaviness ebbs and the tears abate. My eyes are still closed and an image of Jack breaks through into my consciousness. Something deep inside me says, "It's time."

I find the phone, then walk down the hall to my bedroom and take out my jewelry box. In the bottom of the main compartment is a business card. I sigh. My palms are sweaty as I dial the phone, and I can hear my heart beating as if it's inside my head, not my chest.

"This is Jack," I hear, as he picks up and suddenly I wonder if I'm doing the right thing. "Hello?" he asks, softly, and I realize he must know it's me.

I can barely find my voice. "You...you made a promise to me once, Jack, that if I ever needed help..."

"Angela, are you in trouble?"

Goodness, I've worried him. Not what I was trying to do, but it is so scary to be on the phone with him, especially after all this time.

"No, I'm sorry...I'm not in any trouble...I just, well, Wednesday morning is the sentencing hearing for the guy who killed Devin. I have to make a statement and I..."

Oh, this sounds ridiculous! Doubt begins creeping in at the sanity of this phone call and I falter. "You know, on second thought, I shouldn't have called you, Jack. I'm so--"

"No," he cuts me off, "I am glad you did and I would be happy to go and offer whatever support I can, Angela."

"I'm probably going to need a ride home..."

"I can do that," he says, "What time do I need to be at the courthouse?"

"It's 11:15 in room 162."

I can hear him scribbling. "Got it," he says, and then, more tenderly, "Thank you for asking, Angela."

"I...I can't really talk right now, Jack. I just found out and..." My throat feels tight and I can sense a sob emerging from deep inside me.

"I understand. This must be so hard for you. I will offer my Masses for you until I see you on Wednesday."

I managed a strangled, "Thank you." Then I hang up and let the tears come. All the pain I thought I had gotten through, the feelings of loss and anger, all of it are drudged up and churning around inside me like a violent tempest. I cry until I am totally spent. Then, lying on the living room floor, I begin to pray.

"Oh God, help me! You know how I feel. When You stretched your arms out on that cross and called out to your Father to forgive your murderers You felt like I do right now. Help me to forgive! I know I need to because You want me to, but also because I need to be an example to my kids. Please...please help me."

Eyes closed, I lie there, exhausted, and an image comes into my mind. It is of a baby, a newborn, swaddled and held by a lovely woman. I instantly know that this is Mary, the Mother of God, and then I see Jesus come up next to her. He strokes the baby's head gently and holds his finger out. The infant grabs onto it and Jesus laughs with delight. Somehow I am aware that this infant is Richard Jenkins, the man who killed my husband. The knowledge that God loves this man as much as He loves me or my children or anyone else, for that matter, floods my mind.

A long sigh escapes my lips. *Who am I not to forgive?* I feel a sense of peace and a new resolve. I can do this. With God's help, I can do this. And Jack said he will offer his Masses for me. It feels good to know that I am prayed for.

***

There is less than a week to prepare for this statement, so I call Fr. Sean to ask his advice. "Wow...big stuff, Jel," he says, "I'll pray for you. I think you need to ask the Holy Spirit to guide you in this and go from there. Fasting may be helpful as well. Why don't you give something up as a fast? Maybe that afternoon cappuccino?"

This is good advice. Now I have focus.

***

The children have left for school and I'm alone in the house. In my bedroom, I methodically dress myself in the black suit I wore to Devin's funeral. I step into matching platform pumps and question whether I should wear them. It's been a year and a half since I've walked in heels and I'm no longer used to them. But no other shoes complement this suit, so I keep the pumps on and hope I'm not hobbling by the end of the day. Once the hearing is over, this outfit will be history. Part of me wants to hold onto it forever. Part of me wants to give it away and never look back.

My stomach is doing flip flops and the lump in my throat prevents me from swallowing anything of substance, so, once again, I don't eat. I drink a small glass of orange juice to hydrate myself, but I have to struggle to get it down. "Are you sure you don't want me there?" Marissa asks, one more time, as she drives south on 169 toward Kansas City. I know she's a little hurt, but I want to know that the kids will be taken care of after school and, frankly, I want Jack there. Something feels right about it that I can't explain.

"Mar, it's not that I don't want *you* there. Please, it's nothing personal. You understand that, don't you?"

"But what if you break down on the stand? What if something goes wrong?"

I take a deep breath. "Jack is going to be there."

"Oh my word!" she yells, "Honey, I don't know whether to hug you or slap you! You *called* him? You *called* him and you didn't *tell* me?!"

"Something feels right about him being there, Marissa."

"Did you pray?" she says it like it is a question in a pop quiz she is giving.

"I've been praying for four months about this. Yes, I prayed."

"Okay, then I won't be mad at you. So he said yes? Is he driving you home? He'd better be driving you home."

I nod, and she bounces in her seat as she drives. "I got it! I'll keep the kids for dinner tonight!"

"I have a lasagna in the fridge that I put together last

night. Why don't you keep them till dinner time and then you and John come and eat with us?"

"Jack is eating with you?" she asks, incredulous.

"No, Mar! It would be a little inappropriate to have him over for dinner tonight, don't you think?"

"Well, who am I to say?" she answers sarcastically.

I laugh. Well, if anything, she has taken my mind off of what I am about to do.

She pulls up in front of the courthouse. There are no spots, so I open the door to get out. Then I turn around and give her a tight hug. "You have no idea how much I appreciate everything you've done to help me with this. I love you, Mar."

There are tears in her eyes. "Go get 'em," she whispers, and mock punches my upper arm.

I go through security and find my way to room 162. It is crowded and I don't see Jack, but it is still a little early. That's okay. I don't want to see him before my statement. I'm afraid I will lose my focus. I squeeze in between a portly gentleman in an out-of-date suit and a smartly dressed woman who is engrossed in something on her Blackberry. I close my eyes and try to block out the noise. Finally, after what seems like hours, they bring out Richard Jenkins. He looks much the same as he did when his face was plastered all over the news on TV. Dark blonde, greasy hair, watery blue eyes, pock-marked face...the image of a drug addict. I try to reach into my memory of the image of the baby I saw in prayer and I remind myself that this man was created by and loved by God.

They call up the family of Sarah Moss, the college intern that Jenkins also killed. Sarah was the niece of the news anchor at the station, which is why it was a high profile case. Her father is making the statement. He is obviously seething with rage. My heart breaks for him, because I once knew that all-consuming hatred. Silently, I ask God to heal him of his pain. Mr. Moss' statement is a long hate-filled diatribe against Richard Jenkins. I try not to listen because I don't want to falter when my time comes. I decide to focus on Jenkins. I can only see his back, sitting up straight, stiff as a board. He seems frozen. *What would it be like to be hated?* This helps me find compassion for the man and I focus on that. Then I am aware of Mr. Moss being escorted down from the stand. My legs feel like Jell-O and my palms are sweating. "The court would like to call Mrs. Angela Cooke to make her statement." I stand up and walk slowly to the stand, praying all the way there.

The judge is in his mid-60's, with sparse gray hair and a kind face. "You may make your statement now, Mrs. Cooke." I can tell he is bracing himself for another rant.

"Mr. Jenkins," I say evenly, "of your own free will, you took drugs and got in a car and killed Miss Moss and my husband. My husband had a family...me and our three children. Our lives have been changed permanently as a result of your behavior. My daughter and sons have no father now, to guide them, care for them, provide for them. The past year and a half has been a difficult and painful one for us. I know that the pain will never really go away. It is starting to become manageable, but it will never disappear.

"I don't know how many others have been killed or their lives ruined by the drugs you dealt day after day. I would imagine there are many," I sigh and rub my forehead. "You have no power to change the past. None of us do. But we do have control over the future, which is why, Mr. Jenkins, my family and I have chosen to forgive you." At this point I start to sense noise and commotion, but I am focused and push it out of my consciousness. "My children and I cannot live our lives consumed with rage at what you did. It would destroy our family and that would gravely dishonor the memory of my husband. Mr. Jenkins, I want you to know that my children and I pray for you every day."

"Are you insane? He killed your husband!" I hear someone scream.

"Quiet down, now!" says the judge as he brings down his gavel.

Don't listen...don't listen...don't listen... Jenkins looks up at me and our eyes meet. Shakily, I go on. "I...I encourage you to amend your life. If you take advantage of all the opportunities available to you in prison, if you better yourself and face your past, then maybe no one else will be hurt by you. And maybe you will save yourself in the process."

Looking into Richard Jenkins' eyes, I see someone who is lost and in pain. He puts his head down and his shoulders begin to shake. "God bless you, Mr. Jenkins," I say, quietly.

"Are you kidding?" a voice roars, "Damn this monster to hell! He doesn't deserve to live!"

"That is enough!" the judge shouts, "Bailiff, escort the Moss family out of this courtroom please!"

The judge looks down at me from the bench. He runs a hand through his sparse hair and sweeps it over his face. He looks weary. "Mrs. Cooke, I appreciate your courage," he smiles, kindly. "Wait for the bailiff to get back and he will escort you out of the courtroom and past the Moss family."

I stand up to get down from the stand and suddenly I feel faint. My hands are jittery and I realize it is probably my blood sugar plummeting. All I've consumed in the past 24 hours is half a glass of orange juice and the toothpaste I accidentally swallowed when I brushed my teeth this morning. Cold beads of sweat pop out on my forehead and I am fading fast.

The bailiff approaches and grabs the back of my forearm. He steers me toward the door, but it is difficult, because there is a crowd pressing all around. I hear someone shouting at me, asking if I want to make a statement. Weakly, I shake my head. I stumble a bit and fall into the bailiff.

"You okay, Ma'am?" he asks.

"Need a second," I manage to whisper.

Suddenly, I feel a hand on my lower back. Startled, I look up and see Jack.

"I'm driving Mrs. Cooke home," he says to the bailiff.

"I still need to escort her out the door," the bailiff answers, and he and Jack both manage to navigate through the crowd, which has begun to thin slightly. Once we are out, Jack grabs my hand and sprints down the hall to get away from the commotion. I force myself to run with him. He leads me out a doorway and down the stone steps to the sidewalk. I feel my legs buckle and hear Jack yell, "Whoa! Are you okay?" as he wraps his arm around my waist to prevent me from falling.

"Too nervous to eat. Feel sick now," I manage.

"When was the last time you *did* eat, Angela?" he asks, his grip tightening as he realizes I could possibly pass out.

"Yesterday...lunch." I whisper.

"Can you make it two blocks to the car?"

"Slow," I croak, nodding. Jack patiently guides me down the street, but gives up and carries me the last half a block. He gets me into his car and reclines the seat so I can lie down. Almost immediately, I start to sense that light, floating feeling that I get before settling into a deep sleep. At first I fight it, but, believing that Jack will keep me safe, I succumb.

At one point, I become aware that Jack is talking to me, but I can't make out what he is saying. Something smells delicious, though, and a moan escapes my lips in response to my hunger. But the sleep grabs me again and I let it.

The next thing I know I am on my living room couch, swaddled in the throw that I keep draped over its arm. My shoes are off and my bare feet feel luxurious wrapped in the chenille blanket. I feel a strong arm behind my neck and a spoon being tipped into my mouth.

"Ummm..." Warm, fragrant broth spills past my lips and down my throat. The heat is invigorating.

"Ummm..." is all I can manage. I feel awake, but my body doesn't seem to want to cooperate.

Jack murmurs, "Good job, Angela. Keep eating the soup."

After a few more spoonfuls, I am able to lift my eyelids halfway. I see Jack's handsome face slightly above mine.

He smiles. "Your color is starting to come back. Thank goodness. You had me worried there for awhile."

I struggle to sit up on my own and he helps me, propping the pillows behind me. I can feel sleep creeping up on me again, though, and my eyes start to close.

"Oh, no you don't. Come on, let me feed you a little more of this and then you'll be able to eat on your own."

I can feel my eyes rolling up into my head.

Jack pats my cheek. "Angela, if you don't stay awake, the next stop is the ER."

I don't want to go to the hospital, so I fight to keep my eyes open and I eat every spoonful of soup Jack ladles into my mouth. Finally, consciousness wins over fatigue and a little strength comes.

"So hungry," I whisper.

"Can you eat on your own now?"

I nod.

"Good girl!" he says, happily. "I got Chinese. Do you want rice first or chicken?"

"Everything. I'm starving," I can still only manage to whisper.

He laughs and says, "That's what I want to hear," as he fills one of my ceramic pasta bowls with roast pork fried rice and some kind of chicken with vegetables. I attack the bowl as soon as he puts it in my hands, and then notice that he is saying grace. I'm so embarrassed!

"I prayed for the both of us," he grins. "Eat."

Wordlessly, I comply. He refills my bowl twice more and I polish off every bit of its contents.

"More?" he asks.

I shake my head. I cannot believe the volume of food I have just consumed. Compared to me, Jack ate like a bird.

"The only other time I have ever eaten like that was right after I gave birth to a child," I say. "Thank you so much for lunch, for *feeding* me lunch...for everything," I sigh. "I seem to be high maintenance when I am around you, Jack. I'm sorry."

In his best weatherman voice he says, "Well, the incidence of high maintenance is 100% right now, but we've only really spent time with each other twice. I'm confident the percentage will dip significantly with each date." He catches himself. "That is, ah, well, if you *want* to see me...socially...that is."

At this particular moment, the events of the day choose to come rushing at me like a freight train and suddenly, I burst into tears. Poor Jack. I can see the look of bewilderment on his face. Reaching out, I pull him toward me, bury my head in his chest and sob.

"Did I say--" he starts.

"Emotion overload!" I wail, into what was a crisp white shirt before I splattered it with tears and makeup smudges. "It's not you. It's not you at all," I sob.

I feel him relax and enfold me deeper into his embrace. The tears spill out until they are gone and then I rest my head on his shoulder.

"It's all done," I sigh. "Volume I of my life ended today."

Jack moves back a little so that we are face to face. "And what about Volume II?" he asks, earnestly. "Am I in that one?"

"I'm sure the Author would write you in if you asked nicely."

"I've been asking Him since the day I first spoke to you, Angela."

"And have you gotten an answer?"

"Well, He's left me some clues…signal graces; but I want to hear from you."

I want to tell Jack everything that I have been through during the last four months. I need to, but I struggle to find the words.

"Jack," I begin, "when you left me on my doorstep four months ago, I was very angry with you. I'm sorry. I shouldn't have said what I said or done what I did that night. I was wrong."

"You don't need to apologize again for that. I've forgiven you. Let it go," he says tenderly.

"Well, the reason I was so angry was because you had exposed a wound. It was like you ripped off the bandage I had spent years applying and all the bad stuff came spilling out at once. I was scared to face the problems I had become so good at running from, and I was humiliated that someone I barely knew could see me more clearly than I could see myself. It was painful, but it was the start of a healing. When I was in your class I had no concept of God's love for me. I mean, intellectually, I knew that God loved me…but I never personalized it or felt it in my heart. You were right that I had to learn to love myself first before I could possibly learn to love someone else."

"I don't need to hear you tell me I'm right, Angela. That's not what--"

I cut him off. "No, no…you don't strike me as a big, 'I told you so' kind of person, Jack. I just need to tell you this, okay?"

He nods and shifts his position so that he is a small distance away from me, then leans his head in slightly to listen to what I have to say.

"I didn't have a deep relationship with God. I relied mostly on myself to get through life and it was going to blow up in my face. But that night with you...and then Fr. Sean's direction... changed everything. He helped me begin to let go of my fear and trust God. It's been hard. It's no accident that much of this took place during Lent." I sigh and rub my eyes. "Father Sean actually instructed me *not* to give up anything for Lent, but to pamper myself instead. So here it is, Lent, the season of self-denial and what is Angela Cooke doing? She gets a makeover, starts exercising, sells her old furniture and redecorates her house. Let me tell you...there was a buzz in the parish, *that's* for sure."

Jack laughs. "When I saw you walk up to the stand today, I was amazed at the transformation."

"Good makeup and a talented hairdresser can have miraculous effects," I say.

He shakes his head. "What I mean is that instead of a lost soul who has no concept of her own beauty, I saw a confident woman who is comfortable in her skin. You seem to finally know who you are."

I sit up further and Jack helps readjust my pillows. "You sent me Magnificat, didn't you?" I ask.

"I wanted so much to send you a gift...I don't know why I chose that; it just seemed...right," Jack blushes slightly.

"It was the *best* gift. Thank you. It put me in touch with God and it gave a rhythm to my life. God has spoken to me so many times through the scriptures on those pages. It was just what I needed and it came exactly when I needed it."

As I speak, I can see puzzle pieces fitting together and I know that God is showing me a picture here.

"The thing you were most right about, though, was that if I would have started dating you then, the relationship would have been doomed to failure. At the time all I knew was that I was physically attracted to you and that was exciting to me. I was also at a place in my life where I would have expected you to save me from myself. Well, we both know that is an impossible task and too much to expect from anyone, don't we? But now, things are different with me, Jack. I'm working hard at giving up trying to control every aspect of my life and there is a peace that exists that wasn't there before. At this point in my life, I am not completely healed and I'm certainly not perfect, but I am learning to accept God's love and that is a good place to be, I think."

"What a beautiful way to begin the next volume," Jack says.

"But there is the problem of Jack," I sigh. "Where does Jack fit in? There have been times I have prayed and gotten a clear cut answer on things. Really...no doubt. But I've gotten no answers on you, Jack, and believe me, I've asked."

Jack looks crestfallen. "Nothing at all?" he whispers.

"No...not until just now. I never thought about the past few months objectively. I just lived through it and I'm grateful that I am a better person now than before. But one thing I noticed was that it was you who helped me become closer to God. You played a role in deepening my trust in Him and love for Him. He used you as an instrument in all of this and the fruit of that is peace in my life. So, that's what I am going to go by..." I smile. "...and I'll bet that's the longest 'yes' you have ever gotten when you asked a woman out on a date."

Jack is beaming. It warms my heart to see him so happy. He reaches out to take my hand. "May I?" he asks.

I put my hand in his and he gently pulls me to my feet and leads me in the direction of the front door.

"What are we doing?" I ask.

"Turning back time," he says as we walk through the door onto the porch. He steps down one step and I turn around to face him.

"Angela, would you like to have dinner with me this Friday?"

"Very much," I answer, as he picks me up and spins me around. He sets me down and I lose my balance and have to grab onto his arm to steady myself.

"Whoa! Hey, I'm sorry...I should have realized you're probably still weak."

"I am a little woozy," I say, as he helps me walk back into the house. I start to walk into the kitchen, to take out the lasagna, so it gets to room temperature before I put it in the oven, but Jack leads me into the living room.

"I'll take care of that. You rest."

Thankfully, I slip back onto the couch and he drapes the blanket over me. I can hear Jack moving around in the kitchen. Cabinets are opening and closing.

"Need any help in there?" I call.

"Nope. I'm good," he answers. He comes into the living room with a glass of cold water. "Drink," he urges, "We don't want you dehydrated." Then he disappears into the kitchen again. He returns with two cups of cappuccino sprinkled with cinnamon. It smells heavenly.

"I see you found my Mukka."

"I have the same pot," Jack says, as he touches his cup to mine. "To Volume II, Chapter 1."

Jack settles into the arm chair next to the couch and puts his right ankle on his left knee. We silently sip from our cups for awhile.

"Angela, are you doing okay?"

"Yes, I feel much better thanks to you."

Jack's brow furrows and he shakes his head, slightly. "No, I mean how are *you*? I'm just wondering how you're feeling about what went on today."

"My brain feels fried," I answer, massaging the area between my eyes with one hand. "You know, I think it would be best if I just let it be and move on. Like a birth. For nine months of pregnancy the focus is on the labor and delivery and then it happens and it's over with. Your life is completely changed by it, but you don't dwell on the birth process because it no longer has relevance." I nod my head in determination. "Yeah...I didn't think I would feel this way, but the book has definitely been closed on this. I feel free of it. It's a good feeling...but exhausting."

Jack gets up from the chair and sits on the floor next to the couch, so that he is closer to me. "I am so proud of you," he whispers, and I feel myself blushing. Never once in my life did I ever blush until I met Jack Bartolomucci.

***

Marissa insists on doing the kids' after dinner chores so we can chat without an audience. "I know how court went...how did *Jack* go?" she asks, eagerly.

At dinner, I had related the story of the sentencing hearing to the kids, but left out what happened with Jack. I give Marissa all the details I omitted when telling the story to my children. "And he *was* the one who sent Magnificat."

"Honey...he sounds like a perfect gentleman!"

"He is, Mar; and so thoughtful and kind. He's almost too good to be true."

"Or maybe he's a gift from God."

8

As I am leaving Mass my phone beeps. It's Jack.

No meat on Fri?

I text him back. *I give up coffee instead.*

That's a killer! C U @ 5:30

I smile. I can't wait.

Jack adds a bottle of wine to our order and thanks the waiter. "Tell me something about you that I don't already know, Angela," he says. We are at an Italian restaurant in Zona Rosa, of all places, and I am trying to push the unpleasant flashbacks out of my mind.

"You first," I say.

"Hmmm...my birthday is in October; on the 7th."

"The Feast of Our Lady of the Rosary?"

He nods. "So...when is yours?"

I turn beet red and avoid his gaze.

"Angela?" he asks, his eyebrows going up, expectantly.

Sighing, I look him in the eye. "It's...um...June...first."

Jack's eyes grow wide and he puts both hands flat on the table. *"Yesterday?* Angela, why didn't you tell me?"

"Well, what would I have said?" I raise my hand in the air. "'It's my birthday...me, me, me, me, *me*!' Anyway, don't you think what you did for me Wednesday was gift enough? Knowing you were there and praying for me helped me to keep my resolve. And besides, I like Chinese."

Jack laughs and shakes his head as the waiter pours wine into our glasses. He touches his glass to mine and says, "A belated Happy Birthday to a woman that I can't wait to get to know."

As we are finishing up dinner, Jack suggests we go for a walk. He must see the look on my face because he asks,

"What is wrong? You look upset."

I decide to tell him about the bad experience I had with Ted here at Zona Rosa. "It was a one date deal," I say, "which is why I agreed to see him in the first place."

As I recount my date from hell, Jack moves over onto the seat next to me. "Angela, I promise you that I will never, ever treat you like that. I hope you know that you can trust me."

"I do know that I can trust you. After all, I was passed out and defenseless two days ago and all you did was feed me soup. If that doesn't scream 'trustworthy' I don't know what does."

All of a sudden, a terrible remorse grips me.

"Jack" I whisper, "I did the same thing to you that Ted did to me. I treated you terribly."

He gives me a bashful smile. "On the surface it would seem that way, but I think I know why you did that and I don't think it was because you were trying to get some sexual satisfaction out of it."

"No, I wasn't. But I honestly don't know why I...kissed you."

"You were in a lot of pain," he says, looking at me kindly. "I think you wanted to make an emotional connection with me."

I sigh. "Do you do this with all the women you date?"

Jack's eyebrows go together. "Do what?"

"Read them like a book?"

He grins. "Only you, Angela."

Being with Jack seems to have a soothing effect on me; like salve on a wound. I know, deep down, that he accepts me for who I am, with no judgments. This gives me a sense of freedom that I haven't felt with any other man in my life, with the exception of my father.

Jack looks at me and chuckles.

"What?"

"Angela, did you really stuff a twenty in Ted's pocket?"

Looking back on it, I can laugh now. "Yes, indeed."

***

Tuesday afternoon I am slicing cucumbers for our dinner salad, when I hear the doorbell.

"Mama! Someone is at the door for you!" Rosie calls from the landing.

When I open the door, I see a delivery guy standing there with a huge rectangular box in his arms. The box contains two dozen long stem red roses with a cut crystal vase. The card says, "Happy un-Birthday. Fondly, Jack."

***

"He sent you roses?" Marissa asks, excitedly, as she leans in to inhale their fragrance.

Marissa was away for a couple of days visiting her cousin in Des Moines, so we've planned a girls' night. Marissa brought over two loads of laundry. I have about four to fold. If we get finished at a decent hour, we will treat ourselves to a game of Yahtzee and a decaf cappuccino.

"He did! Oh, the date was wonderful, Mar. He was so respectful. He actually listened to everything I had to say."

Marissa laughs. "Honey, that's what he's supposed to do! So, are you going to see him again?"

"Friday."

"The kids will come to us for dinner, then. You enjoy yourself and I'll make sure they get to bed at a decent time."

"I love you, Mar. You're too good to me," I say giving her a quick hug. "Can I ask you something?"

She pulls a dryer sheet off of a towel and balls it up in her fist. "What?" she asks, tossing it into the kitchen garbage pail.

"I feel emotions when I am with Jack that I can't

identify. It's like I don't even know myself and that scares me."

"Well, honey, you were numb for so long that you may be out of practice," Marissa smiles. "I also think this man is awakening something in you. I mean, going back to the winter, you have blossomed since you met him."

I sigh. "It's like I vacillate between attraction and fear when I am with him. On the one hand, I am very comfortable with him; more than I feel I should be at this point in our relationship. But I also fear that he will want more from me than I can give right now."

"Well, what do *you* want out of the relationship?"

"I don't know."

***

Jack parks his car in front of Frankie's and opens the door for me. "I hope this place doesn't give you terrible flashbacks," I say to him as he walks me to the door.

Jack smiles, "No, I have good memories of Frankie's, Angela. It's your front porch that spooks me."

We both laugh as we approach the counter. Frankie is at the register, handing someone a tray. He looks up and sees Jack and me, and then his whole demeanor changes. He doesn't look happy at all. Jack walks over to him, but I hang back. I see a heated exchange between the two men. Finally, Frankie seems to calm down and they both look over at me. Jack holds out his hand and I walk toward him and grasp it.

"Hello, Frankie," I say, nervously. "It's very nice to see you again."

He runs his hand through his hair. "Geez, Angela, I didn't recognize you at all. You changed your hair. You look so different. I thought Giacomo came in here with another woman. I was about to take him out back and teach him a lesson."

I give Frankie a big hug and whisper in his ear, "Thanks for the vote of confidence, Pizza Man."

Frankie smiles. "Go sit down, you two. Dinner's on me."

Jack picks a booth in the corner and sits facing the wall. I noticed he did this the last time we went to dinner as well.

"Do you like to look at the wall when you eat, Jack?" I ask.

He chuckles. "Not particularly. I just like to make sure there are no distractions when I am with you, so I can pay attention and hear what you're saying."

"Really? So you sit that way on purpose then?"

"Angela, everything I do has a purpose."

"This date has a purpose, too?"

"Of course it does. Doesn't it for you?" He sounds surprised.

I sigh. "I don't know. You're the one with all the dating experience. I'm a little rusty."

"I date for two reasons, Angela. One is to make a new friend; the other is to get to know a woman enough so that I can make a decision as to whether or not we should explore the possibility of marriage."

"Are you always this serious?" I ask.

"Only about the important stuff. Look, I'm going to be honest with you. I'm not getting any younger and I'd really like to settle down. I need to date a woman who would be open to that possibility. Are we on the same page?"

A wave of fear washes over me. *What am I getting myself into here?* "Jack, I'm not exactly sure what I want at this point in time. I can tell you that I enjoy spending time with you and I am thrilled that we seem to have so much in common. But...my husband died a year and a half ago and I can't think marriage right now. Friendship I can do."

He sighs and runs his hand through his hair. "Do you mean that this whole thing begins and ends at friendship, or would you be open to something more in the future?"

Frankie appears at our booth with a tray of food. "Fried calamari, Caesar salad and rigatoni a la vodka!" he announces.

"Frankie, I didn't know you did this kind of food. It looks delicious," I say, sincerely.

"We cater, too, so here you go. Eat up...and feel free to stay as long as you want." He winks at Jack, who stands up and embraces him.

"Thanks, Buddy. Appreciate it."

"I'll be back later with dessert," Frankie says, making his way toward the kitchen.

"Should we pray?" I ask, ready to dig into the meal.

"As I recall, you were just about to answer my question."

"I am seriously thinking about my answer, Jack. Maybe the omega threes in the calamari will help my brain work it all out."

Dramatically, I put my hand over my heart. "If I promise an amazingly profound answer, will you let me eat?"

Jack smiles and then leads us in grace.

As we eat, thoughts bounce around my brain like a game of pong. *Enlighten me, Lord. Help me to know what to do in this situation. I am fearful and hesitant. Please help me.*

"Jack, have you ever been in a serious relationship with a woman before?" I ask.

"Once, when I was in my twenties."

"What was she like?"

"Her name was Sharona. She was beautiful, inside and out."

"Sharona is a Jewish name."

Jack nods. "I worked in New York City in my uncle's friend's office during the summers while I was in graduate school. I saw her a few times on the subway. After awhile we started to look for each other. Then we met every day. Eventually, we began a relationship. We both wanted to get married, but my aunt and uncle were against it."

"They didn't like that she was of another faith?"

He shakes his head. "They liked Sharona. They thought she was a wonderful woman. But they insisted that God should be the center of our lives and that I shouldn't put Sharona in a situation where she would need to choose between me and her faith. Her parents were of the same opinion regarding me."

"But you were young and starry eyed?"

Jack laughs. "Yeah...and stubborn. It took quite some time, but Sharona and I finally came to the same conclusion. It was painful, but it was the right thing for both of us."

"I'm sorry, Jack."

"I went to her wedding five years after we broke off our relationship. She has four children now. Her husband is a great guy."

"Jewish?"

"Of course," He smiles. "My experience with Sharona taught me the lesson that just because you love someone doesn't mean you should marry them. There are many other factors that go into a decision like that."

"Such as?"

"Well, faith is a huge one; whether or not both spouses will work outside the home, childbearing, child-rearing, finances. All these things need to be agreed upon before people get married, if the marriage stands a chance; don't you think?"

"Mmm...isn't this the best Caesar salad you've ever tasted?" I ask.

"You're stalling," Jack says, soberly.

I put my fork down. "I'm not stalling...I'm afraid," I say, feeling a lump in my throat.

"What are you afraid of?" he asks, tenderly.

"I can't put my finger on it, but there is fear there. I wish I could explain, but that's the best I can do."

"Do you have reservations about me, Angela?"

"Oh, no. Not at all. I feel very comfortable with you...too comfortable, actually."

"Meaning?"

"Well, my husband just died and here I am with you, feeling emotions that I can't even put a name to...I guess maybe on some level I feel guilty about that, and a little afraid of what people will think."

Jack's brows come together. "And you're going to let those feelings govern your decision about us?"

I feel the color rush to my cheeks. "Well, when you put it that way, it makes it sound ridiculous."

Jack sinks into the back of the booth and gazes at me, saying nothing. Something in the way he looks at me makes me feel like he can see into my soul. I look down at my hands, which are in my lap, wringing my napkin.

"Okay," I whisper, "I'm baring my soul." I look up and into his eyes; then I shift my body forward. Jack leans in toward me so that our heads are so close as to be almost touching. "I want to get to know you, Jack. I know that neither one of us can know what the future holds. But, I am fairly certain that if I don't allow this to unfold in whatever way God wants it to, that I will regret it for the rest of my life. The problem is, I'm afraid to admit that; out loud at least."

"You just did," Jack whispers; amused.

"Right...don't tell anyone."

He laughs. "Angela, you are a beautiful woman; even more so when you allow yourself to be vulnerable."

"It's hard for me to do that. I'm still learning to let go and to stop micromanaging every aspect of my life."

"But I can see that you're trying," Jack says, "and that makes all the difference."

***

Tonight we are at Jack Stack's in the Plaza, which, in my opinion, is the best barbecue restaurant in Kansas City. We both ordered the burnt ends and beans. Jack is washing his down with a beer. I'm sticking with water.

"Angela, tell me something about you that I don't already know," he asks. This has become a regular conversation starter with Jack. I've grown to like it, because we are really getting to know a lot about each other and discussing things that wouldn't normally come up in regular conversation.

"Like what? My favorite color?"

"Favorite color is good."

"Well, I have different favorite colors for different things. Like rooms, for example. I like rich colors for walls: deep reds, golden khakis...jewel tones. But for clothes I prefer light, cool colors like ice blue or a pale mint green. Of course I like to wear black, too, but who doesn't? My favorite color of flower is a salmon-colored rose."

Jack laughs and shakes his head. "You're a complex woman, Angela! Boil it down to one color for me."

"Hmm... I guess I would have to say the palest shade of blue. And what about you, Jack? What's your favorite color?"

"Brown."

"That's it...brown? Any particular shade of brown?"

"No, just all brown...and sometimes blue."

"So, we complement each other then," I say.

"How so?"

"Well, according to you, I'm complex, and I think you are pretty straight forward. Besides, pale blue and brown go nicely together."

He laughs, "And this is the basis for compatibility?"

"Absolutely. Google it. Favorite colors predict compatibility. You will find it in all the scientific journals and, more importantly, in *Cosmo*. I also heard that if you play the soundtrack to *Saturday Night Fever* backwards it says it on there, too. But it's Barry Gibb, so you need a dog to hear it, because the pitch is too high for the human ear."

Jack is cracking up. I love his laugh. It's deep and sincere and masculine. The more time I spend with him, the more I find myself wanting to make him laugh, because it gives me such joy to see Jack so happy.

When dinner is over, we walk down to Brush Creek. It is a warm night, so I slip off the cardigan I'm wearing over my dress and Jack offers to carry it for me. We descend a concrete stairway and find an empty bench. The moonlight glints on the water and a string of lights glows on the bridge ahead. I cannot think of a more romantic setting than this.

We settle down on the bench and I move over to Jack and rest my head on his shoulder. "Angela," he whispers, "may I hold your hand?" I reach over and slip my hand into his.

"Jack, I can't believe how knowing you has completely changed me."

"Uh oh," he says in jest, "Good or bad?"

I look up at him and smile. "You know, just a few months ago I would have been insulted if the man I was dating didn't try to kiss me; especially after seven dates."

"And now?"

"I'm grateful."

Jack shifts his body so that we are face to face. "Tell me why you're grateful," he says, earnestly.

"Well, I think it's because when I look back, at this point in our relationship, Devin and I were practically living together. I mean, we spent most nights at his place right from the beginning. After a month, it would have been pretty messy and painful to end it, because we felt some sort of obligation to each other, because of the physical ties. The decision to spend the rest of our lives together was made with our bodies and not our brains. We just closed our eyes, jumped in and never looked back. Taking the focus off the physical, I think, enables you and me to really see each other." I put my head down and rub my forehead. "I don't know if I am making sense."

"You are making perfect sense," he strokes my cheek. "Would it be too forward of me to ask why you..."

"Jumped into Devin's bed?"

Jack nods.

"I have thought about this a lot since his accident. You know, my father and I were very close. He died when I was 17 and after his death, I felt like there was nobody to love me. Devin paid attention to me; he made me feel special. I guess I thought that was love."

***

Jack had to work late tonight so we agreed to go out for dessert. I have been dressing up for our dates, but since this is just dessert I decide to go casual. I'm wearing a pair of khaki Capris, a knit crew neck tee in black and my black Candie's wedges. Jack had the same idea. He's got on brown Bermudas, a tan Guayabera shirt and brown leather slip-on sandals. I glance at his arms and legs. He's not as hairy as I would have thought him to be, having all that Italian blood in him.

Jack discovered a little gelato place on the Plaza. It's adorable; very tiny—the eating area is about the size of my living room. Counter height bistro tables are scattered throughout. The walls are exposed brick, decorated with vintage ads. The ceiling is stamped copper and a copper chandelier dripping with crystals hangs at the center.

"This gelato is amazing!" I exclaim. "Mmmm...you have to taste mine."

He dips his spoon into my bowl and spoons some into his mouth. All of a sudden I see Jack blush. "What? Don't you like it?" I ask.

"I *love* it...it reminds me of you."

"Coconut gelato reminds you of me? Really?"

"Your perfume. It is...uh... it can be intoxicating at times."

I try to hide my amusement. "I don't wear perfume, Jack, but I do slather on coconut oil after I shower. It's an excellent moisturizer."

"You mean the kind you cook with, that you can buy at the grocery store?"

"Mmm hmm. If it gets hot enough outside you can bread me and fry me."

Jack laughs. "I'll remember that. Here, taste mine," he says, spooning some into my mouth. He ordered half hazelnut, half dark chocolate.

This combination is delectable. The creaminess of the hazelnut and the slight tartness of the dark chocolate complement each other perfectly.

"Oh! This tastes just like a Baci!"

"That was my favorite candy as a kid," Jack says. "My Aunt Philomena always had a stash for when she caught me being good."

"Your aunt sounds like my kind of woman."

"I think you would have liked her, Angela. I know she would have liked you."

"What kind of a person was she?"

Jack tilts his head back as if he is trying to conjure the memories from somewhere far away. "I called her my 'Zia Mina.' She had a very gentle disposition. Her love of God drove everything she did, raising me, teaching, being a wife to my uncle. The best thing about Zia Mina was that she loved me unconditionally and accepted me completely."

He looks down at the table and lowers his voice. "You know, it's hard to be a single, older guy. People push dates on you, they make assumptions..." Jack focuses his gaze on me now and looks deeply into my eyes. "I always knew I was called to the married life, much like a boy who recognizes his call to the priesthood at a young age. She supported me and always told me to pray and God would provide. She died six years ago. I was blessed to be able to be with her when she passed."

My eyes tear up. "She sounds lovely," I say, my voice catching. "I wish...I wish I would have had someone like your aunt in my life."

We are walking to the car now and Jack takes my hand. "What was your mother like, Angela?"

"My mother was a career woman. I...I was what you would call a 'change of life baby.' After my parents married, they had two boys right away. That was enough for my mother. When they got older she went to work at a bank and had a career. Then, when she was in her mid-40's, I came along. My father was quite a bit older than she was and so they decided he would retire from his factory job and she would continue to work. It turned out he loved the situation. He got to spend his days playing with me. We were very close." I smile, remembering the good times we had together while he was still alive. "It was Daddy who taught me how to cook and who took me clamming and out for long rides in his little single engine boat. It was just the two of us, because by then my brothers had moved out and started lives of their own. So, I actually have two brothers who are in their 60's."

"Do you keep in touch?" asks Jack, reaching into his pocket to get his keys.

"Not much. I never lived with them and they were closer with my mother. I was a Daddy's girl. Jimmy, the oldest, checked out of my life completely when my mother died. I mean, we exchange Christmas cards, but that's about it. Tony is sort of an odd bird. He sent me a weepy letter when Devin died apologizing for not being able to afford to come out for the funeral."

"That was thoughtful," Jack says, opening the passenger door for me.

"Absolutely. I wrote him back thanking him and we've written several times since then," I answer, and as I lower myself into the seat, my sandal falls off my foot and right into the storm drain. I look down, dumbfounded, then the absurdity of it grabs me and I burst out laughing.

Jack looks on in surprise. "Did you just lose your shoe?"

I take my other shoe off in a fit of giggles. "This one is useless, now," I say, throwing the remaining shoe over the open door of the car toward a trash bin at the edge of the sidewalk. It ricochets off the rim of the bin and onto the hood of Jack's car.

"Oh my goodness!" I exclaim, "I'm sorry!"

Jack is laughing now. "It's all right," he says, retrieving the shoe and tossing it into the garbage, "I'm getting you another pair because it happened on my watch."

"Don't be ridiculous." I say, "This stuff happens to me all the time. Did I mention to you that I tend to be a bit klutzy?"

He chuckles, "But I feel completely responsible. After all, I was the one who chose to park near the storm drain."

"No worries," I answer, "I do have other shoes, you know."

After we arrive at my place, Jack opens the car door for me, and instead of taking my hand, he gathers me into his arms and begins to carry me up the steps. I shriek in surprise.

"Wouldn't want to damage those pretty feet of yours," he says.

We reach the front door and as I slide down out of his arms, I wrap mine around his neck. "How do you know whether or not I have pretty feet?" I ask, playfully.

"I took a peek when we were in the car," he whispers, "It's official...you are beautiful from your head down to your toes."

9

Can u meet me @ LuAnne's 4 lunch?

It's Jim. We haven't seen each other much lately because classes and youth group broke for the summer. Rosie has ballet camp at 1:00 right near LuAnne's, and I can leave the boys home.

I text Jim back. *1 PM OK?*

C U there

***

There are two local hangouts in Smithville. Hearth & Kettle is where all the older folks go. It's a down-home, diner-type place that serves comfort food like meatloaf, mountain oyster stew and fried catfish. If you live in Smithville and have blue or white hair, Hearth & Kettle is the place to be.

LuAnne's is for the younger crowd. The décor is simple and contemporary, in pale greens and blues. The upholstered booths are covered in a contemporary vinyl print and there are TVs on the walls. LuAnne's has a great salad bar and offers an extensive menu of desserts, gourmet teas and coffees. They sell pizza, Paninis and cold sandwiches as well. Every time I come here, which is infrequently, I always promise myself to come back more often, which I never do, because it's not in the budget.

Jim is already sitting in a booth when I get there. He smiles. "Long time no see," he says, getting up and giving me a hug.

"So true! I've been going through withdrawal, Jim," I joke, as I hold up my hand. "See? I've even got the shakes."

Jim laughs as we walk up to the counter. I fish my wallet out of my handbag.

"Put that away. It's on me."

"Don't be ridiculous," I protest.

Jim presses his lips together and shakes his head. "Your money is no good here," he says, firmly, so I put my wallet away.

We slip into our booth with our lattes and salads, say grace and dig in.

"So, I'm sensing there is a particular reason I am here with you today other than that you miss me," I say, cautiously.

Jim takes a swig of his latte and sits back in his seat. "Jel, we have an odd relationship, you and me, don't we? Almost like a...a..."

I grin. "Father-daughter-husband-wife?"

He laughs. "Yeah, just like that."

"What is it, Jim?" I ask, gently.

He sighs, "Well, you know Katie is pregnant and, normally, in our family, the mother would throw the baby shower. But Chloe is deceased and Katie's in-laws live out of town, so it doesn't look like it's going to happen unless I do it. But I have no idea what to do, and I'm not close enough with her girlfriends to feel comfortable calling them for help."

"Do you want me to help you give Katie a baby shower, Jim?"

He lets out a sigh of relief. "Yeah, I do. Do you have the time?"

"For you, of course I do," I smile, "I'm glad you asked."

After all the help Jim gave me after Devin's accident, the very least I can do is help him with his daughter's shower. We agree to have it at Jim's house next month. I make Jim put a timeline in his Blackberry of what needs to be done and we split up the tasks.

"There's a lot to planning these things, isn't there?" Jim says, shaking his head.

"If you want to do it right, Grandpa," I say.

Jim sighs wistfully, "Yes, a Grandpa without a

Grandma. Things would be so much better with her here."

"Don't worry. Chloe will look down on you that day and be very proud of what a good job you've done for Katie."

Jim stares at me for a few beats. "And I'm proud of you, Jel," he says, "for the work you've done to move your life forward instead of wallowing in self-pity."

"I did that for awhile," I say. "But then God hit me in the head with a two-by-four named Jack."

Jim smiles, "You did get a rough start, but he's good for you. Be open to God's will."

10

Frankie's is crowded tonight. There are lots of young couples here with their children. As I bite into my slice, I notice a family sitting at a table near the window. They have a chubby toddler strapped into a high chair. She is beautiful, with rosy cheeks that are covered in tomato sauce and large, expressive blue eyes. Her mother is breaking off small bits of a slice of pizza and putting them on the tray. The child is picking them up in her sweet little hand, squishing it into a fist and stuffing her whole fist into her mouth.

"That child is adorable," I say, "I can't take my eyes off of her. I remember my kids at that age. It's such a sweet, innocent time, but it goes by so fast. Before you know it, all you have are memories."

Jack glances over at them. "How would you feel about having more children, Angela?"

Wow...food for thought. "Hmmm....I'm definitely willing to embrace any child that God would give me. I have to admit, though, that being pregnant at my age would probably be a bit unnerving at first. But I am sure that if I got pregnant again I would fall in love with the baby and enjoy motherhood to the fullest."

"Your mother didn't feel that way, did she?"

Shaking my head, I say, "I think my mother was scared. My father's job didn't provide a lot of luxuries and she got used to working, dressing nice, having money. I think it was hard for her to give that up. But, essentially, she chose her job over me. Looking back on my life, I wish she had made a different decision, but my father was good to me."

"Is that why you don't work? It seems to me that you struggle, financially, sometimes and it would alleviate that if you got a job."

I'm startled by this revelation. I never looked at my decision to not work as having anything to do with my mother. "How do you keep doing that?"

"Doing what?"

"Know things about me that I don't even know?"

"I listen to you, Angela..." Jack shrugs. "That's all. So, you were saying..."

"Well, after Devin's accident I made three promises to myself and my kids. One was that I would be there when they got home from school every day, at least until Rosie was in middle school. Devin's death knocked them for a loop and I wanted to give them the security of knowing I'd be there. The second was that I would never use a credit card again as long as I lived. The third was that I would learn more about my faith so that I would be able to raise them with a love for the church. Devin's parents were Catholic, but they didn't practice. My parents practiced, but they just went through the motions. Neither one of us knew much about our faith when we met. Consequently, we made some pretty lousy choices. I don't want that to happen to my kids."

"You have good children, Angela. They are growing up well because of you. Some women, and men, don't have a desire to make personal sacrifices for their families."

"I don't know...I'm just doing what needs to be done, Jack. And what about you?"

"What?"

"Kids?"

"I've always wanted more than one child. Being an only child can get lonely sometimes. I wouldn't want my own children to feel that way."

"I hear you." I say, draining my iced tea glass. "But what if those kids weren't biological kids? Would you be able to handle raising another man's children? Would you even want to?"

Jack reaches across the table and takes my hand.

"I wouldn't be here with you tonight, Angela, if I wasn't open to that."

11

There must be a rip in the space-time continuum, because for the first time in many moons, I've found myself completely devoid of children as I prepare for my date with Jack. The boys are at a youth group lock-in, and Rosie is at my friend, Jenna's, place functioning as a mother's helper while Jenna's husband, Dave, is out of town. Marissa has agreed to pick up Rosie when she's done and have her stay overnight. This will be a big treat for Rosie, who loves Marissa probably as much as she loves me.

"All Rosie wants for her birthday is to meet Jack," I tell Marissa. With the kids out of the house, it's too quiet in here, and since I need conversation (like some people need air), I'm on the phone with her while I check my closet for an outfit to wear.

"Wow...do you think it's time?" she asks.

"I do. I want to spend more time with him than just dinner every Friday. I have been praying about this and, I know we've only had about a dozen dates, but I want more out of this relationship than dinner once a week. I have been wondering when to talk to him about it and Rosie seemed to give me the answer today. Do you think it would be too forward to say something?"

"Honey, no. Honesty is never a bad thing in a relationship. Tell him tonight."

"We're supposed to be going to a jazz club. I don't know if I really want to talk to him about this in a noisy, crowded restaurant..."

"When is he picking you up?"

"In a little over an hour."

"I have an idea," she says, "I'll drive you over there so you can talk to him before dinner. If we leave now we'll catch him before he comes to pick you up. This way, you can have a nice talk and then go out."

"You just want to see where he lives," I tease.

"Don't *you*? Come on...you know I love spontaneity," she urges.

"All right...I'll put my makeup on in the car. You better hurry over here or I'll miss him."

I quickly throw a long black and white tunic over a pair of black leggings and the gladiator sandals I bought with the gift certificate Jack sent me to the shoe store at Zona Rosa. The gift certificate was so large that I bought these sandals and each of the kids got a new pair of shoes too.

Marissa hugs me as I get out of her car and approach Jack's building. It is a small, well-kept prewar building that has a lot of character. I look at the mailboxes and note Jack is on the second floor. I'm nervous, so to burn off energy I run up the stairs. There is only one door on the whole floor, so I ring the bell. When Jack opens the door, I can tell he has just been shaving. He is wearing black sweats, a fitted black tee shirt and is wiping his face with a towel. His mouth opens in surprise.

"Angela! Wasn't I supposed to pick you up tonight? What's going on?"

"Jack, I came here because I need to talk to you. Can I come in?"

"Um, yeah...sorry...please, come in." His eyebrows are furrowed and his mouth is turned down at the corners. He looks perplexed.

I hear the door slam and turn to look at Jack, startled. "Sorry," he says, "It's on a spring and if you let go, it slams."

I glance around the apartment. It is so much like I imagined it to be. The décor is simple and masculine. There are beautiful, custom book shelves in deep cherry, lining every wall. On the left there is a galley kitchen with granite countertops and a matching island with two stools.

The granite is a mixture of light and dark gray and burgundy, which accents the color of the shelving in the living area. The kitchen cabinetry is a matte gray with nickel accents...very masculine. The wall opposite the door has two bare, floor-to-ceiling windows that flank a fireplace, above which hangs a haunting image of Jesus in His suffering. I've seen this print in Fr. Sean's office. It was painted by an unknown artist and has the Latin words on the bottom "Sic Deus Dilexit Mundum" which translates to "For God So Loved The World." Facing the mantle is a brown leather couch centered on an oriental rug, between two mission style side tables. There is a bistro table and two chairs placed in front of the left side window. A mission chair and a floor lamp balance it out near the right side window. On the wall across from the kitchen and beyond the living room, is a set of glass paneled French doors behind which looks to be the bedroom. The wall just behind me, with a large carved wood desk, functions as an office.

I sigh. "Jack, this dating situation isn't right for me," I begin.

Shock appears on his face, then hurt. "Wow, Angela," he says, sarcastically, "please, don't sugar coat this. Just come right out and say it, why don't you?" He walks over and lowers himself onto the couch, elbows on knees; head in his hands.

I am horrified. "No, Jack," I yell, "I didn't mean *that*!"

What on earth have I done? What possessed me to phrase this the way I did? Why am I such a screw up at the most important moments in my life?

I walk over to Jack, who slowly looks up at me. "How else could I possibly interpret what you just said?" he says quietly.

My heart feels heavy for having hurt him this way. *God, help me fix this.* I settle down on the couch next to Jack. His head is in his hands and he doesn't look up at all. "I seem to have a knack for really messing things up when it comes to articulating my feelings...may I try again, please?" I ask softly.

He sighs, "If you feel it is absolutely necessary, then go ahead," he says, struggling to keep his voice steady.

I want so much to relax him, so I reach up and begin to rub his back gently as I begin to speak. "Jack," I whisper, "what I meant to tell you was that I...I want *more* than to be your Friday night date. I love spending time with you and I want you to be a bigger part of my life. Would you consider meeting my kids and spending time with us as a family?"

He turns his head and looks at me. "Is that really what you want?"

I nod. "So much so, that I rushed over here to tell you before we went out... but then I screwed it all up. I'm so sorry, Jack, for being such an idiot."

He wraps his arms around me and draws me to him. "You're *not* an idiot," he says, firmly, "I'm sorry, too, for jumping to conclusions and not trying to understand what you were saying."

It feels so good to be here, wrapped in Jack's arms. I rest my head on his chest and snuggle in a bit. He responds by rubbing my back and a feeling of security envelops me.

"So..." he says, "do we forgive each other?"

I look up at Jack and nod and he reaches down and strokes my cheek in that way that makes my insides melt. "There is something I was planning on asking you soon, but almost seems as if you have answered me before I could even ask the question."

Confused, I furrow my brow.

"Angela, I was going to ask how you felt about starting a courtship."

"I've read about it, Jack, but I want your take on it before I answer, okay?"

"Well, it is the next step in our relationship. In a courtship, we are seriously and prayerfully considering whether or not we may be called to the sacrament of marriage."

Oh, my...this is serious. Well, what did I expect the next level of a relationship to be? Still, this talk of marriage is a little unnerving. I need some comic relief, so I widen my eyes in mock innocence.

"To each other or other people?"

Jack bursts out laughing. "Hopefully to each other!"

"So, it means you meet my kids and spend time with us?"

"Yes, Angela, and we see each other more often and we discuss things that will help us determine whether or not we are compatible in areas like finances, household responsibilities, childbearing, childrearing...everything."

Immediately I blush.

"It's okay," he whispers. "Nothing would be off limits. You could ask me anything. If we are going to do this right, we each need to be an open book to the other...totally transparent."

I take a deep breath. "All I know is that I am no longer content to be just friends...but marriage?"

"As far as marriage goes, we aren't making a decision now to get married; we are in a discernment phase. We take all the time we need...no rush."

"No rush? At our ages, Jack, we don't exactly have all the time in the world, do we? Oh my, there is so much to consider, isn't there?" I came to Jack's apartment determined, but now I just feel frustrated and confused.

"Angela," says Jack, gently, "Maybe you need some more time to think about this. That's okay with me."

I close my eyes for a moment to center myself.

God, help me. I came here tonight because I am restless in the relationship the way it is going. I find myself missing Jack during the week and craving his advice and opinion on things that come up in my life. Continuing a casual dating relationship won't satisfy these needs. Deep down I know that You are moving me into another phase with Jack, but I am scared. Help me to get past that fear and do Your will.

I inhale deeply and let out a cleansing breath. "I'm going to be honest with you. I...I feel restless in dating mode, and I want very much to know you better. But there is some fear there..."

He takes my hands in his. "Are you afraid that I will push you into marriage, Angela? Because that wouldn't be good for either one of us. I want to get married, not just to *be* married, but to spend my life with a woman that I love, who loves me and freely chooses to give herself to me." Jack grins. "I'm a little selfish that way."

I study Jack's face. There is no pretense there; only kindness and sincerity. There is nothing in him that I should fear; deep down I know that. Any hesitation or anxiety comes completely from inside me. It is all mine to overcome.

"If I promise to work on getting over my fears, will you promise to be patient with me?" I whisper.

Jack draws me close to him and, in his embrace, my heart quiets and there is peace. "I promise," he says, "I promise."

I tell Jack about Rosie's birthday and he agrees to come for dinner and cake. "Rosie will be over the moon," I remark. *And she's not the only one...*

It's getting late and we've lost our reservations. I tell Jack that I'm too tired to go out anyway. This evening has taken a lot out of me.

He rubs his hands together. "Well, I have a steak in the fridge. What do you say I cook for you?"

"Only if you'll let me help," I say, following him into the kitchen.

Jack takes the steak out and I peek in after him to see

what else is in there. Oooh, Portobello mushrooms! I put them on the counter. Jack puts a head of garlic next to the mushrooms. There is also lettuce, cucumber and tomatoes, so I decide to make a salad, too.

"Are these kalamata?" I ask, taking out a plastic container of olives.

Jack nods as he fires up the built-in grill on his stove. His stove is beautiful. It's a Jenn-Air and it looks like a commercial model. I snoop around and find a cutting board and a large bowl to mix the salad in. Jack hands me a Santoku knife and I get to work peeling the garlic and slicing the vegetables.

"I didn't even ask if you like steak," he says, grinding some pepper onto the meat. "If you want we can have something else instead."

It smells delicious and I have to stop myself from salivating.

"I *love* steak...I just never eat it. I can't really aff--" I stop myself before I say too much. "...cook it well. I usually overcook it and it comes out really dry."

This is not a lie. Steak is the one food to which my cooking prowess does not extend.

I see Jack clench his jaw and press his lips together, slightly. *I wonder what that look means?* He comes over to me and takes me in his arms.

"I can teach you," he says. "How about I bring some steaks on Sunday?"

I thank him and explain that the birthday child gets to pick her meal and Rosie has already chosen hers. Honestly, though, I really don't want Jack bringing steaks for my whole family. I am sure he doesn't make that much money working for the Church. Then I glance around his apartment, with its state-of–the-art kitchen and I wonder how he can possibly afford this place.

***

Back home, I am still on cloud nine thinking about the wonderful time I had with Jack earlier tonight. As I am slipping into bed, my phone rings.

"I didn't wake you, did I?" Jack asks.

"No, I am wide awake, but dreaming about those Portobello mushrooms. They were delicious. Thanks again for dinner."

"Angela, believe me, it was my pleasure," he says. "There was something I didn't get to ask you when you were over here tonight."

"What? If I wanted seconds on dessert?"

He chuckles. "I wanted to ask you if you would be willing to pray together each time we see each other."

"Yes, of course, Jack. I think it's a good idea." I wonder what would have happened if Devin and I had prayed before our dates...or what *wouldn't* have happened.

I can hear the elation in his voice. "Great! There is a prayer I found that I'm e-mailing you right now. It asks for the Holy Spirit's guidance in doing God's will. Thank you, Angela."

"I'll make sure to memorize it tomorrow. See you Sunday, Jack."

"See you Sunday, love."

To: **jellycooke@gomail.com**
From: **giacomob@kcdiocese.org**
RE: Holy Spirit Prayer

Holy Spirit, soul of my soul, I adore you
Enlighten, guide, strengthen and console me
Tell me what I ought to do and command me to do it
I promise to be submissive to all that you ask of me
And all that you allow to happen to me
O Holy Spirit, show me your will. Amen.

12

Rosie is extremely excited about meeting Mr. B. Since I told her Jack would be coming tomorrow, she has been following me around asking question after question. She is also practicing saying Jack's last name correctly...Bar-toe-low-myew-chee. Ben took the news well. He seems intrigued by the idea of Jack and it seems as if he has decided to make no judgments until they meet. Sam is another story. He got very quiet and has spent most of the day in his room.

I knock on his door. "Samwise, you in?"

I hear a grunt from inside, which I interpret as, "Please, do come in, Mother dear."

He is sitting on his bed, back to the wall, reading. I sit down on the bed and scoot back so I that am next to him.

"So you seem uncomfortable with Jack coming to spend the day with us. Can we talk about it?"

Sam sighs. "You know, Mom, you go out with this guy every Friday night and we haven't even met him and all of a sudden he's coming for Rosie's birthday. That's a *family* thing..."

"Well, when we were dating we weren't sure if we would be seriously interested in each other. So, if we went out together for a couple months and decided that we didn't want to continue the relationship, then what would be the point of all of you meeting? But, recently, Jack and I decided that we will continue to see each other long term, so it is time that you meet him and get to know him. Does that make sense?"

Sam picks up a small foam ball and tosses it toward the basket at the top of his closet door. It silently falls into the netting. "Yes...yes it makes sense, but, it's gonna be like he's a stand-in for Dad. It's going to be weird. And I don't really like that my mother has, you know, a boyfriend." He slides down off the bed, pops the ball out of the basket and gets back on the bed next to me.

"Sam, I am not trying to replace Dad. It's not like I realized there was a void in my life and I looked around for a way to fill it. I am in a relationship with Jack because he is Jack and I care about him. If I hadn't met Jack, there is a strong possibility that I would not be dating anyone right now. Respectful, faithful men don't just grow on trees you know, and I would never spend time with someone who wasn't both of those things and more."

Sam lobs the ball and misses this time. "But don't you feel guilty; like you're betraying Dad?"

Reaching out and hugging Sam, I say, "If the tables were turned and I was the one who died, I know that I would have wanted your father to be free to fall in love again, if he found the right person. I wouldn't want him to spend the rest of his life mourning. I would want him to try to find some joy. Don't you think he would want those same things for me?"

Getting up off the bed, Sam walks over and looks out the window. "But he's your boyfriend and what if he, you know...you're my *mom*. "

Now I fully understand what he is worried about. "Sam, do you trust me?" I ask. He nods, slowly, eyes still on the window. "You know that I try to put God first in my life, right? Well, do you think I would do anything to mess that up? You know I would never do anything with Jack that I wouldn't do with you."

Sam wrinkles his nose, "Ewww."

"What, eww?" I ask. "Do I hug you? Hold your hand? Kiss you on the cheek? I do those things with Jack. For Pete's sakes, I do those things with Marissa! Look, if any strong feelings develop between Jack and I, we will keep them in check. We are both making sure of that. And you know that I have spoken to you about how I would like you to treat women. I'm not a hypocrite. I am holding Jack to the same standards."

"Well, I don't trust him."

"Why don't you meet Jack before you make that judgment?"

"I will...tomorrow. And I'll be watching him like a hawk."

***

Jack's car pulls into the driveway and immediately Rosie and Ben appear on the landing near the front door. Sam recedes into the living room.

"Mama?" Rosie looks at me imploringly. I nod that she should answer the door. Jack is standing there with a huge bouquet of red roses. Rosie looks up at him, speechless and wide-eyed. Jack squats down to her level and says, "I'll bet you're the birthday girl, aren't you?" Slowly, she nods. "Well, then, these are for you. Happy Birthday, Rosie. I'm Mr. B." he says and gently places the bouquet in her arms.

Rosie looks over her shoulder at me, beaming. I raise an eyebrow and immediately she looks at Jack and says, "Thank you, Mr. Bartolomucci. It's nice to meet you. Please come in."

"It's my pleasure," Jack says, smiling and then extends his hand. "And you must be...Ben?" They shake hands and Ben says, "Nice to meet you. My mom says you like *Lord of the Rings* just as much as we do."

I can tell Ben has rehearsed this line. He was very concerned about what he would say to Jack when they met.

"I might...do you think you'd like to play a trivia game sometime?"

Ben looks down at his feet. I clear my throat and he instantly looks back up. "Maybe...maybe that would be fun," he says, bashfully.

"Ben? Would you please help your sister find a vase for

these roses?" I ask, and he takes the cue to leave. When the two younger children are out of earshot, Jack takes my hands in his and we both pray. Then he embraces me and whispers, "Why am I so nervous?"

"Don't be," I tell him. "Besides, there are only two of us, but we're bigger. We could take the three of them if we had to."

Jack laughs as I take his hand and lead him upstairs. Sam is standing in the middle of the living room with his arms folded across his chest. He looks so much like Devin right now that it's unnerving. I take a cleansing breath and then introduce Jack. Sam, apparently remembering at least one thing from the lecture I gave him last night on how I expected him to behave today, silently extends his hand. Jack shakes it and says, "I'm glad to meet you, Sam. Your Mom has told me what a great job you have been doing taking care of things around here. I really enjoy hearing what a tremendous help you are to her. You sound like a responsible guy." Sam doesn't know what to make of this, so he just utters a weak, "Thank you."

By dinnertime, everyone is more relaxed. I serve Rosie's birthday choices; breaded, fried chicken cutlets, garlic mashed potatoes, raw vegetables with ranch dressing and a green salad. Ben and Jack hit it off and have a deep conversation on the Christian imagery in the *Lord of the Rings* books. Apparently, Jack once wrote a paper on this subject and Ben is lapping it all up. Rosie is completely smitten and can't take her eyes off Jack. I can see Sam is struggling, but he is being polite. Silently I pray that God remove the bitterness and doubt from his heart.

After dinner and birthday cake, the kids clear the table and go downstairs to watch *The Voyage of the Dawn Treader* DVD that Jack gave Rosie as a gift. The movie had come out right around the time of Devin's death, so we never got around to seeing it and the kids are excited. Jack says he'll help me clean up and follows me into the kitchen.

Once there, he wraps me in his arms.

"You're an amazing cook, Angela. In fact, you're an amazing woman," he says and kisses me gently on the cheek.

Suddenly, Sam appears in the doorway. His eyes are narrowed, his hands are balled into fists, and I can see he is ready for a fight.

"So...so...are you gonna...do you want to...you're *not* going to touch my Mom!" he says, defiantly.

"Samuel Devin Cooke!" I gasp.

"Angela," Jack says, "If it's okay with you, I'd like to discuss this with Sam."

My face is beet red and I am very embarrassed, but I know Jack is level-headed and I trust his judgment. "Yes, that will be fine, Jack, *after* Sam apologizes for his rudeness." Then I shoot Sam a look that says I mean business.

"Sorry," he says, avoiding Jack's gaze.

"I accept your apology, Sam. Look, I know that *how* you said it upset your Mom, but *what* you said was actually a good thing." This gets Sam's attention and I can tell he is really listening to what Jack is saying, although he is still suspicious. "You are the man of the house here, and I'm impressed that you are responsible enough to find out what my intentions are. It is good that you brought this up and I think it is worth discussing."

"You do?" Sam asks, quietly.

"Absolutely. So, from what you said I can see that you love your mother very much, and that you're concerned for her virtue, and you want to make sure she is treated with dignity and respect, right?"

Sam nods, eyes still narrowed.

"Well, we are on the same page there. I care about your mother very much and I would not want to hurt her in any way or do anything that would compromise her values. I wouldn't ask her to lie, I wouldn't ask her to cheat; I wouldn't ask her to steal and I certainly wouldn't ask her to do anything else that wouldn't be appropriate. If I did, it would mean that I actually *didn't* care about her at all."

"Yeah...okay," Sam says, relaxing his fists and crossing his arms across his chest.

"So, since we both care about your Mom and we both want to protect her virtue, it looks like we're actually on the same team, doesn't it?"

Slowly, Sam nods his head.

"As a man of faith, Sam, I am giving you my word that I will treat your mother with the utmost respect," Jack offers his hand to Sam, "Can we shake on it?"

Poor Sam...he wanted a fight, but all he got was a garland of roses. Still, he's not ready to give in and stands there stiffly. Jack takes a step toward him. "I tell you what. Here is my phone number." He hands Sam his card. "When I am out with your Mom, you feel free to call anytime on either my phone or hers to see how she's doing."

"You would...let me check up on you?" Sam looks at me and I nod.

"Of course," Jack says, "I have nothing to hide, so why wouldn't I?" He extends his hand again. "What do you say?"

This time, Sam takes a step forward and completes the handshake.

13

"How would you feel about a double date?" Jack asks. He is calling me on his lunch hour to make plans for tonight. I want you to meet the Chrises."

"The who?"

"My friend Chris Johnson and his wife, Christina: the Chrises. Chris is the guy I play racquetball with on Tuesdays and Thursdays."

"Sure, if they are your friends, that is fine with me. Where are we going?"

"How about Chinese?"

"I'm in."

When we arrive at the Dragon House, there is a biracial couple sitting at a booth in the back, near the window. The woman stands up and waves to Jack. Christina is a very pretty Caucasian woman, with thick, silky, brown hair that cascades down her back past her shoulders. She has fair skin and large brown eyes, set wide apart. Chris is a large African-American guy; built like a football player and his head is shaved. He has a friendly smile accented by deep dimples around his mouth. Together they make a handsome couple.

"Chris, Christina...this is Angela." Jack says it like he is the emcee on a talk show.

I extend my hand, but Christina embraces me and kisses me on both cheeks, European style. Chris shakes my hand. As we settle into the booth, the Chrises sit close together, holding hands.

"So how long have you and Jack known each other?" I ask Chris.

"Ever since Jack moved out here," he glances at Jack. "What? About five years? We met at the gym. I saw him wearing a JP II tee shirt and I figured we had our faith in common, so I struck up a conversation with him," says Chris. "We really hit it off and decided to meet twice a week for racquetball."

"Right," says Jack, smiling. "And twice a week he kicks my butt."

"Don't listen to him," Chris says to me. "Jack can be a formidable opponent...when I'm tired." Both men laugh.

"Well, I don't know about you, but I am starving. Let's order first, then talk," says Christina.

Jack picks up a menu and points. "You like this...and this," he says to me.

"How do you know that?" I poke him in the ribs. "I've never eaten here!"

"You have," he whispers in my ear, "Remember the day I drove you home from court?"

"Kids, if you can't share it with the whole class..." Christina jokes.

I look at Jack. "Go on and tell them," I say, "I don't mind."

The waiter comes and we order our food. I let Jack order for me.

"I want you to tell them, Angela....the *whole* story." he urges. This is not exactly light dinner conversation, but Jack sits there, waiting, so I go ahead.

"My husband, Devin, was Sales Director at the TV station over on Southwest Trafficway, downtown. Two Decembers ago, a drug dealer, who was driving under the influence, crossed the median, drove into the parking lot and straight into Dev, just as he was getting into his car."

Christina gasps and puts her hand to her mouth.

I can feel my throat getting tight. "Devin was killed instantly, and, frankly, I am thankful for that...that he didn't suffer."

"Geez," Chris says, shocked.

"Well, the dealer, Jenkins, didn't stop. He literally

plowed right through Devin and his car, into an intern, a young college girl, who was walking out of the building. She was also killed instantly."

"Oh, my gosh!" exclaims Christina, "I remember this! It was all over the news! How terrible for you, Angela."

I falter a bit. "It was...it...well, the driver got away, hid the car and disappeared for eight months. The police finally caught up with him when a guy he rolled got arrested and turned him in for a plea bargain. But, then a mistrial was declared when it was discovered that some of the jurors were doing their own research on the case."

"Really?" Chris asks, "Why would they do something like that?"

"Apparently they were big CSI junkies," I answer, shaking my head in disgust. "The whole thing was a huge mess. Finally, I just told the DA to let me know when the guy was convicted. I had to stay out of it for my own sanity, and to protect the kids. We needed to heal and getting involved in the trial would have set us back, I think."

"It's overwhelming how much pain there is in the world," says Christina, sadly, shaking her head. Chris puts his arm around her and draws her close to him.

Jack picks up the story with the sentencing hearing. He somehow has remembered every detail of what happened in the courtroom. The way he describes it makes me realize that it touched him profoundly. As Jack speaks, tears begin to roll down Christina's face. "There was so much hate in that courtroom," says Jack. "But Angela was like an oasis of peace and love."

"Hang on a minute," I interject. "That forgiveness was borne of a lot of pain and prayer. It certainly didn't come overnight. I still have bouts of resentment and even anger, but, ultimately, forgiveness is a decision and not a feeling." I see a knowing look pass between the Chrises, and I get the feeling they identify in some way with what I've said.

The mood at the table is so heavy that I start to regret even touching the subject. Jack senses it, too, so he continues with how I passed out and what he had to deal with and in no time we are all laughing. "I still can't believe, after all that, that Jack asked me to dinner," I say.

Christina smiles. "Most people can't see past themselves, Angela," she says. "I'm glad that Jack found someone who can. It's not easy to forgive like that."

I genuinely like Christina. There is a quiet strength about her that appeals to me. At the same time, I can't help but feel like I am meeting my future mother-in-law and that she will give Jack the lowdown on what she thinks of me later tonight.

"Jack tells us that initially you made a mutual decision not to see each other until you worked some things out. That's a good way to start a relationship, I think."

Jack looks stricken. He must have told them about the first time we saw each other. The Chrises are probably to Jack what Marissa is to me. I tell Marissa almost everything. I think he must have told an abridged version that left out my bad behavior; which was very generous of him. This is a man I could definitely fall in love with. I smile at Jack, and then reach under the table and squeeze his hand. "Well, it was Jack's idea, actually. I have to admit that I wasn't really on board at first. But he was right and it was good that we waited. In fact, I am glad we did."

"Ah, wisdom," says Chris, turning to his wife. "Maybe we should have waited till we were older and wiser."

Christina kisses Chris lightly on the lips. "Then we'd still be waiting," she says. "And we wouldn't have any children. Where's the wisdom in that?"

"Jack tells me you have six!" I exclaim. "Do you have pictures?"

Christina takes her wallet out of her handbag. "Here is the one that was on our Christmas card."

"What gorgeous kids!" I say, as I look at the photo of six

handsome children, all with perfect café au lait complexions. The oldest girl is holding a chubby toddler. The child's corkscrew curls frame a perfectly round face that is the palette for huge saucer eyes, a perfect nose and a heart-shaped mouth. "Who is who?" I ask.

Proudly, Christina fills me in on her family. Their oldest, Felicia, is finishing a degree in foreign language at Mizzou. Marcus is 19 and studying computer science at a tech school. Their son, Ambrose, is a sophomore in high school, and another son, Matthias, is in sixth grade. Christina tells me their daughter, Germaine, is about to turn 10.

"But the baby, Nica, started calling her May and it just sort of stuck. Nica is also a nickname. It's short for Veronica."

"The baby is like a little cherub! She is absolutely adorable!" I exclaim.

Jack has told me that he is godfather to the Chrises' youngest child. "Nica and Jack are in love with each other. She calls him 'Daddy Jack.' He spoils her rotten."

I smile. "That doesn't surprise me at all." I can see Jack doting on this adorable toddler. I am glad he has a child in his life on which to lavish affection. "You know, I have two boys and a girl. In fact, they are close in age to three of yours," I tell Christina.

"Chris and I would love to see you and Jack and your kids sometime, Angela. It would be nice for them to get to know each other."

We spend the rest of the dinner talking about our kids and planning to meet sometime, while the guys talk racquetball, politics and everything in between.

***

"So, you and Christina seemed to hit it off," Jack says on the ride home.

"She is great, but I get the feeling that if she didn't like me this relationship would be toast."

Jack chuckles. "Christina is like a mother hen...very protective of the people she loves."

"You're really close with them, aren't you? Like family."

Jack nods. "We've been through a lot together...that can really bond people, Angela."

I know what he means. That's one of the reasons why I am so close with Marissa. She has had a total of eight miscarriages in her life. Since I've known her she has lost four babies and I was there with her through all of those; crying with her, grieving with her, caring for her when she couldn't care for herself. When Devin died, Marissa was the one who came over at the crack of dawn each day and forced me to get out of bed when all I wanted to do was shut out the world. We've held each other and sobbed together more times than I could possibly count.

Jack drives through the entrance to the lake and pulls into a spot by the marina. "Let's walk," he says. The night is clear and warm, with a slight breeze, and moonlight dances on the lake. Jack takes my hand as we stroll on the paved path that hugs the shoreline from the marina to the golf course.

In a quiet voice, Jack says, "Nica means so much to me. She has been the closest I've come to having a child of my own."

"I understand, Jack," I say, gently. Spotting a bench, I lead him over to it and we sit down.

"She is two and a half now. About ten months ago, Christina had just laid her down for a nap, when she got a call that there was an accident during recess at school and Matthias was being rushed to the hospital. She asked a neighbor, who she was friends with at the time, to come sit with the baby while she went to the hospital. Turns out Matthias' arm had been broken in two places and after it was set, Christina brought him home."

I put my arms around Jack to comfort him, because I can tell from the sound of his voice that he is about to reveal something devastating.

"Later that day, she found evidence that Nica had been sodomized," Jack says, his voice breaking. "The neighbor told police her husband was there part of the time. They are pretty sure it was him."

We both start to cry. In the picture Christina showed me, that baby was like a sweet little cherub; so innocent and pure. I think about my own precious Rosie and how I would feel if the unspeakable had happened to her.

"I am so, so sorry," I whisper.

Standing up in front of Jack, I gently draw him toward me and rest his head on my chest. He wraps his arms around my waist and cries. I remember so many times that Marissa held me this way and I sobbed and clung to her in my pain. I have always thought of Marissa as my Simon of Cyrene, helping me to carry my cross. Now I find myself more than willing to help Jack bear his. When I sense that Jack has calmed, I tilt his head up to look at me and wipe away his tears.

"You haven't spoken of this much to the Chrises, have you...because they have been going through their own pain?"

Jack nods his head. "It almost destroyed their marriage," he says, quietly.

"Chris blamed his wife?"

"No. Christina blamed herself. It has taken a long time for her to forgive herself for what she felt was her fault."

"But there was no way she could have known."

"That's true," Jack says. "These people were friends. The Chrises had had them over for dinner, the boys did yard work for them, shoveled in the winter...they trusted them."

"Is the guy in jail now?"

Jack sighs deeply. "No. The police really tried, but the case got thrown out. Not enough evidence." He rubs his eyes. "I know intellectually that I need to forgive him, but sometimes the anger I feel for this guy scares me, Angela."

"What? Like you fantasize about killing him and getting away with it?" I sigh. "Been there, done that and been to confession for it countless times. I remember being horrified at the amount of rage that was inside me. But Fr. Sean pointed out to me that I needed to let myself suffer, instead of fighting it. Once I allowed myself to feel the pain, the anger became more manageable. At that point, I wasn't ready to forgive Jenkins, but I was at least able to pray for the desire to forgive."

I look into Jack's eyes and see that what I am saying is a comfort to him. Somehow, through Jack sharing his pain, I feel that our relationship has changed. There is an intimacy here that didn't exist before now. I can remember feeling this kind of intimacy with Devin at times during our marriage, particularly at the births of our children. There is that emotional connection that strengthens the bond. Fear begins to creep into my heart at the thought of getting closer to Jack, but the tenderness and concern I feel for him overrides it.

"The kids and I were in therapy for the better part of a year after Devin's accident. Talking about it does help," I take his face in my hands and gently kiss his forehead. "Jack, when this overwhelms you, come to me. I know your pain and I want to help you bear it."

Abruptly, Jack stands up and runs his hands through my hair, then draws my face close to his. I can tell he is struggling to hold himself back from kissing me.

"I could fall in love with you, Angela," he says, fervently.

14

Katie's baby shower is this weekend and I have decided to make pignoli cookies as favors. Jim loves these cookies, which are made mostly from almond paste, topped with pine nuts. I used to make them when Devin was alive, but they are costly to make, so this is the first time I'll be baking some in a long while. Jim is footing the bill for this batch, which I will wrap in clear, cellophane bags and tie with pink and blue ribbon. A couple of weeks ago, I ordered the almond paste from a distributor in New Jersey. Today I'm heading out to the City Market to get the pine nuts from a Lebanese vendor that sells bulk nuts, seeds and dried fruit in his shop.

The kids ride with me as we head south on 169 across the Broadway Bridge and into the City Market area. It is a steamy, hot August day and the sun beats down on us as we make our way toward the shopping area. City Market is a conglomeration of food vendors in downtown Kansas City. On the weekends, there is also a farmer's market featuring locally grown, organic produce. Sometimes, after Mass, Jack will drive us out here and buy some vegetables for me to make with dinner. Then he will take us to the bakery for a cupcake. I always get a lemon cupcake with French butter cream frosting. Jack's favorite is a chocolate whoopee pie with hazelnut filling.

I load up two small brown paper bags with pine nuts and pay for them at the counter. The sweet man who owns the shop gives my kids each a small piece of candy after he hands me my change. Politely, they thank him.

He winks at me and says, "That was because they smile. Kids come in here, they never smile."

We walk past the bakery on the way to the car and Rosie says, "Mama? Can we call Mr. B? Doesn't he work around here?"

Jack works very close to this area, in fact; only about four blocks away. "Well, we can just say hello, honey. He is busy working, you know," I say, finding his number on my phone. I call it and hand her the phone.

She bobs up and down as it rings. Her face lights up when he picks up.

"Guess who, Mr. B!" she says, excitedly. Rosie chats with Jack for a minute and tells him where we are and what we are doing. As she talks to him, she practices her ballet positions. My youngest child always needs to be moving.

"Okay," I hear her say. "We will...bye!"

She hands the phone to me and says, "Mr. B says to stay put. He's on his way."

"What?"

"He says he wants to see his most favorite people in the whole world."

The boys have gone for a walk. Rosie and I wait under the awning in front of the bakery where it is nice and shady. Thank goodness there is a slight breeze today or I do believe it's possible that I could melt. About seven minutes later, I see Jack strolling across the parking lot toward us. He looks so handsome in his pale yellow knit Henley shirt and khaki pants.

Rosie runs to meet him and he scoops her up and twirls her around. Jack approaches me and takes me in his arms. "This was a nice surprise, Angela," he says, stroking my cheek.

Coming up behind Jack, I see the boys. They are heading back from checking out the tee shirt shop across the parking lot.

"I didn't mean for you to drop everything to see us, Jack," I say. "I know you're working today."

He shakes his head. "I have a meeting tonight, so I don't have to put in a full day if I don't want to," Jack looks at his watch. "Let's have an early lunch."

He takes my hand and Rosie's as well, and we walk over to a small Vietnamese restaurant on the square. As we relax at the table after dining, an elderly woman makes her way toward us. She has white hair that frames her face in well-coiffed ringlets and is elegantly dressed in a light blue suit. Her white pumps click on the floor as she approaches with deliberate steps.

"You have a lovely family," she says, in a friendly, sweet voice. "It is wonderful to see children and their parents enjoying each other's company. Not too much of that these days."

I blush deeply, realizing that she thinks Jack and I are married; and politely thank her.

"Your children are beautiful," she continues, glancing at Rosie. "This little one looks just like her father with the dark, curly hair. I hope you don't mind that I was enjoying sitting near your family. When I am on my own, there's not much to do except go out and people watch. Can't stand the TV..."

I can see that Jack, who usually can take control of any situation, is at a loss. The boys don't know what to say, either.

Rosie pipes up, "Mr. B isn't my Daddy. He's Mama's boyfriend!"

We endure a moment of awkward silence, which Jack ends by introducing us and inviting the woman to have a seat. Surprisingly, she accepts. Jack moves a chair over from another table and places it between me and Ben. He then allows the woman to grasp his arm for balance as she lowers herself onto her seat.

Her name is Marion Gold and she is a widow from Briarcliff; a mother of four and grandmother of fourteen, with her twenty-third great-grandchild on the way. I explain that I am also a widow, without going into too many details.

At a lull in the conversation, Jack says, "I think these

kids need some dessert. Can I get you ladies anything?"

Both Marion and I decline as Jack gives Sam money with instructions for the boys to take Rosie for a cupcake.

"I'm still driving at 78," she chuckles. "I like to come down here and take a little stroll, and then have lunch. I see all kinds of interesting things. Gives me something to do on the days I don't have visitors."

I'm surprised to hear that she is in her late seventies; she looks more youthful than that. "How long were you and your husband married, Marion?" I ask.

"Fifty-nine years when he died," she says, with a look of contentment in her eyes. "And every one of them hard...but happy. I wouldn't trade one second of my life for anything else. No...no, ma'am, I wouldn't," she says, firmly.

I wish I could pick this woman's brain. Anyone married for that long has got to be doing it right. Marion stands up and tells us she needs to get back home to take her pills. Jack offers to walk her to her car, but I ask him to check up on the kids instead. As Marion and I make our way to the parking lot, I ask, "Is there one thing that you could point to as the source of happiness in your marriage?"

Marion stops walking and cocks her head to the side as if in deep thought.

"Give everything you have to your husband. Don't hold anything back. If either of you gives any less, you start to become selfish and focus only on your own needs, and, pretty soon you don't even know each other anymore. I've seen it happen countless times."

We cross the street and arrive at a navy blue luxury sedan. "Here's my jalopy," chuckles Marion, fishing her keys from her purse.

"How do you do it, Marion? Give everything, I mean," I ask, not wanting to let this woman go. She is so sweet and motherly that I feel loved just being in close physical proximity to her.

Opening the car door, she says, "Trust, pray, jump in with both feet and never look back, dear."

We exchange phone numbers and promise to meet for lunch sometime. As Marion is pulling away, she lowers her tinted window, waves and shouts, "Both feet!"

15

The leaves are starting to turn, but the days are still warm. I love this time of year. The temperatures are mild and nature explodes in one last burst of color before the grayness of winter.

We are spending the day with the Chrises and their kids. Jack likes to drive, so we stuff ourselves into his compact car and head east to a family-owned apple orchard between Smithville and Kearney. Marissa found this place years ago and we have been getting our apples here ever since. She cans hers and makes apple pie filling, apple butter and apple sauce. I am deathly afraid to can anything. I just don't trust myself not to make a mistake that would result in someone getting sick, or worse. So I slice the apples, toss them with some ascorbic acid and freeze them in plastic freezer bags. I also make apple butter in the Crock-Pot and store it in jars in my freezer.

We pull onto the dirt road that leads up to a huge outbuilding on the farm. A shaggy white dog comes over as we exit the car.

"That's Lady," I say to Jack. "She likes to tag along."

Inside, Leah, the owner, is arranging apple slices on a platter. Leah's family is Mennonite, and so we almost always find her wearing a floral cotton dress with three-quarter length sleeves, and apron and a bonnet. Her long brown hair falls in strands out of her bonnet and her full mouth is spread into a friendly smile.

"Jel! It's nice to see you again. I see you've brought a friend."

"This is Jack," I say, as he and Leah shake hands. "We're expecting some other friends as well."

Leah walks us out to the orchard, where Sam, Ben and Rosie have already wheeled two wagons with four buckets.

"Today we have plenty of Honeycrisp and Fuji," says Leah, showing us where in the orchard those trees are located. "When your friends get here I'll have my children direct them to the orchard to meet up with you."

Rosie looks at me with mischief in her eyes. She squeals, then turns and takes off deep into the orchard with Jack in pursuit. I hear whoops and hollers as he catches up with her, scoops her up and spins her around. When I reach them, Rosie is sitting on Jack's shoulders, picking apples from high in a tree.

"Look!" she yells excitedly. "The ones up top are huge!" She has a bunch of them gathered in her shirt, which she is using like a hammock to hold the fruit. When the boys arrive, we put all the apples into a bucket. Ben and Sam go off to climb trees and pick, and Rosie spots Lady, so off she goes to play with the dog.

Jack is standing beside an apple tree. The rays of the sun filter through the branches, illuminating his handsome face and his eyes are alight with laughter. He scoops me up and swings me around. Abandoning myself to the moment, I shriek with delight. Suddenly, Jack loses his footing and we are both on the ground. I am lying on my back in the sweet smelling grass. His left hand is under my head and his right arm is splayed across my midsection. Our faces are so close to each other, and when I look into Jack's eyes, I feel an overwhelming urge to offer my lips to him, to feel his mouth on mine in a passionate kiss. Jack's breathing is heavy and I cannot tell if it is from the exertion of the fall or if he feels the same as I do. He returns my gaze and I see him shake his head slightly, but he doesn't move to stand up.

Softly, he whispers, "Are you hurt?"

"No, Jack," I answer breathlessly. "In fact, it feels good to be here...like this...with you holding me."

A slight breeze moves through the orchard, stirring up the scent of apples and it intoxicates me. I lift my head so that our lips are almost touching.

He shakes his head again and his eyes are wistful. There is sadness in his voice as he says, "There is a time for everything, love, and now is not the time."

Jack moves away from me and extends his hand to help me up. I take his hand and, as I am getting into a standing position, I hear a familiar voice.

"Hmm...what's going on here?" asks Christina, playfully.

"I...I just fell and Jack was helping me back up."

Now that the spell has been broken, I am embarrassed by my behavior. I know how important it is to Jack that we don't have a physical relationship, and it pains me that I lost myself and tempted him.

Chris and the rest of the crew emerge from behind the trees. Felicia is there, with Nica on her hip and Marcus is wheeling a wagon with two buckets on it. I call for my kids and we make introductions. Sam and Ambrose and Matthias and Ben pair off immediately. Rosie and May are a bit shy, but with some coaxing from Christina and me, they begin a conversation about ballet, which they have in common.

Nica sees Jack, puts her arms out and yells, "Daddy Dack!"

Jack laughs and scoops her up. The toddler squeals with delight. He picks an apple from a tree and shows it to Nica. She holds onto it like a prize.

"Let's show Angela, Nica," he says warmly, bringing her over to me. "This is Angela. Say hello, baby."

Her curls bounce as she shakes her head. "No!" she says, defiantly, burying her head in Jack's neck.

"Nica..." says Jack, in a gentle warning.

"No!" she says again, grinning. There is no malice. It is just a game to her.

Christina walks over and plucks the baby out of Jack's arms.

"Nica, when you want to say hello, you can go back to

Daddy Jack. Otherwise, Mommy holds you." She gives me an apologetic look. "No is Nica's favorite word, lately. We're trying to break her of the habit."

"No offense taken," I say, smiling.

Jack and Chris walk off to help the girls pick apples, leaving me with Christina, who says, "Jack told you about the baby?"

"He did," I answer, "I'm so sorry, Christina."

Nica is clamoring to get down out of Christina's arms. "Are you ready to say hello?" she asks the toddler.

"No!"

Christina sighs. "Then you stay with Mommy, Nica."

The child tosses her curls and sulks.

Christina looks weary now. I can see she has been thinking about the situation with Nica and it has stirred up emotions in her. "I want to thank you. Whatever you said to Jack really helped. He didn't talk to us about it. Well, we were a mess for a long time...he was probably afraid to, I guess." Christina shifts her weight so that Nica is on her hip. "He mentioned that he has had some conversations with you that have been very healing for him."

Since I have been involved with Jack, I haven't ever thought of myself as having the ability to give him anything. In fact, sometimes I wonder what he gets out of this relationship. He has been patient with me, is helping me to work on getting past my fears and has taught me how to have fun. I am glad to hear that I have done something to help him.

"I know that talking helps," I say. "When Devin died, my friend Marissa checked in on me every day and let me cry to her if I needed to. Even in my pain I felt loved by her. I wouldn't want Jack to be alone if he doesn't have to be."

She looks at me intently. "You're good for him," her voice is decisive.

"I am?"

"You are."

16

On the way home from pizza at Frankie's, Jack says, "I'm thinking about buying a new car."

Jack's spending worries me. He takes me to expensive places, buys me extravagant gifts and, frankly, I don't think he can afford it. I'd be just as happy getting a burrito at Chipotle as I would at a gourmet restaurant, but Jack insists on wining and dining me.

"Do you really *need* one, Jack? I mean, new cars are expensive..."

He chuckles. "I can afford a new car. Besides, this one can get pretty cramped when the kids are with us."

"You spend too much money," I blurt out. "Gifts, restaurants and now a car...it's too much."

Instead of turning into my driveway, Jack drives past my house and down to the lake. He parks by the marina and then turns to me. "Angela, I can afford all these things. And besides, I have been waiting all my life to pamper a beautiful woman, so why shouldn't I?"

As a single mother, I need to be very careful about my finances. Jim introduced me to Dave Ramsey's books a while ago and I got hooked. Dave Ramsey is a finance guru who has his own radio and talk shows that help people get out of debt and stay debt free. His philosophy is simple; pay cash for things or don't buy them.

I feel very strong emotions for Jack, but this is something I just can't compromise on and it may result in my not being able to see him anymore, so I brace myself for what may be coming.

"Look," I say. "When Devin was alive, I left our finances up to him. I just bought what we needed and didn't give it a second thought. Since he made a good salary, I assumed we were okay. Well, when he died, I was left with an absolute mess. It turns out that Devin liked having cash, so he charged everything he could in order to have a lot of money in his wallet. After paying off his maxed-out credit cards and our mortgage with the insurance settlement, what's left over isn't enough for me to feel secure."

I reach over and take his hand. "I care about you very much, Jack, but I don't think I can have a serious relationship with someone who isn't concerned with being frugal and wise with financial choices."

Jack looks surprised. "You've been worried about this for a while? Why didn't you say something?"

"How do I bring something like that up? Ask for your check register?"

"Come here," he whispers, and draws me to him. "Look at me, Angela. Do you trust me?"

"Yes, Jack, I trust you, but this just doesn't add up. How much money can you possibly make working for the Church?"

He smiles a lopsided smile and then kisses me on the forehead. "The work I do for the Bishop is more like a hobby, love. I don't really need the money."

"Jack, I don't understand you."

"When my parents died, my uncle liquidated their assets and invested the money for me. Uncle Rafael was a smart investor, not only for me, but also for himself. He did well in mutual funds and in real estate. When my aunt and uncle passed away, I inherited their estate, which included several apartment buildings in New Jersey. After I graduated, I saved up and bought some real estate, which I sold in the late 90's and made a nice profit. I still own my aunt and uncle's apartment buildings, because they are doing well. I have someone who manages them, so I mostly just collect checks from the properties."

"So, you're basically a real estate investor?" I don't like the sound of this at all.

"No, not really. I'm not interested in making deals. I'd much rather teach. The money that my uncle invested for me 42 years ago I never touched. When I was a minor, he would roll over the dividends for me and I have been continuing to do that ever since. I do the same with the money I invested on my own. Each time I get a check, I tithe 20% and I put the rest right back."

I remember something that I read in a Dave Ramsey book once, that if you invest $2,000 a year from ages 19 to 27, and don't touch it until you are 65, you will have about a million and a half dollars to retire on. I'm overwhelmed.

"So...what are you telling me?" I ask.

"That I make enough money from my job and my properties to live very comfortably. I have been leaving my investments alone in the hope that one day I would have a family to spend it on. What I am telling you is that I can afford a new car."

He kisses my forehead. "How do you feel about all this, love?"

"Would it surprise you if I said I was slightly disappointed?"

Jack laughs. "You, Angela, are a constant surprise to me! Why are you disappointed?"

I smile sheepishly. "Well, I have always fancied you a penniless academic who wined and dined me, then had to eat rice and beans for a week, because you were sacrificing all so that I would fall in love with you. I was touched. Now I find out that it's no big deal. Seriously, how would *you* feel?"

He looks at me intensely for a long while. "I feel like...I'd better get you home."

"Why, is something wrong?" I feel very close to Jack right now, after sharing about Devin, and I don't really want to go just yet.

"No," he says, huskily, "I'm fighting the urge to take you in my arms and...I...need to get you home."

After we pull into my driveway, Jack walks me to the door and kisses my hand.

"I'm sorry, Jack. I didn't mean to—"

"Angela," he says, firmly, "you did *nothing* wrong."

"Then...what?"

"I'm not sure. I think...well...there have been women who wanted to date me specifically because they knew I had money. But here you are telling me that you almost wish I was penniless. It affected me in a way that I didn't expect."

"Are you going to be okay?"

"Yeah," he looks down at his feet, "The gym is open 24 hours. I'll spend some time on the treadmill." He turns and starts to walk down the steps.

"Jack?"

He looks over his shoulder. "Yes, love?"

"Remember that night we went out for gelato? When I got home I had to scrub my kitchen floor," I say, blushing. "Just want you to know that you're not alone."

17

It's Jack's birthday. He took the whole day off to spend with us. It's a school day, so Jack and I meet for morning Mass, and then we go grocery shopping together.

Jack wants me to make a big Italian meal...macaroni, meatballs, bracciole...the whole nine yards. It's going to take hours, but Jack is constantly pampering me; so I am happy to be able to reciprocate for once.

While Jack finishes unpacking the car, I put a large pot on the stove and pour in some olive oil. Then I add some water to a small pot and put two eggs in it to hard boil for the filling for the bracciole. I'm dicing onions when he walks into the kitchen holding a small gift bag.

"What's this?" I ask, wiping my hands on my apron, "You bought all the ingredients for dinner and now your own gift as well?"

He winks at me, which makes the color rise in my cheeks. "No, Angela, this is for you. I wanted to give you this today," he says, handing me the bag. I'm touched by his thoughtfulness.

In the bag is a small box, obviously made for a piece of jewelry. Carefully, I lift the lid. Inside is a pair of exquisite emerald cut diamond stud earrings set in white gold. They must be at least a carat each. I draw in a breath. "Jack...I don't know what to say..."

"Say you love them," he says.

"I'm sorry. I... I was caught off guard. They are lovely and I *do* love them. Thank you."

He embraces me and tilts my head up to look into his eyes. "I love you, Angela," he whispers.

Tears roll down my cheeks. "Jack, I'm not sure if I'm there yet. I'm not sure if I know what love is..."

Is it possible to be both elated and devastated at the

same time? Knowing that Jack is in love with me sets my heart soaring, but my inability to know my own feelings brings it crashing right back down to the ground.

"I want you to take all the time you need," he says. "I hope you don't think I'm pressuring you."

"No, Jack. I can't imagine you pressuring me to do anything. You have to be the most patient man I have ever known. I'm frustrated with myself, though. I wanted to make this day...everything...special for you."

"Then put these on," he says, taking the earrings out of the box. "I want to see them on you."

I take one out of his hand and put it in my ear. It has some weight to it, but it's not uncomfortable.

"They were Zia Mina's. My uncle gave them to her on her fortieth birthday. She always hoped I would give them to the woman I loved and so I am honoring her wishes."

My hands tremble a bit as I put the other earring in. "Jack, I don't feel worthy to wear these. After all, from everything you have told me about your aunt, she was practically perfect in every way." I sigh. "...and me?"

"You're an angel."

When dinner is done, I put on the coffee and take out the cake. Rosie and I made Jack a homemade chocolate layer cake with a rich chocolate frosting. For the filling, we folded together Nutella and the frosting. I placed individual Baci candies all around the side of the cake as a decoration. On top, I wrote, "Buon Compleanno" in blue icing.

In between the writing, I add 46 candles and manage to burn myself twice while lighting them. I carry the cake into the dining room and we all sing. I can see the look on Jack's face. He is deeply touched. Then I realize it has probably been many years since anyone has baked him a birthday cake. I wonder if the last person to do this was his aunt. Silently, I ask her to watch over Jack and me. It takes Jack two tries to blow all the candles out.

"Thanks," he says wryly. "I had forgotten just how old I was and I'm so glad you reminded me."

"Wait till you see the support hose and cane we got you as a gift," I jest, cutting a slice of cake and handing it to him. "The birthday guy gets the first slice."

"This is delicious, Angela! You made this yourself?"

"I helped Mama bake it. I also cooked the frosting," says Rosie proudly. "We usually put just frosting in between the layers, but Mama said you would love it if we added the Nutella."

"And I do," Jack says, reaching out and mussing Rosie's curls. "But what I like best is that you took the time to bake it for me."

The cake is cut and the coffee is poured. "Present time," I say.

Jack glances at me and clears his throat. "You know, some people like to *give* gifts on their birthday, instead of receiving them, don't they, Sam?"

"Well, yeah...Hobbits," he grins. Sam has warmed up to Jack over the past couple of months and our dinners with him are relaxed and comfortable now.

"Did I ever tell you I was part Hobbit?" Jack tosses Sam his keys. "There are two wrapped gifts on my back seat. Would you boys mind bringing them in?" I look over at Jack questioningly. He winks.

Sam comes in holding a package the size of a cake box and Ben has a small, jewelry-sized gift box. "Ben, that one is for your sister and the other one is for you boys."

"Thanks, Mr. B," the kids chorus.

Rosie squeals. Jack has given her a pair of earrings, each shaped like a pink ballet slipper and a matching necklace. She throws her arms around his neck and kisses him enthusiastically on the cheek. Jack is obviously happy to hug her back.

"Thank you! I love, love, *love* them! Will you put the

necklace on me, please?"

As Jack obliges, I hear Ben exclaim, "This is awesome!" as he and Sam tear into the wrapping on their box.

"This *is*!" Sam adds, and holds up a game of Trivial Pursuit, the *Lord of the Rings* edition. The boys are very excited. They begin to open the box, but I clear my throat. Sam looks up and walks over to Jack. Ben follows and they both shake his hand and thank him.

"Who wants to play?" Jack asks, enthusiastically.

While the boys open the game and take out the instructions, Rosie gives Jack a poem she wrote out on pink construction paper in her curvy handwriting.

Mr. B likes coffee, not tea
And I know he really likes me
He also likes Ben and Samwise Gamgee
But like a sailor who loves the sea
And a bird who loves the tree
Mr. B loves Mrs. C
And that's the way I like it to be

"This is beautiful, Rosie," Jack says and embraces her. "I am going to put this where I can see it every day."

"Mama doesn't rhyme with tree, so I had to put 'Mrs. C,'" says Rosie, looking up at Jack in adoration. Jack leans over and whispers in her ear, "It's okay, I knew who you meant." Rosie climbs into Jack's lap and wraps her arms tightly around his neck and rests her head on his shoulder.

The scene causes a lump to form in my throat. They look so comfortable and content. Just like a father and daughter. Then fear rises in my chest.

Oh, God, I don't think I'm ready for this. It's too big for me to handle right now. Please help me.

I ask the kids to clear the table so we can play the game and then I retreat into the living room for a minute. I was on my feet almost the entire day and I just need a few minutes to recharge. Jack helps the kids and then comes and sits next to me on the couch.

"If I told you this was the best birthday I ever had, would you believe me?"

"No," I answer, smiling. "Because you haven't even opened your gift yet."

"Hey...the deal was that your gift to me would be this huge meal it took you hours to cook."

"I'm sorry, but you didn't read the fine print on the paperwork. The deal also included a cake, a gift and the company of three overexcited children. You really should be more careful about what you agree to, Jack," I say, handing him an envelope. "Here, this is for you. Happy 46th Birthday."

"Do you need to keep mentioning my age?" he jokes, as he takes the envelope and opens it. His eyes grow wide in surprise. "Michael Bublé tickets? Angela, how did you get these?"

"What do you mean how did I get these? I bought them for you. I'm taking you out to dinner that night, too. So save the date...February 17th; that's your birthday gift."

I wanted to do something special for Jack, so to finance the tickets, I sold one of the silver dollars my father gave me, then dug through my jewelry box and sold some broken gold bracelets and a couple of unmatched earrings. They netted enough money for the show and a modest dinner.

"First off, thank you, Angela. This is very generous of you. But I can't help but think that you probably had to make a big sacrifice to do this."

"To paraphrase a sage old man I know, 'I've been waiting all my life to pamper a handsome man, so why shouldn't I?'"

18

We have fallen into a routine. Jack spends Friday nights with me and Sundays with all of us. We meet at Our Lady of the Angels for 11:00 Mass and Jack stays through our family rosary at night. Sometimes he will spend the odd Saturday or weeknight as well. It is an arrangement that seems to work for everyone.

With love and patience Jack has endeared himself to my children. Sam was initially a challenge, but I sense them growing closer over time. Jack and I continue to pray about our relationship. Sometimes it seems to me that he has made up his mind and is just waiting for me to get on board. I try not to talk about marriage too much, because, frankly, the thought of it scares me. I can see all the ways Devin and I messed up our relationship and I'm afraid that the same may happen to Jack and me.

"Mom, check this out," Ben says, standing at the computer.

Jack bought Ben a digital camera and a photo printer for his birthday and Ben has been photographing everything under the sun. Up on the monitor I see a grid of pictures. Ben clicks on one and it looms large on the screen. It is a picture of Jack and I sitting on the couch in my living room. Jack is sitting up straight and I am next to him, with my body slightly facing away from him. I am looking over my shoulder at him, and Jack's head is turned toward me. I was there, so I know we were having a conversation, but in the picture, it looks like Jack and I are leaning in for a kiss. It is a beautiful picture.

"Can you print that one for me, kiddo?" I ask.

***

It's Christmas Eve and Jack arrived at what seemed like

the crack of dawn. I think he is more excited about Christmas than the kids have collectively been for their entire lives. His over-the-top enthusiasm is beginning to irritate me, but I remind myself that he has spent many a lonely holiday in the past and I should be patient and indulgent with him. Still, his behavior for the past couple weeks has reminded me of a new puppy; eager to get into everything. He bought the kids more toys than they even want or asked for. He offered to buy me everything I even glanced at when we were out shopping together. Yesterday he even came over and put up our outdoor lights...I'm afraid to see the electric bill.

"Popeyes for breakfast," I announce to the crowd as I start cutting holes in pieces of Italian bread. I place them into a frying pan with melted butter and then crack an egg into each hole. Jack pours coffee and hot chocolate as I flip the popeyes and then plate them. He leads prayers and everyone dives in. We need to eat quickly because there is so much to do today.

Jack convinced us to celebrate Advent this year and wait till Christmas Eve to decorate the tree. At first I was put off, but I really warmed up to the idea after putting it into practice. This Advent was a quiet time of reflection, and instead of focusing on the Christmas hype, we were able to work on quieting our hearts and preparing our souls for the coming of the Baby Jesus. As we pull out bins of ornaments, I appreciate that we waited and that we are actually celebrating Christmas on Christmas and not for the whole month after Thanksgiving.

While the kids decorate, I go into the kitchen and make a mental list of what food I need to prepare: antipasto, baked clams, calamari, flounder and shrimp. The hardest jobs come first. I'll bread and fry the flounder and calamari and then worry about the rest of it later.

Jack pokes his head into the kitchen. "You're not decorating the tree?"

I sigh. "I have a lot to do in the kitchen, Jack. You do want to eat Christmas Eve dinner on Christmas Eve, right?"

He walks over and takes my hand, "Come with me, love. Everything will get done. Don't worry." He turns to lead me into the living room, but I pull back on his hand.

"Jack, can we talk?"

He nods and sits on a stool at the counter. "Decorating the tree is hard for me. I left it completely up to the kids last year. There are so many ornaments with so many memories... And this year, you are here..."

Jack looks hurt.

"Meaning," I say, putting my hand on his arm, "I want you to spend Christmas with us, of course I do. It's just...I have all these feelings bouncing around inside of me. I feel like a walking, talking, pinball machine. How do I handle this...my happiness at spending this day with you and my children and the sadness of having all of these memories thrust into my face?"

"Oh, Angela, I didn't think about this; that you would be in pain today. I'm sorry."

"I don't want you to be sorry. It has nothing to do with you. I would feel sad about this whether you were here or not. I just...I know that you are so happy about today and are looking forward to celebrating and I'm trying to manage my feelings and not put a damper on yours."

I slip behind Jack, wrap my arms around him and rest my head on his shoulder. He reaches up and squeezes my hand.

"We'll work on it, love," he says, softly. "We'll take our feelings into consideration and we'll care for each other. I won't ask you to decorate the tree."

"You decorate with the kids, and I'll make you a meal you'll never forget," I say, as Jack swivels the stool so that he is facing me. "Have I told you lately that spending time with you is one of my favorite things to do? I'm so glad you're here today...and will be tomorrow, too."

After a morning of slicing, chopping, breading, frying, mixing and baking, dinner is mostly done. All that's left to do is put together the antipasto and mix the salad dressing. I take off my apron and throw it in the laundry room.

"I'm heading to the shower," I tell the crew. "Then we'll eat."

In the shower, I scrub off the fishy smell and the layer of olive oil that has settled on my skin from the frying I did earlier. I quickly slip on my black dress pants and a very old, but not very worn, red crew neck sweater. Now that I'm showered and my hair and makeup are done, I no longer smell like a squid. This helps me to embrace a festive mood.

When I get into the dining room, Jack and the kids have the table set, the candles lit and the food on serving platters. "We put together the antipasto," he says, "but you're a lot better at the salad dressing than I am."

The table looks lovely. "Thanks for your help, guys," I tell them, smiling. "The feast will begin momentarily."

Walking into the kitchen, I notice that the dishwasher has been loaded and started and the counters have been wiped down.

"You look beautiful, Angela," says Jack as I pour white balsamic vinegar onto the salad. "But, I think there is something missing."

"Missing? What?"

He moves behind me and I see that he is putting a necklace on me. Gently, he turns me around to face him. "Much better," he says. "What do *you* think?"

I look down and see a beautiful crucifix on a silver herringbone chain. The corpus is white gold set on a filigreed cross of yellow gold. It is exquisite.

"Merry Christmas, darling," he whispers.

Most men, if they said 'darling' would sound awkward or archaic. But the way Jack says it makes my heart skip a beat. I wrap my arms around him.

"I don't think it is possible for you to spoil me any more than you already do. It is beyond beautiful. Thank you, Jack."

After dinner, we all relax in the living room. The fire that Jack has started in the hearth crackles and glows, while the lights on the tree softly twinkle.

Everyone is drowsy because we got such an early start to the busy day. Sleepily, Rosie walks over and sits on Jack's lap.

"Rosie, why don't you sleep for a while and we'll wake you up for Mass later?"

Eyes half-closed, she gives a nod. "Will you and Mama tuck me in?"

"Sure," says Jack, scooping her up and carrying her down the hall. "Call us when you're ready."

Ben yawns. "Okay if I take a nap, too?" Sam is right behind him.

We plan to leave for midnight Mass in about three hours. I tell the boys we'll wake them and they turn in. Rosie pads toward us in her night gown, rubbing her eyes. Silently, she takes my hand and Jack's hand and leads us into her room.

Snuggling under her blankets, she puts her arms out for a hug. I sit on the edge of her bed and embrace her. "Mr. B, too," she whispers. Jack leans in for a hug, and then, with his thumb, he makes the sign of the cross on Rosie's forehead. Her eyebrows meet. "What was that?"

"I blessed you, Rosie," says Jack. He looks so happy at this moment. I am sure that he must be longing for a child of his own to tuck in and bless and Rosie has, in a small way, fulfilled that longing; at least on this night.

"Daddy never blessed me," she says. "Daddy never prayed. He went to church, but he didn't pray."

"I think he prayed for you. You just didn't see him

doing it. I'm sure he still does, Rosie."

Yawning, she nods. "Mama, how about one song...the one you've been singing?"

I have always sung my kids to sleep. Rosie still asks me to. Usually, she likes the songs from *The Sound of Music,* but lately she has been asking for *O Come, O Come Emmanuel.* I feel self-conscious, singing a capella in front of Jack, but I try to put it aside and appease my daughter.

I lean over and kiss her. "Okay," I whisper, "but lights out and sleep right after."

I flip the switch on her wall and the room goes dark, then I muster up the nerve to sing the Christmas carol.

Outside Rosie's room, Jack takes my hands in his. "Angela, your voice is beautiful. Where did you learn to sing like that?"

I shrug. "Daddy used to have the radio or his record player going all the time when I was a kid. We loved to listen to music. I was in the choir all through grade school and into high school."

We settle down on the couch and the warmth of the fire covers us like a blanket. "I've always loved to sing; most of all to my children. But when I was a kid, my secret dream was to be a wedding singer. I never wanted to be famous. I just wanted to sing and make people happy."

Jack sighs and his eyes have a faraway look.

"What is it, Jack?" I ask.

"There are things I want to say, but I don't want you to feel I am being too forward," he says, hesitantly.

"I thought you said 'total transparency' when we started this relationship, didn't you?"

He nods. "I was just wishing that maybe...maybe you would sing to me on our wedding day."

Sweet Jack. He gives me everything and the one thing he wants from me I just can't give him...at least not right now.

I take his hand in mine. "Music has been something that

causes profound joy in me. Even as a baby, my father said when I heard music, my eyes would grow wide and I would begin to coo and move my arms and legs. After Devin's accident, I could no longer sing. I don't just mean I lost the desire to sing, which I did, but I literally could not sing...not at Mass, not to my kids, not even in the shower. Even listening to music was painful. When I met you, it had already started to abate. I was able to listen to music, but still not sing yet. Then, one day, I was able to hum along to music and then, slowly, my desire returned. It has taken a very long time, Jack, but I can finally sing again."

I pull my legs up onto the couch and drape the chenille throw over Jack and me.

"My life, like everyone's life, is a journey. Right now God has healed me enough so that I can sing to my children. But, Jack," I say, looking into his eyes. "I don't want you to give up on me. Maybe someday I will sing to you, too."

After Mass, Jack drops us home and heads over to Marissa and John's to sleep. They are out of town at John's brother's house for the holidays, but Mar said Jack could stay over tonight so he wouldn't have to make the trip back home at 2 a.m., just to turn around and come back for Christmas Day. The kids immediately exit the car and stagger into the house. As Jack opens the door of the car to let me out, I hand him my spare house key.

"Come over as soon as you get up," I say. "Put the coffee on, but be quiet, otherwise you'll wake the rest of us." I chuckle and wink at him.

He laughs and pulls me close. "I love you, Angela. Merry Christmas."

Fear, once again, rises in my chest. I wish I could say the same to Jack, but I'm not ready and my heart breaks for him. With tears in my eyes, I whisper, "Merry Christmas," and head up the steps to the front door.

After putting the kids' gifts under the tree, I fall into bed, exhausted. Thinking about the day, it occurs to me that I feel like I am standing on the edge of a precipice with Jack on the other side. I want to step off, but fear prevents me.

God, help me to do your will. I'm afraid, Lord, so give me a push if that is what I need...a big one.

***

Consciousness seeps into my brain and I take a deep breath. The aroma of coffee wafts into my bedroom and I realize that Jack must be here. I wonder if the kids are awake yet. Silently I pray my morning offering and then I welcome Jesus to the world. *Happy Birthday, Infant King! You were born to die so that the gates of Heaven would open for me. Thank you!*

Yawning and stretching, I throw the comforter to the side and head into the bathroom. There are bags under my eyes and my hair is mussed. Quickly, I brush my teeth, rub on moisturizer, slather on eye cream and fix my hair. Then I don my bathrobe and head for the kitchen. All is quiet in the house, except for the faint snoring coming from Ben's room. I make a pit stop into the living room and take Jack's present from under the tree.

Jack is sitting at the kitchen counter with a cup of coffee.

"Merry Christmas, Jack," I say, handing him the gift.

"Merry Christmas, Angela," he says, as he tears the wrapping and looks down at the picture in the frame. His eyes light up. "Did Ben take this?"

I nod. "It's beautiful, isn't it?" I wrap my arms around Jack's neck and give him a peck on the cheek. We both take in the photo for a few seconds.

"This is the perfect Christmas gift, love. Thank you."

"It's not much, but it's the best I can do right now."

"I know," Jack says, wistfully.

19

The week between Christmas and New Year's is hard for us, because it contains the anniversary of Devin's death. It doesn't affect the kids profoundly right now; they are still young. Anniversaries don't mean as much when you are younger as they do when you are older and are aware of your mortality. I have struggled with the inclination to retreat into my shell and push Jack away. With hard work on my part and patience on Jack's, we have been able to juggle my emotions and his desire to be a part of our lives this week.

Early this morning, the kids and I went to Mass and then to the cemetery. We prayed at Devin's graveside. Rosie and Ben cried freely as we prayed, but Sam remained stoic. There was a biting wind, so we were unable to linger, but we talked a bit in the car before we headed home. Each of us told a favorite memory of Devin. The boys both chose the time Dev got the three of them box seats at a Royals game. Rosie related how, on the day of her first communion she saw tears in her father's eyes. I never knew that and the thought of Devin becoming emotional on that day touches me, but not enough to penetrate the numbness I woke up with this morning. Driving home, I wonder whether it was wise to ask Jack to come over this afternoon to spend time with us.

***

We just polished off all the leftovers from Christmas and the kids are downstairs in the rec room happily playing with the new Wii games Jack got them for Christmas. Jack is poking the fire he built in the hearth as I wipe my hands on a kitchen towel. I put it down on the counter and walk over to him, wrap my arms around his neck and press my body close to his.

Jack doesn't reciprocate, so I take his arms and put them around me.

"What are you doing?" he asks.

"I'm about to do something really difficult and I need some comfort from you."

Jack puts a small distance between us and enfolds me in his arms. "What is it, love?"

Looking up at Jack, I say, "Would you help me put away Devin's things that are still around? I'm not sure if I can get through it alone, but it's time...overdue, actually."

He kisses me gently on the forehead. "I'm proud of you, Angela."

I send Jack to the garage to get an empty bin for me as I start removing Devin's CD's from the media cabinet. Jack comes upstairs and sits down on the floor next to me. He looks through the ones I have already removed. "You know, I was wondering about those; AC/DC, Megadeath, Metallica...they didn't seem like you," he says, pulling Van Halen's *Diver Down* off the shelf and adding it to the pile. I put my hand on his and take it off the CD.

"That one is mine," I say, "Leave all the Van Halen, Aerosmith and Bon Jovi." I point to the bottom shelf. "These are mine, too."

"Very eclectic," Jack muses. "Etta James, Peter Mitchell, the Cranberries, Smashmouth and Dean Martin?"

"Hey, good music is good music," I say, as we continue to pull jewel cases from the shelves.

When Devin's music is in the bin and mine is rearranged in the cabinet, I get up and head into my bedroom. I come back with a decorative hat box I have been saving for today. Going over to the tree, I begin to remove the ornaments that were special to Devin and me and put them in the box. One of them is a picture frame that encloses a wallet-sized wedding portrait. It says "First Christmas Together." I hand it to Jack.

"That was Jel," I say, dully. "She had no idea what she was doing on that day. She married this man but they never really loved each other. Well, a kind of love developed between them, because they shared a family, but it wasn't the beautiful, sacred love that it should have been. He died without ever knowing that kind of love. Tragic, isn't it?"

A tidal wave of sadness sweeps me away. I feel myself sinking to the floor and then the tears come. Jack pulls me close and cradles me in his arms, rocking me like an infant.

"I wish I could take away your pain," he murmurs into my ear, as he gently strokes my hair. I sob into Jack's chest until I'm spent.

"You can't take away my pain, Jack," I say, wearily. "But you do help me to bear it and that's why I..."

I...what? I think I was about to say I love Jack. Do I love Jack? I have been waiting for love to come, but I don't think it's here yet. I would think that when love arrives it would do so with some fanfare; that it would feel big and momentous. I haven't felt that yet.

Jack gazes deeply into my eyes. I keep mine fixed on his. I feel as if he can see into the very depths of my soul. It is unnerving and I feel vulnerable and naked, but I don't allow myself to look away.

There are footsteps on the stairs. "What's going on?" There is alarm in Sam's voice. "I thought I heard Mom crying."

"Your mother is feeling very sad about your Dad right now, Sam," Jack says, gently.

Sam comes over and kneels down next to me. "Are you okay, Mom?"

I nod in affirmation and Sam's face crumples. "I'm

sorry," he whispers. "We talked about it this morning...I wasn't sure what to do...I...I should have..."

"We're all in pain," I tell Sam. "And we all deal with it in our own way. The important thing is to let it out."

Tears begin to flow from Sam's eyes and I take him into my arms. There we sit on the living room floor; the three of us, each one in another's arms. I comfort Sam and the both of us derive comfort from Jack.

20

"Oooh, pumpkin bars!" Marissa exclaims, looking at the plate in my hand. "You just come right on in! So, honey, what's going on?"

"Jack is leaving for a week," I tell her. "He just called and told me that he needs to go to a class at the Theology of the Body Institute."

"The one in Pennsylvania?" she asks.

"Yes. The bishop put him on the waiting list and an opening just came up. He's flying out tomorrow in the early afternoon. He's spending the day with me," I say, removing the plastic wrap from the tray of pumpkin bars. "We're going to Mass and then I'm driving him to the airport. I feel like an idiot, but I actually started crying when he told me."

Marissa is scooping coffee into the filter of her drip pot. "Why do you think you feel this way?"

I sit down on a stool at the counter and put my chin in my hand. "I don't know, but I don't think I really want to be without him for a whole week. Besides, we were supposed to see Michael Bublé on Thursday and that's shot now, too."

Marissa sits down next to me, puts her hands on my shoulders and looks at me intently. "I'm going to ask you a hard question, honey, but I'm doing it because I love you."

I sigh. "Okay, I'm bracing myself."

"Have you ever thought about the fact that you have known Jack for more than a year, you are in a courtship and you *still* haven't made a commitment to him?"

"But, he said we could take our time..."

"Taking time is one thing. You're procrastinating. He loves the heck out of you, girl," Marissa scolds, giving my shoulders a gentle squeeze. "Everyone can see it. Even your kids can see it. Do you think it is fair to Jack for you to continue the relationship if you can't say you feel the same way?"

Suddenly, I can see clearly that I have taken Jack for granted and have pretty much strung him along. The realization comes like a slap across the face. My heart feels heavy and I begin to cry. Marissa puts her arm around my shoulder.

"Honey, I think it's time for you to either be all in or all out. If you don't love Jack and don't want to spend the rest of your life with him, then let him go find someone who will," her voice softens. "But I know you and I can see that you love him."

I'm sobbing now. Marissa is right. Marissa is always right when it comes to me. "I don't want to lose him, Mar...but I'm afraid to say I love him."

"Why, Jel?"

"Because what if something goes wrong?"

Marissa takes my face in her hands and looks deeply into my eyes.

"Something *will* go wrong," she says, her voice full of emotion. "I've buried more babies than most women give birth to. You and I both have had financial problems, losses, hurts, disappointments...something *always* goes wrong. The question you need to ask yourself is, do you want to weather the storms with or without Jack?"

***

It's 1:30 in the morning and I haven't slept a wink. I pray, silently offering myself to God and lie there in His presence for a while. Eventually I get out of bed and make some herbal tea. Then I sit down at the computer and decide to make a CD for Jack. I'll slip it into his bag tomorrow when he's not looking. I find a blank disc and label it, 'Songs That Remind Me of You.' Then I get on

Amazon and start perusing the song lists. I click on Mariah Carey's cover of Foreigner's 'I Want to Know What Love Is' and listen to the excerpt. Mariah's beautiful voice sings about how she can no longer hide from the love that has finally found her.

Is this You again, Lord, speaking to me through music? This is exactly what I needed to hear. Thank You.

When I am done downloading, I type up and print out a play list, then cut it to fit in the CD case.

I Want to Know What Love Is (Mariah Carey)

Sunday Kind of Love (Etta James)

The Best is Yet to Come (Frank Sinatra)

Dreams (Cranberries)

I've Got the World on a String (Michael Bublé)

Falling For You (Colbie Caillat)

One Alone Is My Love (Peter Mitchell)

All the Way (Harry Connick Jr.)

Don't Want to Miss a Thing (Aerosmith)

The clock says 2:39, but instead of being bleary-eyed, I feel at peace. Turning off my light, I fall into a gentle sleep.

***

I step out of the shower, wrap a towel around my wet hair and start to rub coconut oil onto my freshly shaven legs. Over the hum of the exhaust fan, I hear a knocking at the front door, so I slip my robe on and head down to the landing.

Jack is standing outside, looking annoyed. "Do you know your doorbell is broken?"

"It's nice to see you, too." I say, letting him in. "I'm sorry about the bell. Sometimes things wear out, Jack."

If I would have known Jack was coming so early I would have gotten in the shower sooner. I waited till the kids left, so I could have a luxurious and relaxing scrub; something our morning schedule won't accommodate.

He runs his hand through his hair and sighs. "I'm sorry...I didn't get much sleep last night and that's certainly not your fault. I'll fix the bell when I get back."

I look at Jack sympathetically. "You must be stressed."

Jack leans in to embrace me and inhales. "You smell delicious, Angela," he says, huskily. And then he gives me kisses starting at my forehead and trailing down to my neck. Nerve endings all over my body respond by standing at attention. Reluctantly, I take a step back.

"Danger, Will Robinson," I say. After all, I have only a robe on and we are completely alone. Jack puts his hands up in the air like he's being held up.

"You're right," he says, but his eyes look troubled.

"Here," I say leading Jack into the living room. "You relax on the couch. I'm going to finish getting ready."

While I dry my hair and put on my makeup I pray. *Jesus please give me the time and the words to tell Jack that I love him. And bless Jack. He is troubled this morning.*

Jack is sitting on the couch reading his Magnificat.

"How long till Mass starts?" I ask as I walk into the living room all dressed and ready.

He looks at his watch. "We have half an hour. Listen, after Mass, I want to take you to Sam's Club and buy you some groceries for the week."

I don't want to spend my last couple of hours with Jack shopping, so I begin to protest.

"Oh, for Pete sakes, Angela," he says, testily. "Why can't you just let me love you?"

Immediately I see remorse in his eyes. "I'm sorry," Jack

says, quietly. "I...I don't know what's wrong with me this morning. I feel...restless. When I woke up, I had the distinct feeling that somehow life was going to profoundly change today and I'm afraid--"

I put my finger over his lips. "Shhh," and then in my best John Paul II voice I say, "Be not afraid."

This elicits a half-smile from him. I reach out and take Jack's hands in mine.

"Jack, I'm so sorry. I have been taking you, and your love for me, for granted. It took you leaving to make me realize how strong my feelings are for you. But I'm sure God knew what I needed and arranged that...sort of like a divine two by four to the side of the head."

I can see a glimmer of hope flicker in Jack's eyes. "All this time I have thought that falling in love would be an event...something big, like an earthquake or a strong, driving wind. But, for a while now, there has been a still, small voice inside me; a voice I have been ignoring, waiting instead for that big sign, because, once again, I fell into relying on myself instead of God to direct my life."

I sigh and look deep into his eyes. This time there is no fear, and the words come easily. "Jack...I love you. I love you and I'm *in* love with you."

"Oh, Angela!" he says, fiercely, and crushes me to him. The world seems to recede and all I know are Jack's arms and the beating of his heart.

After Mass, Jack gently squeezes my hand as I begin to exit the pew, so I sit back down again. The sanctuary is empty; we are the only ones here. But the red candle is lit, signifying that Jesus is present in the tabernacle. Jack's head is bowed and he is deep in prayer. As I watch him, joy springs forth from my soul and I almost can't contain it. A prayer wells up from deep inside me.

Jesus, I am in awe of Your goodness and generosity.

Thank You for giving me this man to love. Please give me the grace to honor both You and Jack by loving him according to Your will.

We are walking through the airport holding hands. "I'll e-mail you every day. You don't have to e-mail me back. I know you'll be busy studying."

"I'll try and call you every day, but this is very intensive and I'm not sure how much time I'll have. It might have to be just a good night call."

Jack is about to go through airport security and he wraps his arms around me for the last time.

"Tell me what you prayed about after Mass?" I ask.

"I was thanking God for answering my lifelong prayer," he smiles, "that the woman of my dreams would fall in love with me."

"Really? Who is she?" I jest. "Do I know her?"

Jack laughs heartily. "I'm going to miss you, love."

"Ciao. Te amo," I say, wistfully, as I watch him turn and walk toward the security gate.

21

To: **giacomob@kcdiocese.org**
From: **jellycooke@gomail.com**
RE: Happy St. Valentine's Day
Thank you for the roses! They are so beautiful! Rosie hasn't seen hers yet. She'll get them after school. Pink was a good choice for her. I love you, too, Jack.
Angela
Song of Songs 5:8

To: **giacomob@kcdiocese.org**
From: **jellycooke@gomail.com**
RE: I love you
I hope class is going well. Thanks for the quick call earlier.
I miss you, too.
Study hard...get an A ☺
I love you
Angela
Song of Songs 8:7

My phone is ringing. Rousing myself from a deep sleep, I grope for it and look at the screen. It's Jack. Clearing my throat so I don't sound tired, I answer.

"Jack? It's after midnight by you; is everything okay?"

He sighs. "Angela...I'm...I'm having a bit of a struggle tonight..."

Poor Jack. How can I help him? I'll try to distract him.

"Well...things have been pretty dull around here without you, sweetheart," I say. "Rosie is not thrilled that you left on a moments' notice and didn't say goodbye. She is making a book of all the things you *didn't* do with her this week. Brace yourself for it when you get back. Hell hath no fury, you know... Oh! And you'll never guess what I found at the thrift store on Saturday! An air hockey table and it's in great shape! Someone dropped it off while I was there, so I had to wait for them to process it before I could buy it. John came with his truck and helped me get it home and the boys helped him get it down into the rec room. They have been having a great time using it."

I feel like a chatterbox and I wonder how much good this is doing.

"Hey, Jack? Are you sleepy?"

"Unfortunately, far from it." Jack's voice sounds so tense.

"Then pray a rosary with me."

The blue crocheted rosary that Marissa gave me hangs from a post on my headboard. As I reach for it, I say, "Let's pray the Sorrowful Mysteries." I want to meditate on Christ's suffering while offering up these prayers for Jack in his own suffering.

I can hear Jack start to pray, "In the name of the Father, and of the Son and of the Holy Spirit..."

As we pray I invoke images of Christ in the garden, being scourged, having a crown of thorns pierce the delicate skin of his head; Jesus laboring under the weight of a heavy cross and, finally suffering death on the cross. As I meditate and pray, I ask Jesus to remove Jack's temptations and allow him to sleep peacefully.

Once we are done, I hear Jack say, "I feel much better, Angela, thank you." He sounds better, too. His voice is relaxed and warm.

"Do you think you'll be able to sleep now, sweetheart?"

"I'm sure of it. I love you, Angela."

"I love you, too, Jack. Good night."

To: **giacomob@kcdiocese.org**
From: **jellycooke@gomail.com**
RE: I love you

Thank you for calling last night. I always want to be there to ease your suffering.
I love you.
Angela
Proverbs 18:10

To: **giacomob@kcdiocese.org**
From: **jellycooke@gomail.com**
RE: I love you
Thank you for the flowers and the phone call. Please don't apologize about us missing the show. I don't want you to worry about it. You have always put me first before everything. This was a minor glitch and it couldn't be helped. I gave the tix to Marissa and John. They were thrilled.
I love you, I miss you, I can't wait till you come home.
Angela
1 Peter 4:8

To: **giacomob@kcdiocese.org**
From: **jellycooke@gomail.com**
RE: I love you
Your LAST DAY!!!! I've missed you so much! I can't wait till tomorrow! What do you want me to make for dinner? Call me later when all is done.
I love you
Angela
1 Corinthians 13:7

"I don't want you to cook," says Jack, "Let's go to Frankie's for an early dinner with the kids tomorrow."

I cradle the phone in my ear as I fold a pair of Ben's pants. "You don't have to twist my arm to get me to go to Frankie's," I say. "So, should I do a drive by or park and go into the airport tomorrow?"

"Just pick me up. I've missed you so much, Angela."

"Me, too. I love you, Jack. See you tomorrow."

22

Rosie squeals as she spots Jack on the sidewalk outside Terminal B. “There he is, Mama!”

I’m driving Jack’s new Chevy Traverse. He left it at our house while he was gone and insisted that I use it this week. I pull over and the boys jump out of the vehicle to help Jack load his bags in the trunk. I don’t get out, because I know if I do I will throw my arms around Jack and not want to let go. He slips into the seat next to me, leans over and kisses me on the tip of my nose.

“It’s good to be back, love.”

“It’s good to have you back,” I say, squeezing his hand.

We are driving north, through downtown Smithville, and, as we approach the grocery store Jack asks, “Do you have any tomato juice in the house?”

I never have tomato juice in the house. I hate tomato juice. “No, just apple. Why? Do you have a craving or something?”

“Yeah, actually, I do; for the spicy kind,” he says. “Would you mind? Oh, and I’ve been dying for some of those salt and vinegar kettle chips. You know how I love those.”

“Maybe you should make a grocery list?” I ask.

I pull into the parking lot of the grocery store and Jack hands me his wallet. “I’m exhausted, love. Would you run in for me, please?”

While inside the grocery store, I bump into Jean, from the Blood Drive Committee, who proceeds to tell me, in detail, about her husband’s root canal that he had done earlier today. “I’m here buying soup, protein shakes and pain killers,” she says, “and straws. I can’t forget the straws.”

“I’m pretty sure they are in the aisle with the paper

plates," I say, pointing; relieved to be able to get back to my family.

When I return to the van, my kids look like they have been caught with their hands in the proverbial cookie jar.

"What on earth are you all up to, pray tell?" I ask. "And does it involve tomato juice by any chance?"

The kids just stare as I slide into the driver's seat. When I look over at Jack, his head is lolling.

"This is turning out to be a very odd day," I say, to no one in particular.

Once we are home, I throw Jack's laundry into the washing machine. He and the children are in the living room talking about his trip. Something feels different about them to me. It's almost like, on a dime, they have become a cohesive unit. Is it possible that their relationship has been like this for a while, but I haven't noticed it until today? I don't know, but there is a definite difference.

I ask Jack if he wants to nap first or go to lunch right away.

"Let's go right now!" says Rosie, enthusiastically.

"I'm with Rosie," Jack says. "Let's get ready and then head over to Frankie's."

As I am putting on some lipstick, Rosie appears outside my bedroom door. She has changed from her jeans into a pink shirt dress, brown and pink polka dot leggings and her Uggs knock offs. Her hair is up in a headband and she is wearing the ballet slipper jewelry Jack gave her.

"Mama, Mr. B was away all week. I think we should dress up for him, don't you?"

I look in the mirror at my yoga pants, tee shirt and hoodie...seems fine for a pizza place.

"Sweetie, I am comfortable in this. I'll dress up for Mass tomorrow, okay?"

She frowns and tosses her curls. "But Mr. B is dressed up. We should match him, at least."

Rosie is right. Jack has on a knit collared shirt, khakis and a blazer. I guess I should dress to complement what he's wearing.

"Here," she says, heading over to my closet, "wear this." She pulls out an ice green, three quarter sleeve, v-neck dress top with ruffles that I bought at the new resale shop that just opened in Gladstone. "That's pretty dressy, hon," I say.

"But it looks beautiful on you!"

Well, if I pair it with my good black boot cut jeans and black mules, it won't look over the top. I smile at my little fashion maven. "All right, you got it. Tell Mr. B I'll be ready in five."

After changing my clothes and dressing up my makeup a bit, I add more texturizing paste to my hair. I'm about to walk out of my bedroom and it occurs to me that the earrings Jack gave me would look pretty with this top. I put them on and head into the living room.

"Where are the boys?" I ask Jack, who is pacing around the room.

"Waiting in the car," says Jack, coming over and kissing my hand. "Angela, you look stunning."

"Why, thank you," I smile, as Jack helps me into my jacket. "I got all dressed up just for you. Aren't you glad to be home?"

"You have no idea how glad."

I try to make small talk in the car, but nobody's biting, so I shut my eyes and take a nap. Before I know it, a blast of cold air hits me and I feel Jack's hand on my cheek.

"We're here, love," he says, standing between me and the open car door. I stretch and smile, then take his hand.

Frankie's is crowded. Instead of heading over to the counter to order, Jack leads us into the back room. It's a spacious room that they use for parties or overflow at busy times. This must be one of those times. There are no booths back here, only large round tables of ten. There are a few bare tables about, but just one is set and there is a vase in the middle with a big bouquet of salmon roses in it.

As we take our seats, Jack addresses the boys. Rubbing his hands together, he says, "Guys, I have a problem I'd like you to help me solve. The woman of my dreams just recently told me that she is in love with me and I'm not exactly sure what to do about this. Sam, any pointers?"

Sam is suppressing a smile. "Well, do you have the same views on finances, religion and raising kids?" he asks.

What on earth is going on?

"Yes, absolutely," Jack answers. "Ben?"

"Hmmm...did you pray and come to the conclusion that God has brought you together?"

"Yep."

"Well, then," says Sam, smirking. "There is only one next logical step, don't you think?"

"Ah," says Jack, as he reaches over, plucks a rose from the vase and hands it to me. Then he takes my hand and draws me up to stand. I sense that something is happening here, but my brain just does not compute. The next thing I know, Jack is on one knee in front of me. "I love you, Angela," he says.

My mouth goes dry and I begin to shake. Jack reaches into his jacket pocket, pulls out a ring and holds it out to me.

"Angela, you are the love of my life and the woman of my dreams. Would you honor and bless me by becoming my wife?"

I glance over at my kids. Tears of joy run down Rosie's apple cheeks. Ben gives me a thumbs-up and I see Sam smiling and nodding, his eyes glistening. I can barely think over the beating of my heart and I begin to feel faint. Shifting on my feet, my heel gets stuck in the hem of my jeans, which causes me to fall forward a bit, and I wind up standing against Jack with both of my hands pressing down on his shoulders.

"Are you okay?" he asks, looking up at me.

"Yes," I whisper.

"Yes, you're okay, or yes, you'll marry me?"

I can feel my head bob. "Uh-huh."

Jack chuckles and shakes his head. "That'll do," he says, slipping the ring on my finger. Standing up, he takes me in his arms and kisses me tenderly. The world falls away as our lips meet and we are swept up in the moment.

When I come to, I see Frankie and his sons in the doorway, applauding. It occurs to me that Jack must have been planning this the entire time he was away. I put my hands on his face and draw him to me. Tears flow from my eyes and I sob, "You...you think about me—"

"—always," says Jack and our lips meet again.

Things seem to move in slow motion as the children get up to hug us and Frankie's boys come over to say congratulations.

"You were all in on this?" I say, looking at my kids.

Sam smiles. "Mr. B asked me for your hand in marriage, Mom. You're lucky I said 'yes,'" he laughs.

"And when did this occur?"

"In the car on the way home from the airport," says Ben. "While you were in the store. We all helped him figure out what to say."

"We were afraid to talk to you, Mama. We didn't want to give it away!" Rosie tells me.

"You did a great job, all of you," I give Rosie a squeeze, and then whisper in her ear. "Thanks for convincing me to dress up, sweetie. Good call."

Frankie walks over, beaming. "Giacomo, you finally did it!" he laughs and the two men embrace.

I turn to Frankie and put my arms around his neck.

Pecking him on the cheek, I say, "I still don't know how Jack pulled this off, but I'm sure you played a part in it, Pizza Man. Thank you."

"My pleasure," he smiles. "Giacomo, he would come in

here every week and tell me about this amazing woman and how much he wanted to get to know her, but the odds were against him. Paula and I prayed like crazy for him, and look what happened. I tell you, some day, we'll be canonized!" We all laugh out loud.

"It all started with a slice of your pizza, Frankie."

"Look," he says, soberly. "I know this isn't the fanciest place, but we would be honored if you would hold the reception here...our gift."

I glance at Jack. He nods and winks. "Frankie, just being able to have the reception here would be gift enough," I say.

Frankie sighs. "Let's talk next week." Turning to my kids, he says, "Who wants to see how we make the pizza?"

They all get up and enthusiastically make way for the door.

"Stay here, you two. Have a few minutes of private time." Frankie winks and heads to the kitchen.

Now that I am alone with Jack, the emotions come to the surface and I begin to weep. He envelops me in his arms. "Is it as bad as all that, love?" he whispers, wiping away a tear with his thumb.

I look up at him and shake my head. "It's just...the emotions are so big that I can't contain them. And I am definitely still in shock."

"You had no idea?"

"None. And I still can't figure out how you managed to come up with a ring. You certainly didn't have time to shop when you were away."

"Do you like it?"

I haven't even had the time to take a good look at it. Jack takes my hand and kisses it, and then holds it up so I can inspect my ring. There are three stones. In the middle is a large, princess cut diamond, set high between two smaller, round brilliant diamonds, on a filigreed white gold band.

"It is absolutely beautiful."

"I had it made when I bought your crucifix. The middle stone is from my Aunt Philomena's engagement ring. The two smaller stones are from a pair of earrings that belonged to my mother," he strokes my cheek and looks deeply into my eyes. "I wanted you to have three stones to represent the marriage covenant, between you, me and God. But, love, if it's not exactly what you want, we'll have it redone."

"Absolutely not!" I say, kissing Jack. All sentimentality aside, the ring is gorgeous. But what touches me profoundly is the beautiful representation of love that Jack has created with the three stones and what they symbolize.

"So what, did you just carry it around with you everywhere, looking for the most opportune moment?"

Jack laughs. "No, the Chrises have a key to my apartment. They went and got it this morning and gave it to Frankie to give to me."

"Hmmm, the branches of this operation were far reaching, I see." Looking deep into Jack's eyes, I whisper, "I'm sorry I made you wait to give it to me. I'm sorry for what I put you through and for all the times that you said you love me and I was too scared to say it back."

Jack takes my face in his hands. "Now is all that matters, Angela. I prayed for this day for so long and I'm so glad it has finally come. Now we have a whole life to look forward to."

"So, when exactly would you like to exchange vows?" I ask.

"Yesterday," Jack says, kissing me again.

***

The kids are in bed, there is a fire in the hearth and Jack and I are sitting on the couch drinking a glass of wine. So much has happened today that it seems like Jack proposed days, not hours ago.

"Everything changes now," Jack says, putting his arm around my shoulders.

"Like what?"

"Well, we are engaged, so I am responsible for you. No more putting me off when it comes to helping with bills and anything else."

"Jack..."

"I'm serious. And I'd like to be spending more time here with you and the kids. I think we should be going to daily Mass together, too."

"I have no problem with that," I say.

"Listen, I took a couple of days off. Let's spend them together making plans. Once we have the basic stuff in place I'm going to have to back off for a time because I have a major paper to write for my class that I need to focus on."

"Jack, we don't need to start making plans right away. Why don't you put all your energy into your assignment and then we'll start?"

He shakes his head. "Tell me when you're going to marry me," he says.

"I guess we should look at a calendar."

"Let's look at the calendar now."

I laugh. "I have never seen this side of you, Jack. You've always been so patient..."

"Angela, I've been patient for 46 years. I've officially filled my patience quota. Now I just want to marry you!"

I go into the kitchen and pull my calendar off the wall. Handing it to Jack, I lower myself onto the couch next to him.

"Let's exchange vows on a feast day," he says.

"I like that idea. What's coming up?"

"The Annunciation."

"Jack!" Playfully, I poke him in the ribs. "That's only about a month away! And besides, Sam's confirmation is in March. You're killing me!"

He sighs and flips the page. "No, not during Easter," he says, flipping again. His eyes light up. "Our Lady of Fatima?"

"May 13th?" I glance at the calendar. *"Friday the 13th?"*

Jack laughs, "We'll get married at 3:00, the hour of mercy. What could possibly go wrong?"

"Well, let's see..." I answer. "You're giving us just under *three months*? How will we even pull that off?"

"I'll make it happen," he says. "I'll give the Bishop a call and plead my case. He can't possibly say no. Besides, they normally don't schedule weddings on Fridays, so I know the cathedral will be available."

The cathedral? Who said anything about getting married at the cathedral? "I thought we'd get married at Our Lady of the Angels," I say. "I wanted Fr. Sean."

Jack looks crestfallen. "Oh...it didn't occur to me...I'm sorry, Angela."

I sigh. A conflict. Our first big conflict, really. I really want to get married in my own parish. It's like a second home to me. But, given what I've put Jack through and considering that he always puts me first in everything he does, I think it is time I made some sacrifices for him.

"Why don't we speak to Fr. Sean tomorrow after Mass and ask him if he will concelebrate with the Bishop? Then we can have the ceremony at the cathedral, with both the bishop and Fr. Sean."

Jack puts his arm around me. "Are you sure? May 13th, at the cathedral?"

I smile. "If the Bishop agrees, the planets align and no black cats cross our paths, then, yes, we'll be married on May 13th."

I watch Jack pull out of my driveway and then I throw my jacket on. It's late, but I'm pretty sure Marissa will still be up. The kids are sound asleep, but I leave a note on the kitchen table just in case. Then I lock the door and drive the half mile to Marissa's.

She answers the door in her pajamas and bathrobe.

"Everything okay?"

"Yes, Mar, fine. I'm sorry, but I just could not wait to show you this," I hold out my left hand.

Marissa's eyes grow wide and she shrieks as she grabs my hand and starts jumping up and down. John hears her and comes running. "You ladies doing all right?" he asks, concerned.

"Jack asked Jel to marry him! They're engaged!" she says, half-laughing, half-crying.

John smirks, "Ah, then things will finally calm down around here." And he comes over and gives me a bear hug. "I am happy for you, Jel. All the best. He's a good guy."

"That means a lot to me, John. Thank you."

"And now," he announces. "I am going to bed, apparently alone. You ladies have fun." John and Marissa give each other a kiss and then John heads down the hall.

She sits on the couch and pats the cushion next to her. "Come on over here. I want to know *every* last detail, honey." Marissa fans her face with her hand. "Be still my heart. He really asked Sam for your hand in marriage?"

"He also asked Sam to be his best man. And I wouldn't want anyone else but you to be my Matron of Honor, Mar."

Marissa gives me a big squeeze. "I am here for you, honey. Oh, we have so much to do! We need to look for dresses this week. There's almost no time! Who else is in the bridal party?"

"We wanted to keep it simple. Ben will be a groomsman and Rosie will be a bridesmaid, or junior bridesmaid, or whatever they're calling it these days. And, of course, we'll have Nica as the flower girl. "

"Good," she says, nodding in approval, "We can have a girl's day with Rosie. She'll be thrilled."

My eyelids are starting to get heavy. "Mar, we're going to have to continue this another day. I'm wiped out. Why don't you and John come for dinner this week? I'll have

Jack pick up a bottle of champagne."

***

I slip back into my house, which is as quiet as I left it. As I slide between the sheets of my bed, I go over the details of the day.

Thank you, God, for all the blessings you showered me with today. You are such a generous Father! Please give Jack and I the grace of a holy and fruitful marriage. Your will be done.

23

Marissa and John have gone home, the kids are in bed and Jack and I are relaxing on the couch. Tenderly, he takes me in his arms and kisses me. He has started kissing me on the lips since we got engaged. I must say, I like this new development.

"I'd better go, love," he whispers. "We have a lot to do tomorrow."

"Such as...?" I ask, kissing him again.

"Errands," he says. "I'll pick you up for morning Mass and then we'll go from there."

I answer with a kiss...then another and another one still. Although I am kissing Jack chastely, my body begins to respond to the feel of his lips on mine. My heart begins to beat faster, my breathing becomes shallow and the blood rushes to my cheeks. Imperceptibly, control of my body shifts from my intellect to my senses. Leaning back onto the couch, I lace my fingers behind Jack's neck and pull him down on top of me. We continue to kiss each other and suddenly a moan escapes my lips.

Abruptly, Jack sits up and moves away from me. "Oh, geez, Angela, what are we doing?" he exclaims, his voice full of regret. "Love, look at you. I'm sorry. I should've stopped...I shouldn't have started..."

Jack stands up and paces back and forth for a few seconds. I can see he is angry. This is out of character for him. I have seen Jack irritated before, but not actually angry.

I sit up and try to tamp the feelings of arousal that still linger. "I'm sorry, Jack. I...I guess I...well, your kisses awakened something in me and before I even realized it I had become aroused."

"You're not the only one," he says, going over to the

window and leaning his head against the pane. I hear him mutter a pseudo-expletive and then he punches his fist against the molding. "You are not to blame. I should have nipped that in the bud. I should have protected you, but instead I let myself go." He turns to me and I can see that he is in pain. "I'm sorry, Angela."

I walk over to Jack and cup his cheek in my hand. Looking into his eyes, I say, "I love you, you know that? One of the things that I like best about you is that I can count on the fact that you will think of my well-being in all situations."

He opens his mouth to speak, but I silence him by gently putting my finger to his lips. "Jack, let's put this in perspective. We had a lapse, but when it comes down to it, nothing actually happened. We kissed to the point that both of us became aroused, but we stopped before any more could happen. Please don't beat yourself up over this. We're both sorry. We'll go to confession and make sure to be much more careful from now on."

Jack looks down at me and whispers, "If I hadn't stopped us, love, would you have?"

My brows come together as I ponder his question. "I'd like to say 'yes,' but in all honesty...I don't know. I can't say for sure if my senses would have won over my reason or vice versa," I admit, reluctantly.

Jack is silent for a long moment. "Well, then, maybe we need to just wait until we're married to kiss on the lips," he says, soberly.

The thought of losing the sweet and gentle feel of Jack's lips on mine when it is still so new makes my heart sink. Then again, we have both made a serious commitment to remain chaste until we are married and so his suggestion is valid.

I sigh. "I hate to say this, but maybe you're right. Having a rule about it would eliminate situations like this," I wink at him. "But we don't have to *like* the rule, right?

Just follow it."

Jack chuckles and then his eyes light up. "Here's an idea; let's fast from kissing on the lips until our wedding day and offer it up for the sanctity of our marriage."

I burst out laughing. "Only you would get excited about something like this. You are such a geek!"

Laughing, Jack says, "And if you stop resisting my efforts, it's only a matter of time before you become one, too."

24

Jack merges onto 635 as we head to Frankie's to iron out the details of our reception.

"So, love, we need to have a serious talk about sex, don't you think?" he asks.

Alarm rises in my chest. "Jack, I am not having this conversation with you!"

"Angela! What's the matter?" he asks, bewildered.

"What do you mean, 'what's the matter?'" I am not talking out loud about sex to you. Whatever you want to know, you'll find out on May 13th."

He glances toward me and says gently, "You're really that uncomfortable about it?"

"Keep your eyes on the road; and, yes, I am." I realize I sound testy and I feel bad. "I'm sorry."

"Angela," Jack says, "I want you to be comfortable with me. We need to be completely intimate in every way in order for this marriage to work. That means sharing everything with each other, even the stuff that makes us uncomfortable. You know that, don't you?"

I know Jack is right, but I can't make the leap right now, in the car, in the middle of the day, with no warning whatsoever. "Oh, Jack," I say. "I want so much to do things right this time, but you're pushing me. I'm not ready."

"When will you be ready?"

"May 14th."

Jack laughs. "Most of the wall came down when you told me you loved me and when you accepted my proposal. But there is one more hurdle for you to get over, isn't there? You're afraid to bare all emotionally to me. Why?"

Why, indeed? "I don't know. I'm just not used to talking about it, I guess. The only information I got from my mother was when she told me 'If you get pregnant, don't come home.' So, of course, I went on the Pill as soon as I met Devin. There. That's it. That was Sex 101 for Angela Rezza."

Jack sighs. "You got no guidance at all from anyone, did you?"

"No, Daddy was so sick when I was in my mid-teens that we didn't talk much at all. I kept him comfortable and sang to him, mostly. I had the sense that there were things he wanted to tell me. But they were left unsaid...and then he was gone," I begin to cry, softly. I haven't cried about Daddy in decades. "Jack, I felt so alone and abandoned. It hurt so much. I just poured all I had into school then. When I wasn't at school, I was at the library, reading, and then I would walk home, eat and go to my job at the pizza place."

"I didn't know you worked at a pizza place."

I nod. "After Daddy died I got a job as counter girl during the dinner rush. My relationship with my mother was strained at that time, so it was easier for me to keep busy than to deal with her."

"That seems to be a pattern with you, love," says Jack, as he pulls into a parking space. He turns to me and takes my hand. "Sometimes you remind me of a tiny bird with a broken wing. I want so much to care for you, to soothe you. I want you to know that you can tell me anything, anything at all; and I will never judge you or leave you. I know you haven't really had this kind of a relationship with anyone before, except maybe Marissa."

I lean over, wrap my arms around Jack's neck and put my head on his shoulder. "There are things I haven't shared with her. Stuff about Devin and me. Nothing bad, but I felt embarrassed that we had such a lousy relationship when she and John seem so perfect..."

"How do you feel, love, talking to me right now?"

I look up into Jack's eyes. "Safe," I answer, "and loved."

He strokes my cheek. "This is how I always want you to feel with me. I promise you, the more you share, the more you reveal your emotions to me, the more intimate we will become. Do you think you can do that?"

"I promise you I'll try, Jack. But if I start to shut down, will you help me?"

"Always," he whispers, kissing me gently on the cheek.

The 'open' sign isn't lit up and the door is locked, so we knock. Frankie comes to the door in his usual white pants, white shirt, white apron. "Hey, you two, are you ready to make some plans?"

He escorts us into the back room. "Paula!" he yells. "They're here!"

A petite woman emerges from the kitchen, wearing the same attire as Frankie. She has shoulder length light brown and gray hair, cut in layers. She has a kind face that has the battle scars of motherhood; crow's feet around her eyes and laugh lines around her mouth. A boy who looks to be in his mid-teens follows behind. He must be their son, Freddie, who Jack told me about. The boy is dressed in blue sweatpants and matching sweatshirt and he is bouncing behind his mother in a way that reminds me of Tigger from the Winnie the Pooh cartoons Sam used to love when he was small.

Frankie slips his arm around the woman's waist. "This is my wife, Paula; and this is our youngest, Freddie. Freddie has autism, so he probably won't answer you if you talk to him...but he might. You never know."

Jack and I greet Paula and then I walk over to where Freddie is bouncing. I walk around him until I catch his eye. "Hello Freddie," I say, softly.

He stops bouncing, but looks past me.

"Hello Freddie," he says.

I put my hand on my chest. "I'm Angela." I wait a couple of long beats and then again I say, "My name is Angela."

"Angela, *Beauty and the Beast*, dancing, yes," he says, and bounces again.

Paula walks over to us. "Freddie, you're right," she says, "This is Angela and she is the bride we told you about. She will be dancing on her wedding day in a fancy dress, just like Belle in *Beauty and the Beast*."

I am drawn to this sweet and handsome young man. He is pure goodness and light. There is not a drop of malice in him and I find that touches me profoundly. I want to connect with him.

"Does Freddie like music?" I ask Paula, "The music from the movie?" Rosie loves the movie *Beauty and the Beast* and so I know all the words to every song.

"Oh, yes," she says, "he loves to listen to music. It is very calming for him."

Freddie has bounced over to the far corner of the room, so I make my way over to him. Quietly, I begin to hum a song from the movie. Freddie stops bouncing and looks in my direction again. Then I begin to sing softly. As I continue to sing, Freddie looks me in the eye. Then he starts to sway back and forth. When I finish singing the song, Freddie turns and begins to bounce again, but I feel that I have made a small connection.

"Thanks for looking at me, Freddie," I whisper.

Paula puts her arm around me and says, "I appreciate you trying with Freddie. Most people don't even acknowledge him at all."

I smile. "When my daughter started kindergarten I began working as a part-time aide with a little boy, Joey, who had autism. He was very much like Freddie. I could see the goodness in him and I fell in love with that," I say, sitting down at a table with Jack and Frankie. "I worked with him for two years. Then his parents divorced and his mother moved to California, but she sends me updates sometimes. He seems to be getting good services there."

Jack kisses me and takes my hand. "Frankie was just

telling me that they are planning a fundraiser for Freddie to get him a service dog. I told him we would help."

"Absolutely! So how much do we have to raise?"

"The dog is going to cost us $12,000," says Frankie. "It has to be specially trained just for Freddie's needs. But when we get it, it will be a great companion for him and it will keep him out of danger and also help him be more aware of another creature's needs as he cares for it. We were going to do a silent auction in September to raise the money."

"I have lots of experience with silent auctions from my work at the parish." I put my hand on Frankie's arm. "Call me. We'll talk."

"Frankie," says Paula, "they are here to plan the wedding, remember?"

Frankie and Paula's son, Vince, walks out of the kitchen and nods to us. "Here is the paperwork, Dad," he says and then turns to Freddie, who is bouncing and humming. "Come with me, big guy," says Vince, as he holds out his hand. "Freddie..." And then Freddie walks over to his brother and they head toward the kitchen.

Frankie lets out a deep breath and cracks his knuckles. "Here is our menu, but if you want something else, we can whip it up for our friends," he says, winking.

"Listen, Frankie," Jack says. "I know that you and Paula offered to do this gratis, and that is very generous of you, but Angela and I want to at least pay for the expenses and to hire wait staff so your family can be with us that day."

"It's important to us that you be there," I add. "We really want your family to bring up the gifts at Mass. It would mean so much to us."

After much discussion and negotiation, Frankie caves in and Jack and I are relieved. We decide on a buffet of Caesar Salad, Garden Salad, Shrimp Scampi, Veal Francese, Rigatoni alla Vodka and Eggplant Parmagiana.

Frankie and Paula have catered enough weddings and

formal affairs at their restaurant that they have it down to a science. We work out the rest of the details, taking most of their suggestions. Jack and I both want the reception to be simple, elegant and fun for our guests and I think we will achieve that. It is all coming together now and Jack and I are on a big high.

***

As we are driving home, I tell Jack, "Sweetheart, I read somewhere that in biblical times, it was tradition for the bridal couple to give alms at the time of their wedding."

He glances at me and smiles. "Yes, Angela?"

"Well, I was wondering, if we do the wedding really frugally, can we afford to gift Freddie the money for his service dog?"

Jack reaches over and squeezes my hand. "You have a generous heart, love. I'm glad you brought that up, because I feel pulled in the same direction. I'll take care of it."

"I love you."

"And spend as much on the wedding as you like," he adds.

"Get out of here!" Jack can't possibly mean that. Did he really just give me carte blanche to buy whatever I want? This seems surreal.

"I'm serious. I've been pretty frugal all my life so that I could indulge the woman I love. As a matter of fact, I have always wanted to say this: 'Whatever you want, babe, you got it.'"

I laugh heartily. "Has your testosterone level just increased exponentially?"

"Absolutely," he says, grinning.

"You know I won't, though, don't you? Spend a lot, I mean."

Jack sighs and I notice he has gotten off at the

Broadway exit and is heading into town. We turn onto his street and he parks near his building. "I need to run in and get something. Be right back."

He comes back to the car with a folder. "Let's go have coffee," Jack says, as he puts the car in gear.

When we get to LuAnne's, I take the folder he gives me and open it up. It's full of statements. "What is all this?" I ask, as Jack slides next to me into the booth, with our coffees.

"My assets...*our* assets, Angela," says Jack. "This is what we own and what we have to work with. You see, here is my monthly income from the properties." Jack hands me a bank statement. The amount deposited each month is more money than my family receives from Social Security in half a year. I look up at him, wondering if the shock has registered on my face.

"And this is how much I have invested." Jack hands me several pieces of paper. "See? This is the inheritance from my parents...and here, this is what I have invested on my own. And this is a college fund I started for Nica. I have a call in to my investment guy; I'm setting up funds for Sam, Ben and Rosie, too."

I'm glad I'm sitting down, because I am completely overwhelmed. When Jack told me he had money, I didn't think it was *this* much money. For the first time in my life, I'm speechless.

"Oh, and here," Jack says. "These are receipts from my tithing. Each month I give 10% of my income to the Church and an additional 10% to causes. But we need to talk about where you want some of this money to go, too, because it's ours now, not just mine."

I realize that my mouth is open, so I snap it shut and blink a few times to bring myself back to reality. The possibilities that this money opens up are endless.

I turn in the booth to face Jack. "After the accident,

someone anonymously left an envelope for me at the church office, with a thousand dollars stuffed in it. No note, nothing...just ten one hundred dollar bills in a plain white envelope with my name typed on it. After the tag sale last year, I put ten percent of the money in an envelope for a woman with three kids whose husband has been in and out of rehab with an addiction to painkillers from a work accident he had. I was so happy to help them out." My heart leaps as I ask, "I'd love to be able to do a lot more of that...can we?"

Jack laughs, "We can and we will, love." He puts his arm around me and gives me a squeeze. "Whatever you want, babe, you got it."

25

"Do you have any dresses that aren't strapless?" I ask Ronnie, the sales consultant who is helping Marissa and me. We are at the Wedding Wardrobe in downtown Kansas City, because I heard they have great service and a huge selection of dresses. Initially, Ronnie told me to look through and get an idea of what was available and then we would talk. Most of what I have seen is strapless or low cut.

"I'm an older bride and I want something more modest, especially for the ceremony."

"What cut are you thinking of? Ballgown? Mermaid?"

I shake my head. "How about something simple, like a floor length A-line or sheath? I want simple, modest and elegant."

She smiles and nods. "Why don't the two of you sit and relax while I pull some samples that reflect what you want?" she says.

Eventually, Ronnie comes over, arms laden with gowns. "Let the trying on begin," she announces.

There are several in a Grecian style, with empire waists. "That's big this year," she says. "It is a modest and elegant style that is perfect for a mature bride." I try one on. It is a pretty gown in chiffon, with silver embellishments and an empire waist. "You're so tall and thin, that this would be the perfect gown for you, Mar. But it's not for me," I say, disappointed.

Next I try on a Nicole Miller. It is a simple chiffon floor-length sheath, with a scoop neck.

"It's pretty and looks nice on you, Jel, but it's not elegant enough. I'd say put it in the 'maybe' category," says Marissa.

"This is moving more toward what I want, though."

"Here, try this one. It's not couture, but I have a feeling this is what you're looking for," Ronnie says, slipping a gown over my head. Marissa puts her hand over her mouth and her eyes tear up. "Honey, you look beautiful!"

I turn to face the mirror. This may be the one. It is a simple A-line in taffeta, with a chapel length train. The shoulder straps are so thick that they are almost a cap sleeve. The whole bodice of the dress is ruched, which fades below the waist, into unembellished taffeta. It has a plunging v-neckline, which has a wrap effect.

"Oooh, look at the back!" exclaims Marissa.

Ronnie helps me rotate to the perfect angle. The back is high enough to be modest and it laces up from the waist. "So feminine...so elegant," says Ronnie. "This really suits you."

"I think this dress is perfect, except for the neckline. Is there anything that can be done? I don't want cleavage," I say.

Ronnie checks the tag and tells me that it comes with a matching modesty piece that can be sewn in. No one will know it wasn't originally part of the dress.

"And I will also need a bolero for the church. I don't feel right walking down the aisle in bare arms." Marissa nods in agreement.

Ronnie goes into the back room and comes out with an armful of boleros. "Try these on for style, but, honestly, I would suggest having sleeves made. We can order extra fabric when we order the dress."

Ronnie explains to me that a bolero would cover up the detail in the back of the dress. Instead, the seamstress can remove the straps and add any kind of sleeve I want.

"Here, take a look." Ronnie helps me into a bolero with three-quarter length sleeves. She folds the front of the bolero inward, so it looks like there is just a sleeve.

I like the effect.

I look in the mirror and twirl around. "This is the dress. With the modifications it is exactly what I want."

"I agree!" says Marissa. "You'll look like an angel!"

Happily, Ronnie claps and says, "Let's look for shoes and veil while you have the dress on."

I settle on a closed toe sandal in white silk with pleating and Swarovski crystal embellishments on the straps. I choose the simplest two-layer, elbow length veil. The top layer will function as a blusher.

"Should I even be wearing a veil at my age?" I muse.

"Oh, honey, you know Jack is going to want the whole package. Make him happy," Marissa says, primping the veil.

Ronnie is nodding in approval. "The pleats on the shoe compliment the ruching on the dress," she says, taking my measurements. "You will look stunning, dear."

With my bridal attire chosen, it is time to move on to Marissa's.

"I have a mother of the bride gown that has the same wrap effect with ruching at the bodice. Let's start there," Ronnie suggests.

Marissa takes the dress and disappears into the dressing room. She reappears minutes later.

"I look ravishing, don't you think?" she says, waltzing dramatically through the doorway.

I nod enthusiastically. The gown looks beautiful on Marissa. Her tall, thin frame wears the charmeuse fabric perfectly. Her straps are thinner than mine, but the dress comes with a matching bolero. There are also silver embellishments at the bodice that make it just different enough from mine to complement it perfectly. "Mother of the bride dresses usually come up higher in the neckline," Ronnie tells us, so there is no need for a modesty piece.

The sample is a champagne color, which I don't like. "Does it come in blue?" I ask.

"Two shades...sapphire and seurat blue," she says, showing me the swatches.

I choose seurat blue, because it is a lighter shade of blue.

Marissa selects a strappy silver sandal with crystal accents along the vamp.

"I'm so happy with our choices!" I announce. "This is so exciting. It makes it seem less like a dream and more like reality."

On the way out, I make an appointment with Ronnie for the following Saturday, to choose Rosie's and Nica's dresses.

"You'll get to meet Christina," I tell Marissa. "She and her husband Chris are the closest thing Jack has to family."

"Until May 13th," says Marissa, smiling. I can't help but smile, too.

26

Jack and I pull into the Chrises' driveway. We are having lunch here today. The Chrises live in an upscale subdivision in Gladstone, not too far from St. Andrew's where I take my classes. Christina answers the door and welcomes us into a large foyer that has a curved staircase at the back. To the left, through glass paneled French doors, is a sitting room. Christina shows us into the room. "Lunch is in an hour. I'll try to keep Nica occupied while you talk," she winks. "I'll look in on you in a little while."

After she leaves I ask Jack, "So, this was a bait and switch, wasn't it?"

Jack smiles sheepishly. "You knew we would have to have this discussion sooner or later..."

"And this is the place you wanted to have it?"

"It was either here or on the Mamba at Worlds of Fun," he jokes.

"Right. A roller coaster would be *less* scary," I sigh. "Okay, okay, I promised I would try and I need to make good on that," I say, nervously.

"Let's talk a little about our expectations, Angela," says Jack, as he leads me over to a sofa and we sit down.

"I'm not sure what you want from me, Jack. What do you want me to tell you?"

"Well, tell me a bit about you and Devin. Let's start there."

I look down at my hands, which I am wringing, and force the words out. "Before we were married we had sex as much as possible. It made me feel closer to Devin and I know he felt the same way. After our wedding, though, it fell off pretty quickly. We both were busy and just couldn't seem to connect. Then, after a while, I began to look at it as an obligation I had to fulfill, or as a tension reliever. The last few years of our marriage we had sex probably once a week or less." I catch myself. "Well...much less."

I can see compassion in Jack's eyes as he takes my hand in his. "Would you say that you were fulfilled, Angela?"

I hate this conversation, but I know it's necessary. Fear begins to rise in my chest, though, that maybe Jack will think I am a total freak and not want to marry me after all.

"Fulfilled? Is that a euphemism for...uh, no. My body doesn't seem partial to, uh...that," I admit.

"But Devin took care of you, didn't he, love?" Jack is embracing me now and I know he is trying to be a comfort to me, but my fear makes me want to bolt.

"What do you mean?" I ask, and then the light bulb goes on. "Oh...well, once in awhile, if I was very aroused after he was done he would, you know, help me out."

I can feel Jack tense up and I hear some anger in his voice.

"You mean to tell me that Devin didn't make sure that his wife was fulfilled in the bedroom? He satisfied himself without giving you a second thought?"

No, that's not how it was...was it? "Jack," I say, gently. "You're blowing this out of proportion. He didn't leave me hanging. Most of the time I was no longer aroused. Frankly, I was happy to be able to roll over and go to sleep."

"And this is what...this is how..." Frustrated, Jack lets out a long breath and runs his hand through his hair. "I need to show you something. I'll be right back," he says, and heads out of the sitting room and through the front door. He comes back almost immediately with a packet of papers, which have been stapled together, and hands it to me. "Read this paragraph," he says, pointing.

In his book, Love and Responsibility, Wojtyla stresses that self control plays an important role in how a man expresses tender, sacrificial love for his wife.

> *...the woman's excitement grows more slowly than that of the man. The man must take this difference between male and female reactions into account, not for hedonistic, but for altruistic reasons. There exists a rhythm dictated by nature itself which both spouses must discover so that climax may be reached by both the man and the woman, and as far as possible occur in both simultaneously.*
> *(Wojtyla, Love and Responsibility p. 272)*

Jesus prepared the Church for her birth at his crucifixion. Only when He knew that she was ready to receive Him, did He give His body completely. As a result of this union, the Church was able to bear fruit. These fruits are grace; a participation in the life of God; and salvation; dwelling with Him in heaven for all eternity. Just as Jesus gave His life in order for the Church to grow and be fruitful, a man must die to self to create that holy union which is so divine that it even holds the power to create.

From the cross, Jesus speaks the words, "Today, you will be with me in paradise." A husband's self-giving actions during marital relations should mirror that statement as he helps his wife to experience the joy and ecstasy that God allows here on earth as a foretaste of the joy of heaven. In this way, a husband must prepare his wife to receive him and work to delay this giving until she is ready, underscoring St. Paul's statement that men must love their wives as Christ loves the Church.

"You wrote this?" I ask.

Jack nods.

"This is beautiful," I whisper, as the floodgates open and tears spill down my face. Jack comes to me and envelops me in his arms.

"I never knew this," I say, as Jack wipes a tear from my cheek. "I just assumed that there was something wrong with me, which is why I wasn't aroused much when Devin and I..."

"Angela, lovemaking needs to happen in all dimensions of a relationship. You can't ignore each other all day and then create an instantaneous spiritual and emotional bond in the bedroom. That bond has to already exist and be strong in order to be truly intimate." Jack tilts my head up so that I am looking into his eyes. "I promise you this: that on our wedding night and every time we become one...which will be often..." He smiles and brushes away some strands of hair which have fallen into my eyes. "...that you will have no doubt how much you are loved, cherished and cared for. I will give myself to you completely, both in and outside the bedroom."

"And I want to do that, too. I want to jump into this marriage...with both feet." I smile up at Jack through the remainder of my tears. "So...how often?"

He laughs. "Well, you know that lovemaking is a renewal of wedding vows, so, as often as possible, to strengthen our marriage."

"I need to make a phone call," I say.

"A phone call?" asks Jack, puzzled.

"To the feminists," I say, wryly. "Somebody needs to tell them that when the Church wants them to submit to their husbands, it involves having completely fulfilling sex as often as possible."

27

We are at the Chinese food place downtown, near Jack's apartment. I move my wedding notebook out of the way as the waitress places the Poo Poo platter in front of us.

Jack leads grace and then says, "Whatcha got?" as he bites into his eggroll.

"Marissa gave me the name of the DJ from the Valentine's Day dance she and John went to over at St. Monica's. She said he played really good music and he sang too. I called earlier and he has our date open. We can meet with him this week."

Jack looks weary. I don't think he realized how much work it would be to pull this wedding off in three months. We are in such a time crunch that we agreed to split some of the planning and each tackle it on our own.

"How about I take care of the music, hon?"

He nods, looking relieved. "I got the limo already...did I tell you that?"

I chuckle. "You did. See? I wrote it in my book."

He tells me there is a photographer that the chancery uses for events who also does weddings. I tell Jack to go ahead and book him if he is available. We have a discussion about what kinds of pictures we want and I know Jack will call me with any questions. It feels good to let some of this go. I remember when I married Devin I had to micromanage everything. I couldn't delegate at all. My reception had to be perfect and I made sure it was. This time, I want to focus more on preparing for our life together versus planning a party. I know our guests will have a good time. I know there will be good food. I'm not too worried about the rest.

I let out a cleansing breath. "Okay, you book the photographer and I'll call the DJ. It looks like all our bases are covered: music, food, limo...I go to the florist Tuesday morning. The big stuff is done. High five me," I say, holding up my hand.

Jack laughs out loud and obliges me. "There is one big thing you forgot, love. What about our honeymoon?"

I smile sweetly at Jack. "And what did you have in mind?"

"I thought I would take that on myself, love, and surprise you. How do you feel about that?"

A surprise honeymoon? I look at Jack across the table and I can see it in his eyes that this is important to him. So, I look on the bright side; this is one more thing I won't have to plan.

"You don't want to go to one of those all inclusive beach resorts, do you?" I ask, wrinkling my nose.

He shakes his head. "I know what you would like, Angela, and what you wouldn't."

"You'll at least tell me what to pack?" I ask, before polishing off the rest of my roast pork fried rice.

"Of course, love. It's just...I have some ideas and I'd like them to be a surprise."

"Okay, then," I relent, "but no clues. If it is going to be a surprise, I want you to *really* surprise me."

Jack looks thrilled. I love his smile; so genuine and handsome. My doubts flee and I am happy to make him happy.

As Jack and I walk to the counter to pay the check, I ask, "Do you want to start moving some of your things over to the house soon?"

Jack's eyes become cloudy and his brow furrows. "Angela, we need to talk about this. I don't feel comfortable moving into Devin's house."

He collects his change and we walk outside. At first I am shocked by what Jack says, but then anger starts to well up inside me. *He waited this long to tell me this? Where are we going to move on such short notice?* ***How*** *are we going to move on such short notice?*

Once we are out on the sidewalk, Jack motions to take my hand, but I move away from him.

"What?" he says, perplexed. "You're upset?"

"Uh, yeah," I say, sarcastically. "Did you think I *wouldn't* be?"

He stops walking and turns to me. "You're not just upset, you're downright angry, aren't you?" Jack asks and I can sense some anger in his voice as well.

I want to yell at him: This is ridiculous! We can't just pack up and go. Moving takes some doing and with the wedding plans and the kids' school schedules, it would be nearly an impossible task. I know that yelling would accomplish nothing, however, so I remain silent and try to get a grip on my feelings. We walk for a long time without speaking, but my anger doesn't dissipate; it seems to grow.

Jack tries to take my hand again, but I move away. He turns to me and wraps his arms around my waist. I begin to squirm in the hopes he'll release me and I can dramatically stomp off in a huff.

"Hey," he says, firmly. "I have no idea what you're thinking. Stop playing games and talk to me, Angela."

Now I am ashamed of my behavior and how I let my anger rule my actions. Tears begin to roll down my face. Jack's face softens, too, as he pulls me toward him in an embrace.

"It's too much, Jack!" I wail. "I can't change my whole life by May 13th! Why didn't you tell me before? We could have waited to get married if you wanted to move. Now what do we do?"

Jack's face is grim. "I want us to have our own place, love. I don't want to live in Devin's shadow. I've been thinking about this more and more lately and I just can't bring myself to..."

I cut him off. "It's not Devin's house! It's *my* house! You have an apartment. It just makes logistical sense that you move to Smithville."

Jack shakes his head. He isn't angry, but he's definitely convicted. "No. I'm supposed to take care of you and I want to give you a home that we can share."

"But I already have a home we can share," I say, frustrated. "I don't need a new one...*you're* the one that needs a new one."

"It's just a house, Angela."

I shake my head. "It's *my* house. The down payment on that house was money that *I* saved from working, *not* Devin. And I bought it outright after his accident. My name is on the deed. I own it!" I lower my voice when I notice a group of young adults staring at us. "Jack," I whisper, my voice breaking, "Marissa is like a sister to me. Please don't ask me to move away from her. And the kids...we'd be moving them right near the end of the school year..."

Jack rubs his face with his hand. "Come with me," he says. Numbly, I follow. I see that he is headed toward the cathedral. It is late on a Friday and so it must be locked, but Jack pulls out a key and goes in the door to the cathedral offices and we are able to enter the sanctuary through the passageway from there.

The silence is soothing. The cathedral is dark, save for the red light above the tabernacle and a bank of candles across from it. Gingerly, we make our way up the aisle to the left of the altar and ascend the steps to the chapel that holds the tabernacle. Jack motions to me and we kneel down.

I'm finding it hard to pray, so I just spit out my feelings. *This is crazy! I don't want to have to call off the wedding because we can't come to a resolution. I love Jack and I want to marry him, but he's asking too much.*

A still small voice inside me says, *"Do you love Jack?"*

What a ridiculous question. Of course I love Jack.

The voice prods again, *"Or do you love your house?"*

I wrestle with my thoughts for a while. Ultimately, remorse grips me and I realize that if we are to get married at all, I need to be ready to let this go. I am angry that Jack waited so long to tell me. I am also upset that he seems threatened by Devin. But these things do not trump my love for him.

Jack is deep in prayer. He is kneeling down next to me and his head is in his hands. Taking a cleansing breath, I tap Jack on the shoulder. He turns to me and, in the dim light from the red candle, I can see pain in his eyes. "I'm sorry," I whisper, "that I made it seem like I love my house more than I love you. Let's try and figure out a plan of how we will move in a few weeks. We can maybe rent something for a while. Somehow, it'll work it out."

Even though I am doing exactly what I don't want to do, my heart feels a bit lighter, having accepted this burden, instead of running from it.

"No," Jack says as he embraces me. "I'm the one who needs to apologize, Angela. I've been governed by my pride here. I know it makes sense for us to live in your house, at least initially. I don't want to add to your or the kids' burden by asking you to move right now. I'm sorry...I'm so sorry."

"I forgive you, my love, and I'm sorry for the way I behaved." I lean up and kiss Jack's cheek. I know this was hard for him. "There's no reason for you to be throwing punches at a dead man," I whisper. "It's *you* who captured my heart...remember that."

28

Jack has really been pushing me to ask my brother, Tony, to give me away. I'd rather ask Jim, who has been more of a father to me in the past couple of years than either one of my brothers has ever been. But Jack, who has no family, is insistent. He thinks family should come first. I promised I would pray about it and the notion that Jack may be right keeps nagging at me.

My brother, Tony, is a loner. He never married and seems, from what I can tell, to live hand to mouth. He is the polar opposite of our brother Jimmy, who is a very successful financial planner and lives in Scarsdale. However, Jimmy broke relations with both Tony and me after Mama died. Tony, on the other hand, has kept in contact with me sporadically over the years and has always struck me as having a compassionate heart.

I have a few vivid memories of Tony from when I was a child. In one of them, he came over to the house when I was about five years old. I remember how handsome he looked in his dress whites. He took me out for ice cream and gave me a small stuffed bear that had a white Navy hat sewn onto the top if its head. I still have that bear, tucked away in a box of memorabilia in the attic. After we left the ice cream shop, Tony put me on his shoulders and walked along the beach at Smith Point. It was a balmy day and I loved the feeling of the wind in my hair and the sun on my back. As he lifted me off his shoulders, Tony twirled me around and then drew me close into an embrace. I remember him saying something like he would always love me, even if he was far away. I don't know why this memory has remained after all these years, but it does and I am glad to have it.

As I am praying after morning Mass, another memory

of Tony surfaces. It seems as if he and Daddy had just had a big argument. They were inside the house, yelling, and I went out onto the porch to get away from all the anger. I saw Daddy get in the car, back out of the driveway and peel down the street. Mama was at work, which left Tony and me alone together. It must have been the summer after first grade, because I can remember that he came out onto the porch and teased me about my missing front tooth. He hugged me and told me not to worry, that adults sometimes don't agree, and they get upset, but they get over it. Holding my hand, he took me for a walk around the block and told me how beautiful the sunsets were over the ocean and how much he loved being out at sea. I remember asking him why he didn't want to be with me and Daddy and Mama. He scooped me up into his arms and I think he may have cried some. He told me that people go away, but their love always stays. And then Tony took his dog tags from around his neck and gave them to me. He told me to keep them for him until he could come home for good. I did keep them for a long time.

At one point, I hung them around the stuffed bear's neck, having to twist the chain a couple of times to get it to be small enough. They may still be on that bear in my attic.

With the thought of my childhood toy in mind, I leave Mass and head home. I take the ladder from the garage and climb into the attic. In the dark and musty space, I locate the pink plastic tub I am looking for. Inside, I find my first holy communion dress and veil, wrapped in tissue paper, which is fastened with a ribbon; a scrapbook I put together in the fourth grade, programs from all my choir concerts stuffed into a manila envelope and there, at the bottom, my Navy bear. As I reach in and pull it out, I hear the jingle of Tony's dog tags. Clutching the bear to my chest, I can feel a lump forming in my throat.

Tony is my brother and he does love me. I wish I would

have remembered that over the years. Circumstances always seemed to keep us apart. When Daddy died, Tony was stationed in Italy and a big thing was going on...what was it? A cruise ship, the Achille Lauro, was taken over by PLO terrorists and they killed an American citizen. The plane they got away on was forced, by our military, to land in Sicily and they weren't granting anyone leave. Tony couldn't get away. Then, when I married Devin, he couldn't be there either. Tony did send me a letter apologizing for not being able to come to the wedding. My memory is jogged here, that I was angry at Tony for not being around when Daddy died and I blew him off. I feel terrible for this now. Looking back on my life, Tony tried to connect with me as best as he was able and I didn't make enough of an effort to reciprocate. My heart begins to swell with love for the brother that I barely know and I understand now that Jack is right. I need to give Tony a call.

Holding the bear, I gingerly make my way down the ladder and head toward the kitchen. I look Tony's number up in my address book and dial it as I sit down on a stool at the counter. As the phone rings, my stomach does flip flops. Although we have corresponded lately, I haven't actually *spoken* to Tony in almost twenty years. He picks up on the fourth ring.

"Tony?" I say. "This is Angela."

After two beats I hear him say, "*My* Angela? My...uh...little sister?"

I start to get choked up. "Yes," I whisper, and then I can't speak anymore.

"Are you okay?" he asks, alarm in his voice. "You sound like you're crying."

"I'm sorry, Tony," I say. "I...I just found my bear. Do you remember the bear you got me? I put your dog tags on it."

"You still have that?" he asks, softly.

"I do," I answer. "Tony, I want to apologize for not keeping in touch over the years. Thank you for always being the one to reach out to me."

Now he sounds choked up. "You mostly wrote back when I wrote to you. You sent me pictures of your kids. I'm glad you did."

"But I should have been doing that all along," I clear my throat. "Do you remember me writing you that I started dating someone?"

"Yeah, when you sent me pictures from Christmas you mentioned it."

"Well, he proposed to me and we're getting married on May 13th. Jack and I both would like you to be there. Will you come?"

Silence.

"Tony?"

"Uh...oh, congratulations! I would like to come, Angela, but I'm not sure if I--"

I cut him off. "Jack happens to be a very indulgent man. He told me to tell you that he will take care of all of your travel arrangements because I want you here and he wants to make me happy. Please, Tony, all you have to do is give me your arrival and departure dates and show up at the airport."

"He really said that?"

I chuckle. "He really did. Jack is an orphan and it will mean the world to him to meet his brother-in-law. Please, give him the opportunity to do that."

"I will come, then." I can hear a smile in Tony's voice.

"Thank you!" I exclaim. "Can you make it for a week? Five days?"

"Uh...I think five days would be better for me. I'll fly out of MacArthur."

My heart leaps. I can't wait to tell Jack. "Okay, when I make the reservations I will send you the confirmation. You still don't have a computer?"

"Nah...what do I need one of those for?"

"Lots of things!" I say, laughing. "But that's okay, I can always just call you. Oh, and there's one more thing. Do you think you can get to a tuxedo store and have them take your measurements?"

"How formal is this wedding, Angela?" he asks, sounding surprised.

Working up the nerve, I answer, "Just the wedding party is dressing formally. Um...I was wondering if you would do me the honor of giving me away at the ceremony."

"Hang on," he says, his voice sounding funny.

After a short moment, he gets back on the phone. "I'm sorry, Angela...I just got all...I don't know. This phone call was such a surprise. After all this time, I feel like I have some family again."

I do, too. It feels good. "When I married Devin, Daddy had passed away and so I just marched right down that aisle on my own. But this wedding, for me, is a new beginning. Maybe it can be a new start for us, too. It could be, don't you think?"

"Yes...I...I will call you with the measurements."

"Thank you so much!" I say, sincerely. "Jack will be here soon and we'll make travel arrangements. I'll call you tomorrow with details."

29

Jim picks me up at 11:00 in the morning, armed with two lattes from LuAnne's, and we head downtown to meet with Rick, the DJ. He is a single guy and has a home office in his apartment. I just don't feel right about going to this meeting alone. I didn't want to have to ask Jack, because I promised him I'd take care of this myself, which is why Jim is with me.

"I got you a cinnamon latte, okay, Jel?" Jim groans. "I'm sorry...*Angela*. Need to get used to that."

I've asked everyone to call me Angela. It's a struggle for my closer friends, who have known me for years, but I think that, since Jack calls me Angela, and Jel was Devin's pet name for me, it is appropriate.

Rick lives in an upscale loft in the River Market area, just over the bridge. It is furnished tastefully in blues and grays.

"I have an entire recording studio in here as well," Rick says, as he shows us around.

He is in his mid-thirties and rather handsome. He is tall, has a light olive complexion and shoulder length black hair cut neatly in layers. His brown eyes are set close together and there is a cleft in his chin.

We talk for awhile about the music for the reception. "I really want people to have a great time. I want everyone up and dancing," I tell him.

"My kind of party," he grins.

We settle on lots of 80's club music and also some swing for the dinner hour. He will e-mail me song lists to choose from.

"There's one more thing," I say. "I'd like to sing to my husband at the reception. Sort of a wedding gift."

He wrinkles his nose. "I usually don't encourage that, honestly. In my experience it never turns out the way you want it. I can play a special song, or sing myself, but..."

Wow...this guy is arrogant.

Jim pipes up. "Jel...Angela has an amazing voice. You should hear her before you decline."

Rick shakes his head a bit and I sense he is suppressing an eye roll. "All right," he sighs, "Let's see what you've got. What song did you have in mind?"

"*One Alone Is My Love* by Peter Mitchell."

"No, I don't have that," he says, checking his laptop. "Mitchell...he's the guy that used to open for the Rat Pack in the fifties, right?"

"I'm impressed," I say. "He's pretty obscure. He only made one album. My father had it and played it all the time along with Sinatra, Tony Bennett and Dean Martin."

Rick smiles. "Hmm...I have *Someone to Watch Over Me.* That has the same feel to it. How about you do that one and we'll see, okay?"

He hands me the mike and cues me to start. At first, I am a bit shaky, because I wasn't expecting to have to audition for my own wedding, but as the song goes on, my voice gets stronger. When I am done, Rick is silent for a few beats and says, "You know, I'd like to hear that again...do you mind?"

I shrug and oblige him. The second time I sing much better and I actually enjoy the experience.

At the end of the second take, Rick says, "Can we try something else? How about some 80's...Madonna?"

I look at the list on his laptop and choose *Crazy for You.* Jim's phone rings. "Where can I take this so I can hear?" he asks.

Rick points. "Outside in the hallway, on the balcony or in the bathroom."

Jim answers and walks through the sliding glass doors onto the balcony.

Rick cues the music and I give it all I've got. At the end of the song, he comes over to me and says, "Have you ever sung professionally before, Angela?"

I tell him my only experience was in choir all through school.

"Your voice is amazing. You should sing with me. I've been toying with the idea of bringing someone on. People are really going for the live music and I could use a partner." Rick looks down and taps on his laptop.

I didn't expect this. I've always wanted to sing professionally, but...now? Now is not the time. I want to give Jack all of me after we marry and my gut tells me a job, especially one that takes me away on the weekends wouldn't be a good fit right now for Jack and me or the kids, for that matter. Still, it's so unbelievably tempting.

"Here," he says, "let's do this one; do you know it?"

It's Lady Antebellum's *Need You Now,* a hauntingly beautiful duet.

"I love this song," I gush, "I sing it in the shower!"

Rick raises his eyebrows. "Sing it with *me*."

As Rick cues me, Jim walks back into the loft, sits down on the sofa and listens. We do a fairly good job on the song. I'm pretty happy with the first-time results.

Jim has a troubled look on his face. "When I walked out you were saying you didn't like brides to sing, and when I walked back in you two were doing a duet. Apparently I missed a lot out there on the balcony."

Rick shakes his head. "Just messing around," he says, dismissing Jim's concerns.

"Angela, I'll download *One Alone Is My Love* and we should start practicing immediately. Can you come a couple times a week?"

I shake my head. "My schedule is really busy. I can probably make it once a week," I turn to Jim. "Does that work for you?"

Rick's mouth turns down in a frown.

"Of course," Jim turns to Rick, "this day and time works best, if you're open."

He sighs and runs his hand through his hair. "Yeah, yeah. That would be fine."

***

"Rick is rather pushy, don't you think?" says Jim, as he pulls out of his parking spot and into the flow of traffic.

"Yes," I say, "He's pretty forward...but you have to admit, he does have a great voice."

"I think he wants to do more with you than sing, Jel." Jim sounds concerned.

"He asked me to work for him, actually. I think he's interested in me professionally, not personally, Jim."

"He knew you for twenty minutes and he offered you a job?! I'm not crazy about this guy. I don't think you should be spending too much time with him," says Jim, turning right onto the Broadway Bridge.

I laugh. "I think he's harmless. But, just to be on the safe side, I'm bringing my body guard, okay?"

Shaking his head, Jim says, "Well, the next time we go over to his place, I'm turning off my cell phone and staying put."

30

It's Saturday and Jack is over. At his suggestion, we decided to take today off from making wedding plans, because we are both exhausted and need a break. I am thrilled at the prospect of hanging out with Jack and the kids and doing nothing but relaxing.

The five of us are playing *Lord of the Rings* Trivial Pursuit, when the phone rings. I am tempted to let it go to voice mail, but Rosie grabs it and hands it to me. It's John. He sounds upset.

"What's going on?" I ask, concerned.

"Marissa's having a hard time here, Jel. I can't calm her down. Can you come by?"

I tell him I'm on my way and then ask Jack to hang out with the kids while I'm gone. I grab my keys and drive to her place to save time. I have no idea what could possibly be wrong, but I know I need to get over there right away. The fact that John called me must mean it is something serious. Could she have lost another baby? She would have told me she was pregnant, though, wouldn't she?

Out of breath, I run up the steps to Marissa's front porch and burst through the door. "Mar?" I yell, "Mar, what is going on?"

"We're down here, Jel," John calls, so I head downstairs to their basement, which is actually a beautiful den, with comfortable chairs and a hand carved bar that John built himself. When I get to the bottom of the stairs, the lights are off. Suddenly, they go on and I hear "Surprise!" chorused by my friends. Marissa is standing next to me, smiling, and when I see that she is okay, I burst out crying.

"You scared the heck out of me!" I yell, wrapping my arms around her in a hug.

"But I surprised you, didn't I?" she cracks a smile.

John comes over and gives me a hug. "Sorry to be an accomplice, Jel...Angela."

"You!" I say, exasperated, and give him a light punch on the upper arm.

"That's my cue to leave," John grins. "Have fun, ladies," he says, disappearing up the stairs.

Surveying the room I see that Jim's daughter, Katie, is here, with her infant son, Mike Jr. She is chatting with Christina and Felicia and Paula, Frankie's wife. Gina, from the Women's Auxiliary, sits in the corner, in a rocking chair. Gina and her husband are Natural Family Planning teachers and they have been giving Jack and me a private refresher course before the wedding. Denise, who I know from the Elizabeth Ministry, is sitting on the hearth, having a conversation with Gina. Denise is a very loving woman, who is great at helping the mothers who have suffered some kind of tragedy. She has the knack of gently coaxing people to open up and share their feelings. Also in the conversation is Samantha, who oversees meal delivery for the Elizabeth Ministry. That used to be my position, but she stepped up and took it over for me back when I resigned from all my ministries. I don't see Wendy, who does the scheduling for meals and babysitting for the Elizabeth Ministry. Then I remember her telling me she had her high school reunion this weekend.

Jenna stands off to the side, next to Marissa. Of all the women in the room, excluding my BFF, I am closest with Jenna. She and her husband, Jeff, have four children under the age of eight, but they made themselves available to me after Devin's accident. Jenna helps me out sometimes by picking up or dropping off one of my kids when I have to be in two places at once. I return the favor by watching her children once in a while so she and Jeff can get away on their own.

"Wow," I say to everyone, "Thanks! You guys really got me." I reach for my phone. "Let me give Jack a call and tell him to bring Rosie over."

"Oh, no," says Jenna. "This is strictly a women's only bridal shower...no men and no one under twenty-one."

I blush. "What on earth do you ladies have planned, pray tell?"

Jenna leads me over to a chair that is draped with feather boas. "Pick one," she says. "We all get one." Everyone dons a boa. I choose a light blue one and sit in the chair, which still has a few feathery wraps left on it.

"We know you and Jack don't actually need anything," says Marissa, "So we decided to have fun and throw you a lingerie shower."

I burst out laughing. "My, my, you are creative," I exclaim.

After a delicious lunch of Marissa's home made chips and salsa and enchiladas, we settle down for the opening of the gifts. The first gift I open is a beautiful peignoir set from Christina and Felicia. It is a lovely pale pink lace gown and matching robe. There is also a pair of feather high-heeled mules to go with it. "This is absolutely beautiful!" I exclaim. "But I guess it's strictly for the bedroom. I can't wear this while frying eggs for breakfast, huh?" I say and everyone laughs.

Katie hands me a small, wrapped gift. "This is from my Dad," she says. It is a book, *The Five Love Languages*, and there is an inscription inside.

Dear Angela,
This book helped keep Chloe and I focused on each other and our marriage. I pray it does the same for you and Jack.
In Christ,
Jim

My eyes tear up. "He gave Mike and me the same book for our bridal shower," says Katie. "We keep it on our night stand and refer to it a lot. I highly recommend it."

"So, does it contain some amazing secret about marriage that we all should know?" asks Denise.

Katie chuckles as she cradles her sleeping infant in her arms. "It's not rocket science. You just figure out in what way your husband likes to receive love; either through physical touch, through gifts, words of affirmation, acts of service or spending time together. Once you know his love language, that is how you relate to him and he will always feel loved...and vice versa, of course."

"I need to read that book," says Jenna. "With four little ones, sometimes Jeff and I can be like two ships passing in the night. Maybe that would help."

Katie's gift is a set of three large pillar candles on a mirrored tray. "Romantic ambience," she smiles. I thank her sincerely. "These will go beautifully on the dresser of the new bedroom set Jack and I ordered."

Jenna and Gina pitched in together for a luxurious set of Egyptian cotton sheets. Lifting the flap on the package, I run my hand over them. They are the softest sheets I have ever encountered. "These are like buttah!" I say, in my best New York accent.

There is a gift bag from Paula. It is full of scented soaps, shower gels and lotions in all my favorite flavors. "How did you know I love Coconut Lime?"

"Jack thought you would like that," Paula answers.

"You mean *Jack* thought *he* would like that," says Christina and we all laugh.

In the gift box from Denise is a short, black lace nightgown with spaghetti straps.

"Ooh la la!" exclaims Jenna. "Girl, you're all set for the honeymoon!"

"Wait a minute, don't forget mine," says Samantha, handing me a gift box. Inside is a pretty, light blue teddy with white lace trim.

"This is beautiful," I say, and as I lift it out of the box, something falls from it onto the floor. I reach down to pick it up and realize it is a package of condoms. The blood rushes to my cheeks. I sure hope this is a gag gift.

"You're such a joker, Samantha," I say, slipping the package discreetly back into the gift box.

"What?" she deadpans.

Could she be serious about this? As I am debating what to do about the situation, Christina says, "Is there a gift we aren't privy to?"

"Don't be so prudish, Jel," says Samantha. "Really!"

There is an awkward silence in the room as the other women realize what the gift is. I learned a long time ago that just because someone is Catholic, not to assume they know Church teaching. I was in the dark about it once as well. I know Jack has told me to always stand up for the Truth, so I decide to have a discussion with her, since the opportunity has come up.

"Samantha, I appreciate the thought, but Jack and I will be planning our family naturally --"

She cuts me off. "At your age you're not planning on having kids, are you?"

I can't believe she is so pushy about the subject. Now I feel the need to defend myself. "There is no good reason why Jack and I shouldn't. We're both healthy and we have the means to take care of another child."

I look up at Gina for some moral support. She gives me an encouraging nod.

"But you could have a Down Syndrome baby. Surely the Church wouldn't want *that,* would it?"

"If we happen to have a child with Down Syndrome, we will happily accept that child as we would any child," I say, gently. I am worried about the turn the conversation is going because, frankly, I don't want Paula to be offended.

Paula speaks up, "Frankie and I have a son with autism, Samantha. He is just as much of a blessing to us as our other sons. And, to be honest with you, living with Freddie has taught us all to get over ourselves. We have definitely learned to be more loving and less selfish because of him. Freddie has probably taught us more than we have taught him."

I can see by the color that has rushed to Samantha's cheeks that she is embarrassed. "Well, I just meant...am I the only one here who uses—birth control?"

"I was on the Pill for most of my marriage with Devin," I say. "I can tell you that it did nothing to bring us closer together. In fact, I think it drove us apart. We were selfish with each other. We didn't put each other first or consider each other's feelings in any of our decisions."

Samantha's eyes mist and she looks moved. I can see I've struck a chord with her.

"Even after I came off the Pill, we used Natural Family Planning," I continue. "But we didn't truly understand Church teaching, so we used it like birth control; only to avoid getting pregnant. Looking back on our lives, we didn't really have a serious need to avoid pregnancy." I sigh. "If I had my life to live over again, I never would have gone down that road."

"So...so, what are we supposed to do, just pop out one kid after another? That doesn't seem fair," says Samantha, looking flustered.

Christina laughs, "Chris and I have six kids, but we have been married for almost twenty-five years. That's an average of one every four years. If you look at it that way, it's really not a lot of kids."

"True," Gina pipes up. "We are called to prayerfully consider, month by month, whether or not God is calling us to have another child. Praying together and keeping track of our cycles creates a beautiful intimacy between us and our husband that will actually enhance our relationship."

Samantha's eyes narrow in suspicion. "You're telling me that not using birth control is actually better for your marriage? I find that hard to believe."

I am dismayed by the tension in the room, but I hope Samantha has at least listened to what we have said and will think about it. As I am trying to figure out a way to steer the conversation in another direction, Marissa comes to the rescue.

"You know," she says, "This seems like the perfect time for *my* gift." Marissa hands me a small, wrapped package.

I eagerly tear at the paper, grateful to be out of the conversation. It's a book.

"My, my!" I exclaim, holding it up for everyone to see, *Holy Sex! A Catholic Guide to Toe-Curling, Mind-Blowing, Infallible Loving,* by Dr. Greg Popcak.

"John's brother gave us a copy of this book as a joke for our anniversary last year," laughs Marissa. "Little did he know he was doing us a favor. This book is amazing."

I'm enthusiastically flipping through the pages. "Mar, this is like a how-to manual," I say, blushing.

"Ed and I own a copy. In my opinion, every couple should," says Gina.

"What is so great about this book?" Samantha asks.

"It explains Church teaching on marriage and how to live it out in your everyday life and in the bedroom," Marissa says. "I agree with Gina. All of you need to read it."

"Can I see that?" asks Samantha. I smile and hand her the book. She takes it, sits on the hearth, opens it and begins to read.

"Who wants cake?" asks Marissa.

***

I should be exhausted, but instead I am energized by the events of the day. Climbing into bed, I open the book Marissa got us for the shower and begin to read.

At 12:38 a.m., I finish the book. I have to talk to Jack about this while it is fresh in my mind, so I dial his number.

"Mmm...everything okay, Angela?" he answers, sleepily.

"Oh, Jack," I say. "I'm sorry to wake you, but I need to tell you that I finally get it. I finally get what you have been trying to tell me about sex."

This seems to wake him up quickly. "Get what?"

"I understand now why I shouldn't be embarrassed to be vulnerable with you. Because we need to have a complete union, in every aspect of our lives, body, mind and spirit. God wants it all from us. He wants us to be as selfless and passionate with each other as He is with us."

Jack clears his throat. "This was a revelation you had at one o'clock in the morning?" he chuckles.

"It was the book Marissa got us. Haven't you read it?"

"I haven't had the time to read every book on the subject of Theology of the Body, love."

"It talks about how sex is sacramental and good and created for us by God to help us to grow closer to each other and closer to Him."

I hear amusement in Jack's voice. "And somehow the author of the book got through to you, but your favorite teacher didn't?"

"I'm sorry, Jack. I guess I was so busy being uptight that I wasn't able to process what you have been telling me. With this book, I had nothing to be embarrassed about. I just opened it and started to read."

"Then maybe we should start texting more," Jack jests.

I smile. "Everything that I learned in your class, all the things you've been trying to teach me; they all came together for me tonight like one big puzzle. I also finally understand why you wouldn't date me initially."

"Ah, love," he says. "That's water under the bridge..."

"But I completely get it now!" I say, excitedly. "If I couldn't accept God's love for me, then how could I possibly understand *how* God loves? And if I didn't understand how God loves, then I couldn't possibly love someone else the way He does! And that is, ultimately, what you and I are supposed to be doing, right? Loving each other the way God loves us...making a gift of ourselves to each other in everything we do, both in and out of the bedroom. And when we hold back from each other in any way, physically or emotionally, then we are not cooperating with His plan for marriage."

"You get an A+, Angela." I can hear in Jack's voice how proud of me he is. "Did you read the whole book tonight?"

"I did! I couldn't put it down. After I read the first two parts it was like the whole world suddenly made more sense to me."

"And what comes after the first two parts of the book?"

"Ooh la *la*!"

31

I crane my neck to look through the people standing outside Terminal B, while I cautiously steer the car along the ramp. All of a sudden, my heart skips a beat. I see a handsome man with a full head of thick, silver hair, holding an olive green sea bag. It's got to be Tony. I ease the car over, open the door and step out. "Tony!" I shout and our eyes meet. He stands there, frozen, staring. I smile sweetly as I approach him and take his arm. "I knew it was you, Tony. You look just like Daddy."

I gently steer him toward the car and open the trunk.

He seems to come to and throws his bag in; then he looks at me, shaking his head. "I...I can't believe it's you, after all this time."

I laugh. "Let's catch up somewhere other than here. The police don't let anyone linger."

The closest place to the airport to get coffee is a gas station, so instead I head to LuAnne's in Smithville. After I ask Tony about his flight, we mostly remain silent on the ride there. At LuAnne's I order us both coffee and a slice of chocolate pudding cream pie. The wedding is in three days, so I figure one piece of pie now won't make or break me.

"I thought we would catch up a bit before you meet the kids. They are excited that you're coming, so there may be some commotion when we get home. Actually, I think Jack may be more excited than they are to meet you," I chuckle.

"This guy, he's good to you all the time? He treats you right, Angela?"

"Jack puts God first in all things, and that reflects in how he treats me and the kids. He's a good man."

Tony sighs. "You guys are religious? Does that mean you're having a Mass on Friday, not just a ceremony?"

I remember that Tony was brought up as I was, going through the motions and not really understanding his faith. I don't know that part of Tony at all. If I had struggles, though, I am sure he has had the same.

"Yes, we are. Our faith is really important to us. What about you? Do you still practice?" I ask, gently.

He shakes his head. "Nah...God doesn't want me. I haven't been, you know, what they call a model son."

My heart breaks for Tony. I know how he feels; like he's not loved, and that is a lonely place to be.

"I have felt that way as well," I reach out and take Tony's hand. "But I realized that God doesn't feel that way. He loves us no matter what."

Tony looks down and shakes his head again. "Angela, I've done some pretty bad stuff in my life. If you knew, you'd probably hate me for it."

I can see his pain and I remember so well the guilt I felt about Devin's death and our marriage. "Tony, I am your sister. I will never hate you, no matter what you've done. I promise you that. Truly."

He looks up at me and his eyes are moist. "I don't know."

"Well, you knew that we'd be in church on Friday, have you thought about this at all; about making things right with God?"

Tony sighs and shakes his head. "How is that even possible?"

"Look, if there are things you have done that you're sincerely sorry for, go to confession. Another name for confession is reconciliation; there is a reason for that, Tony. You reconcile with God."

"So, I confess and I'm good? That's it?"

I smile. "If you are truly sorry for your sins and want to make amends, then yes, absolutely. Jack and I have made an appointment to go to confession on Thursday afternoon with the kids. You may come along, if you like," I squeeze his hand. "Think about it, okay?"

Tony offers a weak smile. "I will."

When we walk into the house, there is a homemade paper banner draped over the landing. It says, "Welcome Uncle Tony!" Rosie squeals and runs over to us. I introduce Tony to her and the boys. Jack introduces himself and escorts Tony into the living room. Jack, being Jack, read up on some of the military events that occurred when Tony was in the Navy and brings them up immediately, to make Tony feel at ease. The boys are very interested in the conversation and Rosie tags along, just happy to be near her newfound uncle. I excuse myself to the kitchen to start dinner. After preheating the oven for the lasagna I put together, I go over to the computer and do a search for *Catholic examination of conscience.* I find a thorough one that goes through each of the Ten Commandments. It has an extensive list of questions that will help a penitent determine how he has broken his relationship with God. After printing it out, I write on top *Just in case...* and I fold it in half. Slipping downstairs to the guest room, I lay it on the dresser top. Maybe this will help Tony make the decision to come with us on Thursday. Silently, I ask God to inspire him to do just that.

***

After dinner, Tony takes two bakery boxes out of his sea bag. "This is for your mother," he says, handing me a smaller box. "And this is for the rest of you."

I open mine and my eyes grow wide. Inside are half a dozen black and white cookies. They were my favorite as a child. These are large vanilla cookies, iced half-white, half-chocolate. Anyone who took me to the bakery knew to buy me one of these. "You remembered!" I exclaim, as I throw my arms around Tony's neck. Honestly, I am more grateful that he remembered than for the cookies. How touching it is, that Tony made the effort to bring me a childhood memory.

The kids dig into the other box. It is full of butter cookies; some with sprinkles, some chocolate dipped and some with maraschino cherries on top.

"I would have brought pastries, but I didn't think they would travel well," says Tony.

"I have some memories of you taking me to Romano's for a black and white cookie on occasion," I tell him."I was so in love with you. I felt like a princess being escorted into the bakery by a handsome prince."

Tony looks into his coffee cup. "I never knew you felt that way, Angela," he says quietly. "I should have come around more."

"When I was a teenager, especially around the time Daddy died, I have to admit, I was pretty mad at you. I put a cookie on my plate and break it in half on the line between the black and the white icing. "I'm sorry, Tony. I was selfish back then, and I refused to see that you had obligations that made it difficult for you to come home."

"But that's water under the bridge," Jack interjects. "What matters is you're talking now, right?" he asks, breaking off a piece of the chocolate side of my cookie and dunking it in his coffee.

I go into the kitchen, retrieve the coffee pot and refill Tony's cup. "You know, I had forgotten so much about you and lately, the memories are coming back. They are good memories of my big brother, the sailor, who would come home on leave and sweep me off my feet, and then go off into the world to have another adventure," I smile at him. "And now you're here, and I'm glad you are."

32

The bedroom set is arriving tomorrow, so Jack, Tony and the boys made plans to paint today. I told Tony that I would take him downtown for a tour of the city while the guys painted, but he insisted on helping. This is touching to me, that he would spend his time here working instead of relaxing.

I go into the kitchen to make iced tea while Jack and Sam move the dresser and chest of drawers out of the room and into the garage. I plan to give this set to a family Fr. Sean knows who is in need of it. John is coming later and the guys will load it into his truck for delivery later today.

I hear Jack call from the bedroom, "Angela, would you mind coming down here, love?" His voice sounds tense. Jack is in the room alone when I walk through the door. The mattress has been removed from the box spring and the rest of the crew must be in the process of bringing it down to the garage. He has an envelope in his hand.

"This was between the mattress and box spring when we pulled the mattress off the bed," Jack says, offering it to me. Before I reach out and take it, I can see Devin's messy handwriting on the envelope. "Jelly Bean," it says.

"Wow," I joke. "I guess you know how often I wash the bed skirt now, huh?" But a lump forms in my throat before I get all the words out.

Jack smiles, hesitantly. "You're supposed to wash those?"

Our eyes meet. I wish I knew what he was thinking. It is days before our wedding and here is a reminder of Devin just when we are moving forward and making a new life for ourselves. This has got to be unnerving for him.

"I...I guess I will leave you on your own to read that now."

"No, Jack. We're getting married on Friday, for Pete's sakes. Whatever Devin had to say to me, he can say to you, too."

I can see in Jack's eyes how grateful he is that I didn't ask to be alone and I am glad I don't want to be. He moves behind me and wraps his arms around my waist. The envelope has not been sealed, so I lift the flap and remove the card inside. There is a picture of a tropical beach on the front, with an orange and pink sunset in the background.

Jelly Bean,
Happy New Year, baby. Can you believe in a couple weeks it will be 20 years? Remember how it was for us in the beginning? All those romantic nights? Let's get away and try to get some of that back. You pick the place and I'll make the reservations.
Love,
Dev

I hear Jack exhale, as if he had been holding his breath all this time. Closing the card, I turn and let his arms envelop me. Jack entwines my hair in his hands and kisses my forehead.

I look up at him and smile through my tears. I hadn't expected this one final moment with Devin, yet I am glad it happened. I realize now that Devin felt that there was something missing from our relationship and was searching for more. Deep down, I am sure he was searching for intimacy, for the sanctity that didn't exist between us. I know he loved me in the best way he knew how and that's enough for me now. I have no regrets about this part of my life anymore. I was a different person with Devin and I gave him what I could at the time. I have sadness over what could have been, but I am so thankful that I have been given a second chance with Jack.

"I love that you're here with me right now," I whisper to Jack. "Here we are in the room we will make love in, and possibly conceive a child in. It is our room, Jack. I look forward to the memories we will make here. I don't want to look back. I only want to look forward."

***

Every one is asleep. I turn on the dishwasher and pad down the hall to my bedroom. I wash up and put on a pair of pajamas; long sleeve, because, despite the ninety degree weather at the beginning of the week, there is a chill in the air and the promise of cool temperatures for the weekend. Typical Missouri weather.

The furniture was delivered today. Carefully I make up the bed that Jack and I will share as man and wife. We will be spending tomorrow night, our wedding night, at his apartment, but this will be our marriage bed. I smooth down the light blue sheets and then top them with the comforter. It is a light blue with a dark brown border. The guys painted three walls light blue and the wall the bed is on the same shade of brown as in the comforter. The room looks and smells brand new. There is no trace of my old life here.

I walk over to the closet. Jack brought over most of his clothes and they are hanging on one side, beside mine. Last weekend, Jack and Sam moved two of his bookshelves over to the house. Now they are in this room, filled with Jack's favorites. I smile as I survey the shelves and imagine Jack lying in our bed, reading. I make a note to run out as soon as we return from our honeymoon and purchase a reading lamp for his nightstand.

I am tired, but I can't stay in this room. I don't want to

be here without Jack. I go into the closet and pull out a blanket, then I grab my pillow and head to the couch.

As I am snuggling in, I hear footsteps on the stairs and then the kitchen light goes on. Sitting up, I adjust my eyes and see a shadow on the kitchen wall.

"Tony?"

He peeks out from the kitchen into the living room. "Angela! What are you doing on the couch?" Tony asks, coming over and sitting down on the living room chair.

I explain to him that I want to wait until Jack and I can share the bed, instead of sleeping in it alone.

"That's sweet," Tony smiles.

"And what are you doing up? Are you not comfortable? Can I do anything for you?"

"No, not at all. I just couldn't sleep. I was...thinking."

"Well, I'm here, Tony, if you'd like to talk," I say, getting up and walking toward the kitchen. Tony follows. "How about some herbal tea with honey?"

He grins. "How about a glass of milk and a leftover cookie from Romano's?"

"Sounds good to me," I chuckle, pulling two glasses from the cupboard.

Tony removes the bakery box from atop the refrigerator and takes out a black and white cookie. "Want to split?"

"Sure," I say, putting the glasses of milk on the counter and sliding onto a stool. Tony sits beside me and we munch for a minute, in silence.

Quietly, Tony says, "I'm sorry I bailed on confession today. I know you wanted me to go."

My heart breaks when he says this. I did want him to go. I was crushed when he chose to stay at the house.

"Tony," I answer. "The decision has to be yours. You can't just go to please me. You have to really want to confess on your own."

The tip of Tony's nose is red and his eyes become moist. "I just...I just couldn't do it. I thought about all my screw ups and all the problems I've caused...even in your life... and I couldn't bring myself to go."

He looks so much like my father that I get a flashback of holding Daddy not too long before he died. He was crying and telling me he had so many regrets, but I told him never to regret how he loved me.

"What problems have you caused in my life, Tony?" I ask, gently. "It was I who behaved badly toward you. I should have understood you had obligations and not expected you to be there at specific times. You were defending our country, after all."

"But you were too young to have all that on you...caring for Daddy, taking care of the house. I didn't know Mama was—wasn't..."

"Look, Mama was basically a selfish person. I hate to put it that way, but she was. I don't know how it was with you, Tony, but when it came to me, she did the bare minimum. I fended for myself, especially after Daddy died. But it turns out that I've had a pretty good life. I'm happy; and I've forgiven Mama. "

He looks at me and wipes his eyes with the back of his hand.

"Tony," I say, gently. "Deep down, I always knew you cared."

"I did," he says, quietly. "I do."

"Look, I don't know you well enough to know which specific demons you wrestle with, but the past is over and done. Right now you can be here for me, and you can be an uncle to my kids. That's a good place to start, isn't it?"

"Yes," he says, with conviction. "Yes, it is."

I reach over to the counter, take hold of my milk glass and raise it up high. "To new beginnings," I announce.

Tony smiles and clicks his glass on mine, "Salut!"

"Salut!" I respond.

33

Marissa, Rosie and I arrive at the cathedral and assemble in a small room, off the vestibule. I look through the doorway, which has a clear view of the side aisle in the sanctuary. There are a lot of people already here.

"Mama, I have to make a pit stop," says Rosie. She's a bit nervous about walking down the aisle and has spent the better part of the day in the bathroom. She hands Marissa her bouquet and makes her way through the sanctuary to the stairway that leads to the restrooms.

Then I see Sam emerge from the sacristy at the far end of the sanctuary, beyond the altar, and walk down the side aisle toward me. He looks so incredibly handsome in his tuxedo, that I immediately start to cry. "Don't cry, Mom." he says. "Brides are supposed to be happy."

"You look so much like your father, Samwise; so grown up."

"That's because I *am* grown up. You just refuse to see that, most of the time," he smiles, and hands me a small, purple nylon jewelry bag. "Pop wanted you to have this."

"Who?"

"Uh...Mr. B. We didn't feel right about calling him Dad, because, you know...*Dad.* But Rosie wants to call him Papa, so Ben and I decided on Pop and he's okay with that."

More tears come as I face the beautiful reality that not only is Jack becoming my husband today, but a father to my children as well. Sam heads back towards the front of the cathedral.

Marissa comes over with a tissue. "I'm glad we brought your makeup with us, honey," she says, dabbing at my eyes.

Gingerly, I open the bag and take out a small, folded note, hand-written on vellum.

Dearest Angela,
Today, on our wedding day, I want you to have this rosary. I know you have a generous heart and pray for us, whom you love, daily. Each decade of this rosary is dedicated to the people in your life whom you love the most. May all of us benefit from the prayers that spring forth from your loving heart.
All my love, on our wedding day and always,
Jack

Reaching into the bag, I pull out the rosary. The crucifix is made of sterling silver and mother-of-pearl. The silver 'Our Father' beads are crafted to look like blooming roses. Each decade has a name, spelled out in silver beads. The remaining beads are blue Swarovski crystal. I hold it up and read the names: Samuel, Benjamin, Rosa, Giacomo and Devin.

My heart swells with joy, as I realize this is Jack's way of telling me he has reconciled with the fact that Devin shared my life before he did. I wrap the rosary around my left hand. I want to have it while we exchange vows.

Looking down at the crucifix in my palm, I pray silently to be worthy of the sacrament I am about to receive.

Marissa comes and puts her arm around my waist. I hand her the note.

"There are very few things in my life, honey, that have given me more joy than to see you and Jack; and your love for each other."

"I love you, Mar. Thanks for caring enough to smack me upside the head and help me get over myself."

Marissa laughs and plants a light kiss on my cheek.

Rosie walks through the door. "Are you okay?" I ask.

"Fine, just a little jittery, Mama," she says, plucking her bouquet from Marissa's hand. Marissa and Rosie are carrying bouquets of white roses that have been teased open and the stems tied with silver ribbon. They are full and beautiful. My bouquet is also white roses, but the edges are dyed a light blue, so that it is just a hint of color. I am carrying the stems across my arm and pale blue ribbons cascade from them, almost down to the floor.

Suddenly, I spot Jim heading toward me, wearing an alb.

"What are you doing?" I ask.

"Serving," he answers cheerfully.

I push him on the chest with both hands. "You are *not!*" I say, incredulous. "I didn't know you could do that!"

Jim grins, "I can. Now that I am in the diaconate program, I have served at a couple of Masses with the bishop. I asked if it would be okay to serve at your wedding. You don't mind, do you?"

"Mind? I'm *honored!*" I hug him tightly. I'm so glad Jim was able to arrange this. It adds more to the day for me, knowing he will be such a special part of it.

Fr. Sean arrives, vested for Mass and gives me a hug. "You look beautiful, Jel...I mean, Angela," he says. "Are you nervous?"

"Only about flubbing my vows, Father. Otherwise, I am ready," I answer, with conviction.

The bishop now comes in and I am a little flustered. Bishop Flanagan is in his mid-60's, but looks much younger. He has clear, blue, expressive eyes and a thin, but friendly mouth. He is a very tall man, over six feet. He puts me at ease by saying, "Today is a great day for the sacrament of matrimony, don't you think? The weather is cool, but clear, and the sun is shining. God is good."

I kneel down on my left knee and kiss his ring; no small task in a ball gown with a train. As I am on my knee, he places his hand on my head. "May the Lord Jesus cover you in His Precious Blood and strengthen you for what you are about to do."

Then he offers me his hand. Gratefully, I take it and struggle to my feet.

"Thank you so much, Bishop Flanagan."

"You're welcome," he chuckles. "Now let's unite you and Jack, shall we?"

Tony and Ben enter the vestibule. Jack came by this morning and picked the guys up. They all got dressed at his apartment, so this is the first time I am seeing my brother and my younger son in their tuxes. I give each a tight, teary hug.

The music begins and Bishop Flanagan processes in, followed by Fr. Sean and Jim.

With minimal prompting from Christina, Nica begins to walk down the aisle, just like we showed her at the rehearsal. I hear a collective "Awww" from the crowd as the toddler makes her way toward the front pew, where Felicia is beckoning her. I hug both Rosie and Ben and they turn and wait to make their way toward the altar.

Marissa comes to me. Placing her hand on my cheek, she says, "Goodbye, Jel Cooke," as tears stream down her face, and then she turns and begins her walk. I dab at my eyes with the handkerchief I stuffed up my sleeve.

"You okay?" Tony asks, looking a little shaky himself.

I nod and, taking a cleansing breath, I ready myself. I want to look all the way down the aisle to see Jack, but I stop just short of doing so. I want to enjoy the anticipation. When we hear the beginning strains of the *Trumpet Voluntary*, Tony offers me his arm and we take the first steps toward the altar.

Although I cried nearly the whole day about one sentimental thing or another, the urge to shed tears leaves me, and a profound peace enters my soul. I keep my eyes downcast, until I am at the very first pew. We stop and Tony turns toward me. As he lifts my veil, he embraces me. He is too choked up for words and so he simply moves into the pew, next to Chris and his family.

Next, I focus on my firstborn standing beside Jack. My breath catches slightly as I once again recognize his uncanny resemblance to his father and I offer a silent prayer of thanksgiving for the life of the man who sired my son. I manage a perfunctory smile, which Sam quickly returns before he glances away. It is unspoken that if we linger we will both be overcome by emotion.

I turn my eyes to Jack. My heart skips a beat as I see him for the first time today, the day we will be united forever. Jack is wearing a black tuxedo with a gray silk tapestry pattern vest and matching long formal tie. His deep brown eyes are alight with joy and I don't think I have ever seen him look as handsome as he does at this moment.

Jack smiles broadly and extends his hand to me. We both genuflect and then walk up onto the altar to sit in the chairs that have been placed there especially for us.

Marissa takes my bouquet and I lower myself into the chair on the left, with Jack to my right. He takes my hand again and squeezes it three times. I glance toward him and he winks at me. I can feel color spread across my cheeks and I wonder if, when I am eighty years old, a wink from Jack will still make me blush. I certainly hope so.

The bishop stands and we all rise as he begins the Mass. Jack is still holding my hand and, I'm sure, has no intention of letting go.

"Father," prays the bishop, "when you created mankind you willed that man and wife should be one. Bind Giacomo Gabriel Bartolomucci and Angela Marianna Cooke in the loving union of marriage; and make their love fruitful so that they may be living witnesses to your divine love in the world. We ask you this through our Lord Jesus Christ, your Son, who lives and reigns with you and the Holy Spirit, one God, for ever and ever."

We sit down and Marissa's husband John approaches the altar. He fishes his reading glasses from his breast pocket and perches them on the bridge of his nose.

"A reading from the Book of Tobit," he says, and proceeds to read the account of Tobiah and Sarah's wedding night. Jack insisted on this scripture to be read today. He wanted all the witnesses to our sacrament to hear Tobiah's intentions for his wife, which are Jack's intentions for me; that he takes me, not out of lust, but for a noble purpose and he asks God's blessings on us for a long and happy marriage.

After we all sing verses from Psalm 148, which praises God's name, Chris approaches the altar and turns the page in the lectionary. "A reading from the Letter of Saint Paul to the Ephesians," he reads. He seems emotional and struggles to keep his voice even as he repeats the instructions that St. Paul wrote in ancient times to the church in Ephesus. When he comes to the part where it says, "Wives, submit to your husbands," I squeeze Jack's hand. Later in this scripture, when St. Paul instructs the husbands to "love their wives as Christ loved the church," Jack squeezes back.

Next, we all stand as Fr. Sean says, "A reading from the Holy Gospel according to Mark.

Jesus said: 'From the beginning of creation,
God made them male and female.
For this reason a man shall leave his father and mother
and be joined to his wife,
and the two shall become one flesh.
So they are no longer two but one flesh.
Therefore what God has joined together,
no human being must separate.'"

Bishop Flanagan steps up to the ambo to begin his homily.

"When I met with Angela for the first time, to interview

her in preparation for her marriage to Jack, I asked if she had a favorite scripture about marriage. Immediately she said, 'Ephesians 5; you know, the one that talks about wives submitting to their husbands.' I can't tell you how surprised I was, because I actually have gotten hate mail from people—men and women alike—that call me all sorts of things because I dare to allow this 'sexist' and 'archaic' nonsense to be read at a wedding here, in the 21st century.

"Well, I prodded a little and Angela revealed to me that she understood that this same scripture calls for husbands to lay down their lives for their wives and to love them as they love their own bodies. She said that she read somewhere the root 'sub' means 'under' and that the word submit or submission means to 'come under the mission;' in other words to cooperate with it. Then she announced that if Jack's mission was to treat her as well as he would his own body and to die for her, she had no problem whatsoever cooperating with that!" Laughter comes from the pews and I can hear Jack chuckling as well.

The bishop adjusts the microphone slightly and continues, "When I asked Jack the same question, he answered that the entire Song of Solomon, particularly the parts where the man refers to the woman as 'my sister, my bride;' speak to him. Society views women through a lens tainted by lust. This imagery of a sister-bride illustrates that it is beneficial for a man to love a woman like a sister before marriage so that lust cannot enter into the relationship."

He lifts his head and scans the pews for a moment.

"Who, honestly, would feel lustful toward a sister? No, a man would have tender, loving and protective feelings toward her. Jack understands this; and he honors Angela by loving her as a brother loves a sister. He has lived a life of virtue in preparation for this day. In effect, he has been loving Angela for over forty years, even though for most of that time he didn't even know her."

I gasp. This is true! Jack remained chaste for *me*! He has been preparing his wedding gift to me for his whole life. My heart swells with love for him. I look over, but Jack's head is bent, as if in prayer and I cannot get his attention. I long to hold Jack, to thank him for his selflessness, but that will have to wait until later.

"Jack and Angela will shortly exchange their vows. They have requested to incorporate a Croatian tradition into their ceremony, which will involve this crucifix."

Bishop Flanagan holds up the exquisite crucifix Jack had purchased years ago while traveling in Italy. It is about twenty-four inches long and the corpus is hand carved and, while being accurate in reflecting Christ's suffering, it also has an ethereal beauty to it.

"Instead of kissing each other, they will kiss this crucifix as a public act of accepting the cross given to them by Christ in the sacrament of matrimony. When you have both a woman and a man who truly understand the mutual sacrifices that must be made, before and after their union, in order to fulfill their roles in marriage as ordained by God, it is truly humbling. So, after talking with both Angela and Jack, I thought it wouldn't hurt to go ahead and waive the marriage prep classes." Again, laughter erupts from the pews. I find myself chiming in.

"But in all seriousness, Angela and Jack understand that marriage is, ultimately, a cross. Most of the time, it is a light one and easy to carry. But there will be times when it gets heavy and they will have to shore each other up. There may even be times when one person is doing the carrying and the other is adding to the burden or vice versa. However, most likely it will be the little things that they will encounter on a daily basis, like the age old arguments about toilet seats or toothpaste caps...those minor sufferings to be united with the cross of Jesus that will ultimately unite Jack and Angela with God, in heaven, for all eternity. Amen."

Rising from his chair, Fr. Sean says, "Please stand," gesturing with his hand.

He comes to us, holding the crucifix and a stole. I grasp the cross with my right hand and Jack puts his left hand over mine. The cross is then laid on our forearms and we grasp our free hands underneath it, as we face each other.

As Fr. Sean binds the stole around our hands and the crucifix, Bishop Flanagan says, "My dear friends, you have come together in this church so that the Lord may seal and strengthen your love in the presence of the Church's minister and this community. Christ abundantly blesses this love. He has already consecrated you in baptism and now he enriches and strengthens you by a special sacrament so that you may assume the duties of marriage in mutual and lasting fidelity. And so, in the presence of the Church, I ask you to state your intentions."

Then he asks us a series of questions regarding our freedom of choice in uniting in marriage, our intentions to be faithful and to accept children as given to us by God, which we both answer in the affirmative.

"Since it is your intention to enter into marriage," says the bishop, "declare your consent before God and his Church."

Still bound to the cross, Jack and I exchange our vows. As Jack promises to love and honor me, his voice is quiet and even, yet there is strong, underlying emotion. His voice breaks, however, when he says, "All the days of my life." I know that he is feeling his mortality. Approaching 50 years old, Jack has often wondered aloud about how much time we will be blessed with. Standing here, before him, I know that any time we have will truly be a gift to cherish.

Bishop Flanagan nods at me, and I begin to bind myself to Jack, body and soul. I whisper, because I am afraid if I add any volume to my voice it will break.

Breathing evenly and steadying myself, I say, "I, Angela Marianna take you, Giacomo Gabriel, to be my husband."

Jack's eyes are fixed on me and joy radiates from him, bathing me in a warm light.

"I promise to be true to you in good times and in bad," I continue, "in sickness and in health. I will love you and honor you all the days of my life." I squeeze Jack's hand lightly as I conclude my vows.

Fr. Sean's voice echoes through the cathedral as he raises his hands in blessing. "You have declared your consent before the Church. May the Lord in his goodness strengthen your consent and fill you both with his blessings." He is beaming and, now that I think of it, I can feel a wide and joyful smile on my face as well.

"What God has joined, men must not divide," he declares.

All of us in unison respond, "Amen."

"And now," announces the bishop, "You may kiss the cross."

Jack pushes the crucifix up to a vertical position and we both lean in. I go up on my toes, but Jack must stoop down and our lips both touch the feet of the corpus. I have been focused and calm through the whole Mass, but now, at this moment, I begin to weep. Fr. Sean removes the binding from our hands and passes the crucifix to Jim, who places it on the shelf under the ambo.

Tears are running down my face as I look up at Jack. He reaches out and takes my face in his hands, wiping away my tears with his thumbs. His eyes are moist as well, as he silently mouths, "I love you...my wife."

Sam comes over and gives Jack the rings, which Fr. Sean blesses with the words, "May the Lord bless these rings which you give to each other as the sign of your love and fidelity."

Jack slips my ring on my finger, vowing to love and be true to me. My ring is a simple circle of diamonds set in white gold, symbolizing the eternal nature of our love.

I take Jack's hand in mine. "Jack," I say, and then I catch myself. I wanted to use his given name today. "Giacomo, take this ring as a sign of my love and fidelity, in the name of the Father and of the Son and of the Holy Spirit." Jack chose a white gold ring that has a design on it that looks like a braid. He said it resembles the Crown of Thorns and every time he glances at it, it will remind him of the awesome responsibility he has to help us both live lives worthy of Heaven.

As we kneel and Bishop Flanagan says the words of consecration, my hand is still in Jack's. When the host is elevated and the bishop says, "This is my body, which will be given up for you," it occurs to me that what Christ says to His church, I can say to Jack and he to me; because in marriage we are united in a mutual giving and taking of our bodies in both a spiritual and physical union. Jack's hand grips mine so tightly; it nearly crushes it. I look over at him and he is wracked with sobs. He turns his face toward me and I know instinctively that his thoughts mirror mine. Yet, his are more profound because of the lifelong commitment he made to me and all the preparation he has undergone to give himself to me fully and freely.

We receive communion kneeling, hands still linked. I unite myself now to Jesus and joy wells up from my soul in a wordless prayer of thanksgiving.

The Mass ends and Bishop Flanagan gives the final blessing. Marissa carefully hands me my bouquet and then Jack and I process out, followed by Jim and the clergy. In the vestibule, we are bombarded by friends wishing us well. Our hands are still linked, but I long to be alone with Jack, even for a moment, to tell him how much I love him. The moment doesn't come as we are then whisked out onto the steps of the cathedral for pictures with the priests and the bridal party.

34

Jack takes my hand and assists me into the limousine, then gets in the other side.

"So, when did you add a separate limo for the bridal party?" I ask, hearing the vehicle start up and feeling it begin to move forward.

Jack takes me in his arms. "I love them dearly, but sometimes it's appropriate for a husband and wife to be alone," he says, leaning in and kissing me passionately. This leaves me breathless. He pulls back and looks deeply into my eyes. "I know the reception will be exciting, and I am looking forward to it; but I wanted us to have some quiet time before that, just to hold each other."

"You think of everything," I sigh, snuggling close to Jack and reveling in the feel of his arms around me.

"Of course I do," he says. "I'm your husband...it's my job to think of everything."

Silently we ride in the limo, relaxing before the events that are to come. I am so comfortable that I begin to drift off; then I hear Jack say, "There's something I wanted to tell you, love."

I look up at him and my eyebrows come together. "About?"

"My aunt. I've told you about how she was a very prayerful woman. Well, she was a charismatic. She was baptized in the spirit in her early twenties and received the gift of prophecy."

"Your aunt was a prophet?" I ask, stretching, and then laying my head on Jack's shoulder.

"Well, she didn't just go around making prophetic announcements. Things would come to her in prayer. Anyway, the day she died, I was with her. There were so many things I wanted to tell her, because I knew it would be the last time I ever saw her on this earth. One of my biggest regrets was that I hadn't married and given her a grandchild," says Jack, kissing the top of my head through my veil. "I was very emotional about it and there she was, on her deathbed, comforting me. One of the last things she said to me that day was, 'Giacomo, un giorno ti sposerai un'angela.'"

"Meaning?" I ask. I wish I had learned to speak Italian, but all I know are a few phrases and the names of foods.

"Well, it means, *Someday you will marry an angel.* Except the word *angel*, in Italian, is masculine, so she *should* have said *un angelo.* But she created her own word, *un'angela.* She was trying to communicate something to me, love, don't you think?"

My eyes grow wide and I sit up, so I am facing Jack. "But you didn't know my name when you met me."

"No, but the night you walked into my classroom, I noticed you. Actually, it was like my soul noticed yours, Angela. It confused and frightened me, because, frankly, I thought you and Jim were married."

I throw my head back and laugh. "Jim and me?"

"Yes, Jim and you. I'll admit that when I collected your registration forms I looked to see if you had the same last name."

"Jack! I didn't know you were even interested then."

"Well, I was. I mean, I felt drawn to you and you seemed familiar to me in a way, even though I knew nothing about you. My spiritual director said that it may be the Holy Sprit at work, so I began to pray that if somehow we were meant to be together, that God would remove the obstacles that were in the way," Jack says, as the limousine pulls up in front of Frankie's.

"And then you were moved out of the Lay Formation Institute and became free to date a former student."

Jack leans over and nuzzles my neck. "Yes, and now you are my wife."

"And what if my name had been Matilda or Nancy or Gwyneth?" I ask playfully.

"Or Jel?" asks Jack.

"Touché," I answer.

Frankie greets us at the door, and then leads us into the reception hall. It looks lovely. Paula and some of my friends came here yesterday and decorated. There is pale blue and white tulle draped from the light fixtures, giving an effect of inverse arches all around the room. The tables are clothed in simple white, with low arrangements of blue roses in the center. Silver glitter is sprinkled on the tablecloths, which seem to sparkle and shine under the dimmed light. Along the very back wall, there is a long, narrow table covered in white butcher paper and strewn with crayons, markers, small bottles of bubbles and other small toys for the children. There is no gift table. We requested no gifts on our invitations because, honestly, we are not in need of anything.

Jack and I hug Frankie and Paula and thank them. I tear up a bit as I think of how much work they have done to prepare for this day.

"Let us get everything set up in the kitchen and then I will take off this apron and enjoy the party!" exclaims Paula.

Rick comes strolling into the hall now, holding some cables. I introduce him to Jack. "We're going to make sure everyone has a good time," he assures us.

Jack excuses himself to the restroom and I survey the room one more time. The cake is over in the corner, near the dais, where Jack and I will dine. It has four tiers and is covered in white fondant and decorated with fresh white, lavender and pale blue roses. It is exquisite.

"I've never done a party here before," says Rick. "This place is great. Good space. And the food smells terrific." He reaches under the table that he has his equipment on and produces a pair of sunglasses; mine. "By the way, you left these at my apartment last week."

"I was wondering where those were!" I exclaim, as I cross the room to his table. "Thanks," I say, reaching out to take them from him. He hangs on to them and pulls, forcing me to step closer to him.

"Angela, have you considered my proposal?"

I sigh. We have had this same conversation several times and it doesn't seem to have made a difference. Rick is relentless.

"I have, and I told you I want to give all my time to Jack now. I need to focus on my marriage, Rick. I can't do that and also be spending several nights a week with you."

"But, I love you, I need you and I can't live without you, Angela," he says, being overly dramatic. "Give it a few weeks and reconsider. We make beautiful music together. We shouldn't just let that go to waste."

I yank my glasses out of Rick's hand, chiding myself for allowing us to become too familiar. Rick is basically a nice guy. He just doesn't understand boundaries as well as I would like him to.

Across the room, I see movement in the doorway and Jack is there, his face grim. I walk over to him and embrace him. Jack looks down at me and his mouth is a horizontal line. "What," he whispers, hoarsely, "was that conversation all about, Angela?"

Oh, no! Jack heard us! If I tell him it will ruin his wedding gift. I decide to try and shrug it off.

"What? Oh, I don't know. Rick and I were just talking..."

"First off, I can tell you are not being completely truthful. Second, it sounded like a lot more than talking has been going on..." He glances over at Rick who is in the far corner of the room sound-checking his equipment. "You were at his apartment making beautiful music together?"

Quickly, I replay the conversation in my head. *Oh, my.*

"Jack, I just vowed to love you and be faithful to you. Surely you don't think..."

Jack shakes his head. "I know I should believe you and I want to, but it doesn't add up. You're too familiar with this guy. Have you been seeing him?"

"He's the DJ, Jack. I had to meet with him to plan for the wedding."

"At his *apartment*?"

"He has a home office. Look, I promise you with all my heart there is a very reasonable meaning to that conversation. I also promise that it will all become clear to you in about an hour or two, but I can't talk to you about it right at this moment."

Jack's brows are furrowed and his mouth is still linear. Yet, he yields readily when I lean up and kiss him passionately. There is a supply closet down a short hallway next to the doorway in which we stand. Jack takes my hand and leads me inside. It smells pleasantly of lemon and olive oil and it is neatly organized with shelves full of cans of ingredients, disposable tableware, folded aprons, towels and tablecloths. All the shelves are labeled with the names of their contents, written in large black, block letters. Several mops and brooms are propped in a corner.

"Angela," he whispers, as we continue to kiss each other.

"Oh, Jack," I say, breathlessly. "I'm so sorry that I've worried you. Forgive me and don't doubt me...please."

"I won't, love. I'll trust you when you tell me there is an explanation," responds Jack, kissing my neck and tightening his embrace so there is no space between us.

Suddenly, the door to the closet opens and Freddie walks in. He looks on the shelf and finds a stack of aprons, gathers it up and walks right back out. Jack and I burst out laughing.

"I guess that's our cue to leave," he chuckles.

We bump into Frankie as we walk out of the closet. He cocks his head to the side and says, "Sorry, guys. No more time for privacy. The guests are arriving. It's show time."

Frankie brings us into the front of the restaurant where the booths are. He has set up a small antipasto and some beverages on a table for the bridal party.

"The limo just pulled up. Eat a little something. In about fifteen minutes the DJ will announce you."

Jack walks over and pours me a glass of seltzer. "Drink, love. Stay hydrated," he says.

"You're not afraid I'll pass out, are you?" I ask, playfully.

Jack smiles, bashfully, "Honestly? Yes, I am."

The door bursts open and Marissa and John, the Chrises, along with Nica, and my children arrive all chattering like chipmunks.

"Mama! Papa!" Rosie bounds up to Jack and me. She throws her arms around us both. "Group hug!" she says, excitedly.

"How was the ride, Rosebud?" I ask, smoothing a stray strand of hair off her forehead.

"Good...fun, especially with Nica," and then sounding serious, "I'm glad I had fun in the limo, Mama. Now I have a *good* memory."

The only other time Rosie ever rode in a limousine was the day of Devin's funeral. I marvel at the difference in my daughter's life and how the two car rides took her from profound grief to heartfelt joy in just two-and-a-half years. Frankie comes in from the hall. "Ready?"

One of the double doors that lead into the catering hall is closed and Jack and I take our places behind it. Rick's voice booms. "Let's hear it for our lovely Matron of Honor and Dashing Best Man, Mrs. Marissa Sanchez and Mr. Samuel Cooke!" They both walk in, beaming. There is a window on the upper half of the door and from my vantage point, I can see Sam do a fist pump in the air, which makes me chuckle. "And now, introducing our bridesmaid, Miss

Rosie Cooke, and groomsman, Mr. Benjamin Cooke!" Rick continues.

Rosie is holding onto Ben for dear life. For a child who loves to be on stage, she sure dislikes having the focus of attention all on her. Ben also does a fist pump. I smile as I think of how the boys must have planned their entrances together. "And last, but not least, our adorable flower girl, Miss Veronica Johnson!" There is a collective "Awww" from the room as Nica toddles in holding her little white basket followed immediately by her parents.

Jack and I link hands as we stand in the open doorway and hear Rick announce, "Ladies and gentlemen, for the very first time, Mr. and Mrs. Jack Bartolomucci!" Everyone cheers as we stroll into the room and make our way to the edge of the dance floor.

"And for their first dance as husband and wife, Jack and Angela have chosen the very special, *All the Way*, sung by Ol' Blue Eyes himself, Mr. Frank Sinatra."

Jack takes my hand and leads me to the dance floor. For the entire song, we look deep into each other's eyes. The lyrics mean so much to us, knowing that we have promised to give ourselves completely to each other.

As we hear the crescendo of the final note, Jack dips and kisses me, as everyone applauds. Immediately comes the sound of spoons tapping glasses, so Jack and I oblige by kissing each other until the sound dies down.

"Now, folks, let's get this party started!" says Rick, as I hear the pounding beat of the Black-Eyed Peas. Sam runs to the dance floor and so do Marissa and John, followed by most of our guests.

I love this song and long to let loose and dance, but Jack looks as if he's at a loss. I take his hands in mine. "Dance with me!" I shout over the music.

He shakes his head. "I don't think I..."

"Just copy Chris and John," I say, nodding my head toward our friends who are dancing with their wives.

I reach up and pull him by the tie into the middle of the floor and begin to dance. Jack looks hesitant. I try to draw him in and I am just about to give up when Chris and John come by on a rescue mission. Christina and Marissa come over as well and whoop it up. The men show Jack how to dance and he tries his best to do as they tell him.

Next, *All Star*, by Smashmouth, one of my children's favorites, begins to play. I hear Rosie squeal and turn to see her, Sam, and Ben running over to us. The boys show Jack some dance moves and he falls in with the rest of us.

When the song is over, I lead Jack to the dais. He pulls the chair out and motions for me to sit. Feeling flirtatious, I push him down onto the chair instead, and I slide onto his lap.

"Thank you for dancing with me," I whisper as I nibble Jack's ear lobe.

He looks stunned. "If...if this is the reaction it brings, I'll take more lessons."

"Mmm hmm," I purr, kissing his neck, "I guess a little positive reinforcement doesn't hurt after all, does it?"

Jack laughs, "Let the manipulation begin!"

But I know he's joking. I pull back and smile.

"In all seriousness, thank you for stepping out of your comfort zone, Jack. I know you don't usually dance to this kind of music."

He reaches up and entwines his hand in my hair, drawing me closer to him, and kisses me. "The first of many new experiences, then," Jack says, huskily.

"And all of them with your wife," I whisper in his ear.

***

I am chatting with some of the women from my ministries at church, when I see Rick signal to me. My stomach does a back flip as I excuse myself and head over to him.

"Ready for this?" he smiles.

"If you're asking if I am nauseous and my mouth is dry, then yes, I am completely ready," I answer.

"Look, you nailed it all last week. Hang onto the microphone if you need to, or close your eyes at first. You'll be fine."

I am thankful for his encouragement, but I am still a nervous wreck. Walking over to the microphone, I look around the room and realize that I won't only be singing to Jack, but everyone I know. No pressure there.

"I'd like to ask our groom to come to the dance floor, please," says Rick. I see Jack emerge from a group of teachers from the institute. He has a confused look on his face. When the crowd notices me standing at the microphone, they move back and leave Jack standing in the middle of the dance floor by himself. He notices me and starts to walk toward me until Rick says, "Your lovely bride has prepared a very special wedding gift for you, Jack. Ladies and gentlemen, Mrs. Angela Bartolomucci..."

I hear the strains of my song, but I am so nervous that I completely miss the cue. The music goes off. "Sorry, folks," says Rick, "technical glitch. Let's try that again."

I turn and shoot Rick a grateful look. He gives me a thumbs up and begins to count the beats. I close my eyes, so it is just me and the music and I hang onto the microphone for dear life. Then, channeling Peter Mitchell, I start to sing to my husband...

One alone is my love
A love that was sent from above
On the wings of an angel
In the song of a dove

Memories of my life since I met Jack play in my mind

like a movie as I sing. The more I think of my husband; his patience, his love and his selflessness, the more my feelings are reflected in my song.

Embrace me
Embrace me
I give you my heart and my soul
Embrace me
Embrace me
Hold me close and never let me go

Opening my eyes, I can see that Frankie and Tony are standing next to Jack. It looks like they are holding him up. Both Jack and Tony have tears in their eyes. I close my eyes again, quickly, because I don't want to cry, too, and mess up my wedding gift to my husband.

One alone is my love
More delightful than wine
You are the joy of my heart
A love forever divine

I hold the last note until my lungs ache. There is silence in the room when it is over. I look around and everyone seems stunned. My heart sinks. Maybe I did a terrible job. Then I hear Father Sean yell, "Go, Jel...I mean Angela!" and start to clap. The whole room erupts into applause. Jack rushes over to me, takes me in his arms, dips me and kisses me. Once again, someone starts to tap a glass with a spoon and then others chime in. The whole room is a cacophony of spoons on glasses. We continue to kiss each other until the music starts and people abandon their glasses and spoons and begin to flock to the dance floor.

Jack takes my hand and whispers in my ear, "Come with me." I follow him into the kitchen, through the service entrance and outside. It has been a beautiful day, but now, at the first hint of dusk, there is a chill in the air. Jack takes off his tuxedo jacket, puts it over my shoulders and draws me to him. Then he leans in and kisses me passionately.

"So that's what you've been doing with Rick all these weeks?"

"Of course, what else would I possibly want to do with Rick except work on singing my husband a love song? And besides, Jim was there with me every time." I wrap my arms around Jack and kiss him again. "Rick wants me to come work with him, Jack, to sing with him. I told him no."

"But it's your dream, remember? You told me that you wanted to be a wedding singer and here is the opportunity, falling right into your lap, love."

"At this moment in time, I feel called to focus on your wishes and put mine aside, or on hold, at least. Remember, when I sang to Rosie, you wished I would sing to you on our wedding day? I made a promise to myself that if I ever got up enough guts to marry you, that I would make your wish come true."

"Hmm...and is this the *only* wish you'll grant me?" Jack says, with mischief in his eyes.

"Oh, no," I answer, seductively. "You get *two* more...so choose wisely, my love, choose wisely."

Jack laughs heartily and then we both turn in the direction of the sound of the door creaking open.

Frankie's head pops out of the service entrance. "Hey, you two," he says, "save it for later. Half the guests think you bailed. Let's get moving."

I make a pit stop to the restroom before I go back into the reception hall. Jack goes in without me. The accessible stall, which is the only one my gown will fit into, is way in the back of the restroom, past all the other stalls. As I enter, I realize I should have asked Marissa to come with me and help. The dress is cumbersome and I'm afraid it will get wet. It occurs to me that I should just throw the entire skirt over my head and try to manage that way. As I am struggling to do this, I hear voices.

"...makes you wonder why he's in his mid-forties and never married. Is he hiding some deep, dark secret? Maybe he's using Angela as a cover."

I cover my mouth to stifle a gasp. The voice belongs to Wendy, one of the ladies from the Elizabeth Ministry.

"Oh, no, not at all. I've spent time with Jack and Jel...Angela. They are very much in love, believe me."

That's Jenna. God bless her for defending me.

"Well," Samantha is talking now. "I can't believe he can't even buy her a house. I think it's pathetic that he is moving in with her. Honestly, I think he may be using her, like Wendy said."

"If you think about it," Jenna says testily, "it makes sense for them to be in her house at least until the end of the school year, for the kids' sakes. They have a beautiful relationship and, frankly, I am *happy* for them."

I am seething. These women are supposed to be my friends, but I guess out of the three I can only count Jenna in that group. *How dare they!*

"Don't you think," Wendy scoffs, "that he's just a bit too...um...perfect? I mean, the impeccable clothes, he cooks, he ballroom dances. Really...it does make you wonder *why* he never married."

The automatic flush sounds as I am straightening my dress. I hear a collective gasp from the ladies. They know *someone* heard them; just wait until they see who. Taking a deep breath, I release the lock and walk out of the stall. Wendy sees me and starts to open the door, but Jenna blocks her and says, "Hi Angela! Great reception!"

The other two women just stand there, beet red and motionless. I force a smile.

"I hope all of you ladies have a wonderful time," I respond, rubbing liquid soap onto my hands and working as hard as I can to keep my voice even. "You know, Jack and I wanted to be surrounded by the love of our good friends on our wedding day," I look directly at Jenna.

"Thanks for being here for us." Then I wad up the paper towel I used to dry my hands, toss it into the trash, breeze past Wendy and out the door.

I am so angry that I don't watch where I am walking and I crash right into Fr. Sean.

"Hey, I've been looking for you! I wanted to ask you..." His voice trails as he sees the upset look on my face. "Are you okay?" Fr. Sean asks softly.

I shake my head silently for fear that if I speak, great sobs will come gushing forth. He motions for me to follow him and we wind up in the hallway in front of the supply closet.

"Talk to me," he says.

Tears spill down my face as I tell the story of what happened in the bathroom. "I'm so angry, Father," I sob, "I know I should forgive them, but..." I lower my head and continue to cry.

"I know it's painful to hear friends gossiping about you." He leans back against the wall and folds his arms across his chest as I look up at him. "You kissed the cross a few hours ago, now it's time to embrace it, hmm?"

Reluctantly, I nod. "You'd think that God would fly the white flag just for the reception, at least."

Fr. Sean laughs heartily. "He's just showing you how much He loves you."

I nod and smile, feeling much better now. "You said you wanted to ask me something?"

His eyes light up. "Right...*why* aren't you in the choir?"

Blushing, I say, "I don't know...singing for God seems a bit daunting."

He shakes his head. "Don't bury your talent. Use it for the glory of God. I'd love it if you would consider joining the Advent/Christmas choir."

Jack appears around the corner, sees me and his face lights up. "There you are!" he says, and then his face falls when he notices I have been crying.

"I'll leave you two," says Fr. Sean, winking.

Jack puts his hands on my shoulders and leans back to survey me. "I don't want my wife to be sad on our wedding day. What's wrong, love?"

"I heard some women gossiping about me...about us."

"Wh-- what did they say?" Jack asks, surprised.

Taking a cleansing breath, I answer, "It doesn't matter. None of it's true, anyway. Come on. Let's have some fun."

"Ladies and gentleman, if you would turn your attention to the microphone, our Best Man has a few words he would like to say," Rick announces as Jack and I are sitting and sharing a plate of food.

Sam looks nervous as he grips the microphone and turns his gaze toward us. He spent the better part of the last two weeks working on his speech. We told him that if he wasn't comfortable, he didn't have to speak, but Sam insisted it was his duty as the Best Man.

"Wow," he says, "I need to say something really good, now, don't I?"

I catch his eye and blow him a kiss. He smiles back.

"I...I have to admit, I wasn't too happy when Mom told me she had a boyfriend. I mean... I'm just a kid and here I was, having to make sure she got home in time for curfew!" This elicits a chuckle from the crowd.

"I gave Mr...uh, Pop, a hard time at first," Sam looks at Jack, blushes and says, "Sorry."

Jack holds up his hand and shakes his head in a gesture of forgiveness.

"But when I saw how he treated Mom; like she is the only woman in...in the world, I knew that I shouldn't worry. I know Mom would have done a great job raising us on her own. But I'm glad she has Pop now to help her."

At Sam's statement, Jack reaches over and squeezes my hand.

"It was hard," I see Sam swallow, "for all of us, when—after Dad's accident," Sam's voice breaks. "When Pop showed up, we still felt sad, but we were able to be happy, too. So, Ben, Rosie and I just want to say that we love you and we are glad we are a family."

Jack stands up and walks over to Sam. I follow, amidst applause by all our guests. Rosie and Ben join us and we cling to one another in a hug.

"Thank you," says Jack, meaningfully. "I love the three of you as much as I love your mother."

Rosie throws her arms around him. "That must be a LOT!"

The coffee and cake have been served and Rick is playing more subdued music so our guests can relax while they eat. Jack and I are at the dais, picking at our slices. The cake is delicious, but neither of us has been inclined to eat much today. I've had a glass of wine, though, which was just enough to calm my nerves.

"Look at Tony," Jack says. "He seems to be having a good time."

We sat Tony at a table with the Chrises, who have Nica in a high chair, Marissa and John, Frankie and Paula and Jim. Freddie and his assistant are seated there as well. Paula explained that, when they attend large affairs they have an assistant come with them, to make sure Freddie is safe and his needs are met.

Tony and Frankie are having a conversation, which is obviously hilarious, because both men's faces are bright red and they are guffawing loudly.

"Angela," Jack says, gently, "why don't you ask your brother to dance?"

I had special dances with Sam and Ben, but I didn't plan one for Tony because, honestly, we just don't know each other well enough yet and I wasn't sure what kind of song would be appropriate.

Dean Martin begins to croon, *Return to Me,* as I stroll across the hall to Tony's table. His conversation with Frankie has hit a lull and the men are sitting, quietly, drinking glasses of wine. I put my hand on his shoulder and he looks up at me.

"Would you care to indulge me with a dance?" I ask.

Tony's face lights up as he leads me to the dance floor.

"Are you enjoying yourself, Tony?"

"I am," he smiles. "Your friends are good people, Angela. That Frankie is a riot."

"I'm glad you're getting along with them. They are our family, really, since we have no one else. Except you, now."

We dance, in silence, for a few moments.

"You did a good job on your song. I never realized you could sing like that."

"Yeah, well, I certainly didn't get that gene from Daddy, did I?" I laugh. "He loved music, but he sounded like a dying rooster, remember?"

Tony cracks up. "I do. It was painful. I'm glad he mostly sang in the shower. He was a pretty good artist, though. I mean, he had a talent for sketching. He didn't do it all that often."

"My Ben got that gene. He is very creative. He writes, sketches and does photography."

"I dabble."

"Do you, really? I'd love to see your work, sometime, Tony. Maybe on your next visit you could even give Ben some pointers."

I look into Tony's eyes. "Would you like to visit again?"

"This has been a good visit, Angela. I'm glad to be here. I'll try and save up to make another..."

Cutting him off, I say, "We will always take care of the travel arrangements, Tony. You just let us know when you want to come out, okay?"

"That's...that's generous of you," he says, bashfully. "It would be good to come for a holiday, maybe, if you and Jack don't mind."

"Of course we don't!"

The song changes, but we keep dancing.

"Tony," I ask, "have you ever thought of moving out of New York? Maybe your pension would go farther."

He shakes his head. "I get by. I do odd jobs sometimes. I don't need much."

"How do you spend your time, then, if you don't work much?"

"I ride the train, bring my notebook and sketch. Sometimes I go to the library and read. I fill my days."

"I think we both got the bookworm gene, then," I say as I feel a tap on my shoulder.

"Would you mind?" Jim asks Tony.

"Not at all," Tony says, and excuses himself to go back to the table.

"I just wanted to say that I am so happy for you and Jack, Angela."

"Thanks, Mr. Matchmaker. I appreciate the sentiment," I jest.

Jim smiles. "You know, on the first night of class, when I saw you hand your registration form to Jack I had this glimpse, almost a premonition, if you will, that somehow you belonged together. There is something so right about the two of you."

My eyes tear up. "Thanks for giving me some gentle, but not-so-subtle, pushes in Jack's direction. You're a good friend."

Jack comes strolling over to us, with two glasses of champagne in hand. "Do you mind if I steal my wife?" he asks Jim.

Jack hands me my glass and leads me over to the microphone.

"I just want..." The talking in the room dies down when Jack's voice is heard.

"I just want to thank our guests for spending this memorable day with us. Everyone here has a special place in our lives and we are blessed by your presence."

I scan the room and find no trace of Samantha, Wendy or their husbands. Jenna and Dave are still at the table, though, sitting close to each other, hand in hand. Their children were welcome to the reception, but they chose to get a sitter so they could have a night out on their own. Denise and her husband, Steve, are there as well, enjoying a glass of wine.

"Today, my life changed profoundly," Jack says, sliding his arm around my waist. "My lifelong dream of marrying a loving, faithful, generous and beautiful woman came to fruition this afternoon. All these years God heard my prayers and he answered them by not only blessing me with a wife, but an entire family. I want to say, publicly, that I am honored to be the stepfather to Sam, Ben and Rosie."

"Yay!" Rosie shouts, bouncing in her seat.

"I would like to toast my wife and children and vow to live up to the great responsibility God has given to me in caring for all of you."

"Salut!" Frankie yells.

Jack smiles and touches his glass to mine. "Salut!"

The bubbly champagne tickles my throat and I immediately feel its effects, as a warmth spreads over my body.

"And now, if you don't mind, Angela and I will be on our way..."

"Jack!"

"It's not like they don't know what comes next, love," he says, gently.

"But you're broadcasting..." I stop myself, realizing that everyone can hear us.

Jack is so uninhibited about our wedding night that he doesn't even realize I'm embarrassed. I look down at the rosary I still have wrapped around my left hand and give the crucifix a gentle squeeze. I spy Fr. Sean at his table, sitting next to the bishop's assistant, Fr. Diaz. He winks at me.

"Please continue to dance and have a good time," Jack continues, "Thank you and good night, everyone."

35

I don't know if it is the champagne, or the nervous tension I feel on my wedding night, but I am fighting the urge to laugh. The elevator door slides open and we step out into the hallway. Jack unlocks the apartment door and throws my overnight bag inside, then scoops me up off my feet. As he turns to carry me across the threshold, the door slams shut. This triggers a fit of giggles on my part. Jack is struggling to get the door open again and winds up having to put me down in order to do so.

He sighs, puts his hands on his hips and shakes his head at me. My giggles begin anew as Jack opens the door. He shoves his foot in to prop it open and puts his arms out.

"A little help, please?"

Still laughing, I stagger over to him and he sweeps me off my feet.

"And the humiliated knight carries his queen into her bridal chamber," he announces. Then he quiets my giggles with a kiss as he brings me to his bedroom. Gone is the brown comforter. The bed is draped with a white coverlet on the center of which rests a large bouquet of salmon colored roses. The rest of the coverlet is strewn with rose petals which trail onto the floor.

I gasp. "Oh, Jack, it's lovely."

As I look into his eyes, I become so overwhelmed by the significance of what is about to take place that I start to tremble.

"Shhh..." He kisses me tenderly, whispering, "You have ravished my heart, my sister, my bride; you have ravished my heart with one glance of your eyes."

Jack gently lowers me down from his arms, and then he takes my hand, kissing it. He guides me to kneel next to him at the foot of the bed and he begins to pray.

> *"Now, Lord, you know that I take this wife of mine not because of lust, but for a noble purpose. Call down your mercy on me and on her, and allow us to live together to a happy old age. Amen."*

...and the two become one flesh.

***

Morning light dances on the window panes as I am pulled into consciousness by the delicious feel of Jack's lips on my neck. Stretching, I smile and open my eyes to see my husband lying next to me, propped up on one arm.

"Good morning, love," he says, tenderly, stroking my cheek.

"Mmmm..." I breathe, stretching once more, "I had the craziest dream last night."

"Really?" his eyebrows go up.

"We got married."

He chuckles and reaches over to his bedside table. "Coffee?" Jack asks, handing me a mug. "Light, one stevia, just the way you like it."

"You spoil me," I say, gratefully, propping myself up on my pillows and accepting the mug. "So, when do we need to be at the airport?" I ask. "I just need some time to shower."

"Tomorrow," Jack grins. "About 5:00 in the evening."

My mouth opens in surprise. "We are spending almost two days *here*? Or do you have plans?"

"Yes we are spending them here," he says, kissing me. "And yes, I have plans," says Jack, kissing me again.

"You're going to spill my coffee," I giggle, as he wraps his arms around me.

"Never mind...forget the coffee," I say, handing the mug to Jack, who transfers it to the night stand, then enfolds me, once again, in his arms.

"Do you hear that?" I whisper in Jack's ear.

He pulls back and looks at me, suspicious, "What?"

"I thought I heard a choir of angels singing, 'Encore.' We really should oblige, don't you think?"

Jack looks at me, intensely, and in the depths of his eyes I see profound love and desire. Then he reaches up and, with his thumb, makes the sign of the cross on my forehead. "Now, Lord," he says, "You know that I take this wife of mine not because of lust..."

The waves of pleasure that completely engulfed me are ebbing as I lie cradled, breathless, in Jack's arms. He is nuzzling my neck and murmuring softly.

"Angela, my beautiful wife...my lover...my friend; how blessed I am to love you."

Jack's love enfolds me like a velvety blanket and I feel content to be in his embrace.

Suddenly, I have a flashback of my first wedding night. I had forgotten most of it, because, frankly, it was just one of many similar nights that came before.

After we finish, Devin immediately gets out of bed and fixes himself a drink from the hotel minibar.

"Want something?" he asks.

I decline.

He plops himself back on the bed and grabs the remote. Turning to me and smiling, he says, "Mind if I check the highlights of the game?" I shake my head and grab the magazine I bought to read on the plane.

I didn't realize it at the time, but, on my first wedding night, I felt tossed aside; used, actually. This experience continued throughout my marriage, although I never consciously perceived it. I wonder if Devin felt that I was using him as well. When I reflect on this, and on the physical pleasure coupled with the profound spiritual joy I experienced in giving myself to Jack last night, so completely; there is no comparison.

A lump forms in my throat as I lean up and kiss Jack desperately. "Thank you," I pray, my voice deep with emotion. "Oh, God...thank you!"

Jack strokes my cheek and looks slightly amused. "I guess I should thank you, too, then, shouldn't I?"

"No," I say. "Well...yes, I guess...no...*no.* What I mean is, thank you for holding me and caressing me, even after you were satisfied. Thank you for giving all of yourself to me and not holding anything back. Thank you for making me feel loved and wanted, before, during and after we make love, and throughout the day, every day."

"Angela," Jack says, tenderly, "that's what I'm supposed to do. It's ordained by God; He wants it that way."

"Yes," I whisper. "But I wouldn't have known this if I hadn't met you...because you, Jack, truly know how to love."

Acknowledgments

There are so many people whose love and support helped make this novel a reality. I'd like to thank:

My husband, Joe, for believing that I could fulfill my dreams and allowing that to happen by picking up the slack in the household when I went on my writing binges.

My children, whose creativity awes and inspires me on a daily basis.

My parents for making great sacrifices to send me to college, where my love of writing began to blossom.

All my Marissas: Cindy, Denise, Donna, Kerry, Linda, Peggy, Shannon and Suzanna. Your faith and grace under pressure are an inspiration to me.

Fr. Carl E. Beekman for spiritual direction and for advice regarding the theological aspects of the story.

Fr. Greg Haskamp for not batting an eye when I asked you to pray over my flash drive, for spiritual direction and for assistance with the wedding scenes.

Jonathan Mincieli for your help with the legal aspects of the story and to Kim DellOlio for polishing up my rusty Italian.

Kerry Knott and Shannon Hansen for your valuable feedback on the storyline and character development.

My cheerleaders: the ladies of the Mom's Book Club and all of my relatives who originate from the East Coast.

Those who helped with proofreading, including Dianna Wormsley, Donna Doherty and Annamarie Barvick.

Delena Soukup, for your creativity and talent in creating the cover photo for this novel.

Ellen Gable Hrkach for sharing your amazing editorial talents with me. You make me a better writer! To James Hrkach, for his beautiful cover design. And to Ellen and James at Full Quiver Publishing, for believing in the message of this book enough to want to publish it.

Appendix

Resources to help build relationships:
Heaven's Song by Christopher West
Theology of the Body for Beginners by Christopher West
For Better...Forever by Dr. Greg Popcak
Holy Sex! A Catholic Guide to Toe-Curling, Mind-Blowing Infallible Loving by Dr. Greg Popcak
Men and Women Are From Eden by Mary Healy
Love and Responsibility by Karol Wojtyla
The Five Love Languages by Gary Chapman
Pure Love by Jason Evert
Theology of His/Her Body by Jason Evert
Theology of the Body for Teens by Jason Evert, Crystalina Evert and Brian Butler
Pure Manhood by Jason Evert
Pure Womanhood by Crystalina Evert
How to Find a Soulmate without Losing Your Soul by Jason and Crystalina Evert

Resources to help with faith life:
10 Habits of Happy Mothers by Dr. Meg Meeker, MD
Be A Man by Fr. Larry Richards
A Book of Saints for Catholic Moms by Lisa Hendey
Wrapped Up: God's Ten Gifts for Women by Teresa Tomeo and Cheryl Dickow
www.magnificat.com
www.catholicsistas.com
www.ignitumtoday.com
www.catholicmom.com

NFP Resources:
www.ccli.org (The Couple to Couple League)
www.creightonmodel.com (Creighton Method)
www.woomb.com (Billings Ovulation Method)
www.serena.ca (Serena - Sympto-Thermal Method)

Catholic Fiction from Full Quiver Publishing:
Stealing Jenny by Ellen Gable www.stealingjenny.com
In Name Only by Ellen Gable www.innameonly.ca
Emily's Hope by Ellen Gable www.emilyshope.com

About the Author

AnnMarie Creedon is wife to Joe and mother to their five children, ages 8-21. She home schools her younger children and is involved in the Respect Life and Elizabeth Ministries in her church, where she also sings in the choir. AnnMarie is inspired by the writings of John Paul II, the creativity of her children, the love of her husband and the faith of her friends. She lives near Kansas City, Missouri. AnnMarie is currently working on her second novel. Contact her at annmarie.creedon@gmail.com

AnnMarie's blog: *The Roman(tic) Catholic* (www.annmariecreedon.com) and is an occasional contributor to www.catholicistas.com

Look for AnnMarie Creedon, Author on Facebook, Awestruck

twitter.com/annmariecreedon

For more information on the settings and foods mentioned in the novel, check out AnnMarie's Pinterest board: http://pinterest.com/annmariecreedon/angela-s-song-a-novel-by-annmarie-creedon/

www.angelassong.com
www.fullquiverpublishing.com